FIRE F

THE SKY: EMBERS

Creative Texts Publishers products are available at special discounts for bulk purchase for sale promotions, premiums, fund-raising, and educational needs. For details, write Creative Texts Publishers, PO Box 50, Barto, PA 19504, or visit www.creativetexts.com

FIRE FROM THE SKY: BOOK 12: EMBERS
by N.C. REED
Published by Creative Texts Publishers
PO Box 50
Barto, PA 19504
www.creativetexts.com

ISBN: 978-1-64738-045-8

FIRE FROM THE SKY: EMBERS
N.C. REED

For those who were here before,
For those who have gone ahead,
And for those who remain.

FIRE FROM THE SKY

Dramatis personae

THE SANDERS FAMILY AND FARM

GORDON SANDERS – CURRENT PATRIARCH OF THE SANDERS FAMILY

ANGELA SANDERS- WIFE OF GORDON SANDERS, MOTHER OF THEIR THREE CHILDREN

ROBERT SANDERS – OLDEST SON OF GORDON AND ANGELA

PATRICIA SANDERS- WIFE OF ROBERT SANDERS, MOTHER OF THEIR TWO CHILDREN

- ABIGAIL SANDERS – OLDEST CHILD OF ROBERT AND PATRICIA
- SAMANTHA WALTERS – ABIGAIL'S BEST FRIEND, CURRENTLY LIVING WITH THE SANDERS
- GORDY SANDERS – YOUNGEST CHILD OF ROBERT AND PATRICIA

ALICIA TILLMAN – ONLY DAUGHTER OF GORDON AND ANGELA, SECOND CHILD

RONNY TILLMAN – HUSBAND OF ALICIA TILLMAN, FATHER OF THEIR THREE CHILDREN

- LEANNE TILLMAN – OLDEST OF TWINS BY TWO MINUTES
- LEON TILLMAN – YOUNGEST OF TWINS BY TWO MINUTES
- CLAYTON 'FUSSY' TILLMAN – NEWBORN ADDITION TO THE TILLMAN FAMILY

CLAYTON SANDERS – YOUNGEST SON AND CHILD OF GORDON AND ANGELA

LAINIE HARPER – CLAYTON'S GIRLFRIEND

GREG HOLLOWAY – CHILDHOOD BEST FRIEND OF CLAYTON AND JAKE SIDELL. DEPUTY SHERIFF OF CALHOUN COUNTY, NOW LIVES WITH GORDON AND ANGELA

JAKE SIDELL – CHILDHOOD BEST FRIEND OF CLAYTON AND GREG HOLLOWAY. MECHANIC AND BUSINESS OWNER, NOW LIVES ON THE SANDERS' FARM WITH HIS SEVEN-YEAR-OLD DAUGHTER JACQUELINE (JAC)

- JACQUELINE SIDELL – DAUGHTER OF JAKE SIDELL WITH HIS LATE WIFE, KAITLIN

MEMBERS OF CLAY'S OLD UNIT

JOSE JUAREZ – CURRENT SECOND IN COMMAND OF CLAYTON'S SECURITY DUTIES FOR THE FARM

MARTINA SANCHEZ – JOSE'S FIANCE

- ROBERTO SANCHEZ – SON OF MARTINA SANCHEZ, 8

- RAE SANCHEZ – DAUGHTER OF MARTINA SANCHEZ, 6

SHANE GOLDEN – CONSIDERED THIRD IN COMMAND, NORMAL GO-BETWEEN FOR THE GROUP AND NEW PEOPLE

JODY THOMPSON – SNIPER FOR THE GROUP

NATHANIEL 'NATE' CAUDELL – SCOUT FOR THE GROUP

CRISTINA CAUDELL – NATE'S WIFE

- BABY JOHN CAUDELL – NATE AND CRISTINA'S NEWBORN SON, LESS THAN A YEAR OLD
- KAITLIN CAUDELL – NATE'S OLDER SISTER, AND REGISTERED NURSE
- NATHAN CAUDELL – KAITLIN'S SON, 16

STACY PRYOR

KEVIN BODEE

TANDI MASEO – MEDIC

ELLEN KARGAY – TANDI'S GIRLFRIEND

MITCHELL NOLAN

BEVERLY JACKSON – MITCHELL'S GIRLFRIEND

- JONATHON 'JJ' JACKSON, BEVERLY'S SON, 14

XAVIER ADAIR

FRIENDS OF GORDY'S WORKED INTO THE UNIT
ZACH WILLIS

TITUS TERRY

HEATH KELLY

COREY REYNARD

KURTIS MONTANA (NEWLY ARRIVED WITH SHANE'S GROUP, BUT NORMALLY FITTED WITH THE OTHER TEENS)

AMAZON SQUAD (BUT DON'T CALL THEM THAT)
TALIA GRAY

KIM POWERS

AMANDA LOWERY

DANICA BENNET

FREDA FLETCHER

DEVON KNOWLES

PETRA SHANNON

HEATHER PATTON

EVE ALBERT

JENA WALLER

MIKKI REEVES

GAIL KNIGHT

SAVANNAH HALE

CARRIE JARRETT
EUNICE MAYNARD
CAROL KENNARD
JANESSA HAYNES

ORIGINAL HILLTOP COMMUNITY AND OTHER NEWCOMERS
GARY MEECHAM – GUNSMITH, SHARPSHOOTER, ONE OF THE GROUP LEADERS
DIXIE JERROLDS – SCHOOLTEACHER
-   ASHTON JERROLDS – DIXIE JERROLD'S SON, 7
MARCY GEORGE – 'EMANCIPATED TEENAGER' 17
SAMUEL WEBB – CURRENT 'PATRIARCH' OF THE SURVIVING WEBB FAMILY MEMBERS
LUKE WEBB – BROTHER TO SAMUEL
SETH WEBB – BROTHER TO SAMUEL – 16
LILA WEBB – SISTER TO SAMUEL – 15
DAISY WEBB – WIDOW OF MICAH WEBB
JASMINE WEBB – WIDOW OF MATT WEBB
DARRELL GOODRUM – BLACKSMITH
CARLENE GOODRUM – WIFE OF DARRELL AND MOTHER OF THEIR THREE CHILDREN
-   ANTHONY GOODRUM – SON, 16
-   JAMEY GOODRUM – SON, 10
-   CARA GOODRUM - DAUGHTER, 8
VICTORIA TULLY – FORMER NATIONAL GUARD MEMBER, EOD SPECIALIST
BYRON 'BRICK' HOUSE – FRIEND OF LEON THE ELDER WITH MURKY PAST
TERRI HARTWELL – VETERINARIAN STUDENT CAUGHT BY THE STORM, NOW PART OF THE SANDERS' FARM
OLIVIA HALEY – 17, CLASSMATE OF GORDY'S, ORPHANED BY STORM, NOW LIVING WITH GORDON AND ANGELA
-   CAROLINE – SISTER, 7
-   LIBBY – SISTER, 5
AMY MITCHELL – RESCUED FROM ATTACK SOON AFTER STORM
-   LISA – DAUGHTER,9
JANICE HARDY – 18, CAME WITH LAINIE HARPER, HAS AN EIDETIC MEMORY
CALLIE WESTON – RESCUED FROM ATTACK ON THE FARM
-   CARL – SON, 4
TAMMY DENMARK – RESCUED FROM ATTACK ON THE FARM
-   DIANE – DAUGHTER, 3

NEW MEMBERS OF HILLTOP COMMUNITY
KANDI LEDFORD – FORMER 2ND LT., U.S. ARMY

SIENNA NEWELL – FORMER 1ST LT., U.S. ARMY
VIRGIL WILCOX – FORMER SSG, U.S. ARMY
JAYLYN THATCHER – SURGEON, FORMER CAPT., U.S. ARMY
  – RODDY THATCHER – HUSBAND OF JAYLYN, TRUCK DRIVER
CLIFFORD LARAMIE – FUEL TRUCK DRIVER
MOSES BROWN – BUTCHER/MEAT CUTTER
TRUDY LEIGHTON – SHANE GOLDEN'S COUSIN
  – GWEN PAIGE – TRUDY'S GIRLFRIEND
MILLIE LONG – TEEN PICKED UP BY SHANE'S GROUP ON THE WAY EAST, NOW
LEON SANDERS GIRLFRIEND
DOTTIE GREER – HUSBAND JAMES, TRUCK DRIVER, WORKING WHEN STORM
HIT, INVITED TO LIVE AT FARM
  – HELENA – DAUGHTER, 9
  – QUENTIN – SON,9
EVELYN LACEY – SOAP MAKER (NOT ACTUALLY A PART OF THE SQUARE BUT
LISTED HERE FOR CONVENIENCE

NATIONAL GUARD CONTINGENT
2ND LIEUTENANT FARON GILLIS
SERGEANT FIRST CLASS SHAUN GLEASON
STAFF SERGEANT LOWELL MARTINSON
PFC Truman Toller
PFC Elijah Brigham
CPL Zane Parris
PFC Beau Abramson
PVT Donovan Jordan
PFC Matthew Kenny
PFC Jared Samuels
Specialist Brannon Howard
PFC Richie Millard
PFC Jeffrey Herbert
PFC Vince Hathoway
CPL Carly Isaacson (medic)

LIEUTENANT GILLIS' ORIGINAL PATROL
STAFF SERGEANT LOWELL MARTINSON
CPL RAVEN ELLIOT (MEDIC)
CPL THANE TANNER
PFC DEZI MARTIN
CPL Lynden Witherspoon
PFC Keely Irwin

PVT Parnell Plank
CPL Ellis Gates
PFC Keir Welch
PFC Palmer Lovell
PFC Stanley Clarkson

Author's Note: Those listed as part of the Hilltop Community may or may not actually be staying on the Hilltop at any given moment. All are listed with them as either those who arrived at the farm just before the disaster struck, or were invited to stay afterward, and are not part of the Sanders' family group or extended family (or part of Clay's old outfit at the Troy Farm). For instance, Brick and Janice live in Leon's old house due to their connection to Leon but were not a part of the Sanders' group beforehand. The Guard contingent may seem too NCO heavy, due to Gleason's men having been there for training in equestrian skills and care. Gillis' team was an actual fire team, on patrol, when the virus hit.

TABLE OF CONTENTS

CHAPTER ONE

Christmas and New Year's had come to the Sanders' farm with little fanfare and no celebrations. Small groups gathered for mealtime and to be thankful for what they had, but there was no celebration as there had been the year before. There was no laughing, playing children, romping in the newly fallen snow. No merry making.

There was in fact little enough to be merry about. The plague sweeping through the area had wreaked havoc on those who had survived so much since the disaster that was the Storm. Those who had made it through starvation, dysentery, violence and bloodshed had in the end fallen prey to a killer they couldn't see, and ultimately couldn't fight.

Clay's last orders from the Area Commander of the National Guard, and they *had been* orders as Captain Adcock had stressed Clay's former rank in addressing him, were to close the farm to all traffic in order to preserve the resources the Sanders' farm represented to the future, assuming any of them had one. In the end, one of Adcock's subordinates along with two seasoned NCOs and a short platoon of troopers that had not been exposed to the virus had been given shelter at the farm as well, with orders to answer to Clayton Sanders in all things until ordered otherwise by Adcock, or by his own superior, Major Whitten.

The manpower had eased some strain on the farm's own security forces but was seasoned with the fact that no one had heard from Adcock or anyone else in over two weeks. The only information they had received from Jordan had been in the form of information passed on by a former constable who wanted food to try and make the trip south to safer conditions. If there was such a thing at this point.

So, there had been no merry making. Instead, there was hard work. Including the training of all the school age children in how to survive in the new world they found themselves living in.

-

The truck rattled along the back road, wind whipping around the cab and buffeting the teenagers in the back. All were huddled together for warmth, packs clutched tight as they waited to arrive at their destination.

Finally, with ears threatening to turn frostbitten in the windchill despite scarves and caps, the truck slowed and came to a stop.

1

EMBERS

"End of the line, plebes!" Mitchell Nolan declared as he stepped out of the warm truck cab. "On the ground! Let's go! Hustle!"

Nathan Caudell, JJ Jackson, Seth Webb, Janice Hardy, Anthony Goodrum, Lila Webb and finally Millie Long all disembarked, slinging sparse packs onto their backs even as Mitchell continued to harangue them.

"You've got a map, you've got a compass," Mitchell told them. "You've got a sleeping bag, food and water for two days, and the ability and means to get more if you need it, providing you can manage it. You know your starting point, and there are eleven fixed navigation points along your way. You must identify them all and return to Building Two in forty-eight hours. Note that I say, 'Building Two', and not 'the Farm'," he stressed. "The farm is a huge area and Building Two is not near the edge."

"Once we leave, you are on your own," he warned. "You better learn to depend on one another and to work together, and I suggest you do it in a hurry before you freeze to death, or starve to death, or the wolves get you. Any of the above happens, you will of course be given a failing grade for this excursion. Any questions? Excellent!" he clapped his hands without giving anyone a chance to ask. "Get moving! Clock starts now."

With that he slapped the tailgate, got back into the nicely warmed cab, and rode away, returning to the farm.

Leaving seven teenagers behind to cope with the winter and everything else around them.

-

"There ain't a wolf within a thousand miles of this place, man," Kevin Bodee chuckled as he drove them back to the farm. "At least not one that wasn't in a zoo."

"And how do you know that some eco-nut didn't release said wolves into the wild to keep them from starving?" Mitchell asked. "Now did you think about that, Kev? No, you didn't, did you? But *I* did," Mitchell jabbed his own chest with a thumb with that proud proclamation. "Besides, they need to be a little bit afraid. Though that Webb kid almost certainly knows there's no wolves around here," he admitted. He paused, reaching for his radio.

"Chip, this is Thug. Hand-off complete. Repeat, hand-off complete."

"Roger that," came the short reply. *"Hand-off received. Out."*

The teens weren't quite as alone as they had been led to believe.

"Did he say wolves?" Anthony Goodrum asked, looking wildly around them.

"There ain't no wolves 'round here," Seth Webb told him flatly, already studying the map they had been provided. "Ain't been in over a hun'erd years."

"How do you know that?" Nathan Caudell asked, though curious rather than challenging.

"Made my way trapping before all this," Seth replied calmly. "Whole family did. Ain't no wolves. Plenty of other stuff, though," he allowed.

"He's correct," Janice Hardy shivered beneath her jacket and pulled it tighter around her. "The Red Wolf, or *Canis lupus rufus*, was a common inhabitant of this area in previous centuries but was hunted to near extinction due to predation on livestock and the value of the fur. Reintroduction attempts have been made, most notably in the mountains of North Carolina, but attempts in this state have been unsuccessful. The likelihood that we will encounter one is all but nil."

"'All but'?" Millie Long asked with a raised eyebrow.

"How do you know all that?" Nathan asked, incredulous.

"Oh, I just read it once," Janice replied, once again the stereotypical blonde. "I'm sure lots of people know that sort of thing," she waved away the irrelevancy.

"All but nil?" Millie pressed, becoming concerned.

"There were a great many predators being held in zoos throughout the south, including both Tennessee and Alabama. It is possible that an animal friendly group might have sought to release them from captivity to prevent them from starving," Janice replied. "Similar incidents are recorded throughout the twentieth century in far less trying circumstances."

"Perfect," Millie drew the word out, looking out at the snow-covered landscape. Even as she did, a large snowflake came drifting by her, heading sedately toward the ground.

"Absolutely perfect."

"Anything yet?" Gordy asked.

"*Nah,*" Corey Reynard replied softly. "*Still just standing around. Seth Webb is studying the map, though. He at least should know what to do.*"

Gordy Sanders, Corey Reynard, Heath Kelly and Kurtis Montana were arrayed around the teens in a diamond, there to protect them in the event of any sort of threat. Otherwise, they were to let the teens sink or swim on their own merits.

-

"I don't suppose we've heard from Adcock or Whitten today?" Clay asked as he stepped into Operations. Leon Tillman shook his head slowly.

"Sorry, Uncle Clay. Not a peep."

"How many days is that now?" Clay asked, frowning.

"Nineteen, I think," his nephew replied, looking at a small record book, then at a homemade calendar.

"No, it's twenty-two days," the teen corrected himself. "Three weeks yesterday."

"And we're monitoring everything, right?" Clay checked.

"We are," Leon assured him. "Scanning several frequencies in fact. If he talks to us, we'll hear it."

"I wish he'd do that," Clay muttered, more to himself than Leon.

"We all do," Leon replied. "I'd even settle for hearing from Jordan, to be honest. It's creepy, it's so quiet."

-

"It's quiet," Zach said softly, scanning the area before him with binoculars. "Nothing moving anywhere that I can see."

"It's snowing again, too," Stacey Pryor sighed. "And cold. This wind would cut through butter, man."

"Sure enough," Zach nodded, lowering the glasses. "This is a week today, I think, since we've had anyone try to get onto the farm. Right?"

"Don't jinx it, kid," Stacey warned, though not harshly. "Voice of experience talking, here," he chuckled darkly.

"No, I don't want to jinx it," Zach agreed absently. "I'm just wondering what's going on in Jordan."

"Ain't we all?"

-

"I would love to know what's going on in Jordan right now," Greg Holloway noted as leaned back in his chair. He was sitting in Clay's

4

office, hoping the quiet would continue. Clay was behind his desk, looking at figures provided by Kandi Ledford.

"Wouldn't we all," he stated rather than asked. "I'd love even more to know what's going on with Adcock. Or even Whitten, if nothing else."

"Still nothing, I take it?" Greg asked.

"Not a peep," Clay nodded. "From them or anyone else. We're still getting reports from the stations you set up, but that's it. The little bit of traffic the kids had been picking up in the weeks before the plague has dropped off the air."

"Maybe they're just laying low, like we are," Greg offered hopefully.

"Let us all pray so," Clay sighed, stretching his shoulders before leaning back to brace himself against the wall. "This was not supposed to be so difficult," he sighed.

"You say that like you rehearsed for all this or something," Greg snorted.

"I don't mean the plague," Clay shook his head, his hand making a swiping motion as if to push the comment away. "I really thought I had planned all this down to the wire, man. Leon helped, then Dad got into the mix, and finally the twins. In fact, had Gordon not insisted we bring the twins in we would have really been in a fix. Those two were like hounds, sniffing out any and everything they could find. There's no telling how many tablets, smart phones and hard drives there are around here with gigabytes of information about everything they could think of, read of or find on the internet."

"I've seen it," Greg nodded. "Some of it, anyway," he amended.

"Once things happened, we were all supposed to just hunker down here and wait for things to calm down, assuming they did," Clay continued. "Besides the family and my old team, I made plans for you, Jake, though I didn't know he had a kid to be honest, and Leon for Marla, ungrateful heifer that she was, while making sure that Robert and Alicia and even Gordon didn't run around warning all their friends the sky was falling."

"Good way to get sent to Downey's," Greg agreed.

"Right?" Clay nodded. "Anyway, my idea was to eventually close the roads in and just...sit here. Preferably quietly. That lasted about, oh, twenty minutes or so," he sighed. "My parents were off to the races trying to help people. I told you about our trip to the church, yeah?"

"Yep," Greg nodded once. "I'd love to say I was surprised, but honestly? I've lived there, well had lived there anyway, for over three years. Jordan isn't the nice little place you may remember, my brother. Or wasn't, anyway. No telling what it's like, now."

"Too true," Clay replied. "And I didn't plan on Jordan one way or another. I had a handful of people I was trying to save, and that was all I concentrated on. Leon, bless his departed soul, agreed with me completely, but there was still no stopping Mom and her mission of mercy. I warned them how it would be, and both flatly told me there was no way it could or would happen."

"But it did," Greg punctuated his statement with a firm nod.

"In spades," Clay set forward again. "Anyway, there's no sense rehashing all that crap. Compared to what's happening now, that was nothing. A hiccup."

"There hasn't been any traffic for almost a week," Greg tried to lighten things up. "Not along the freeway or from Jordan. That doesn't mean there won't end up being trouble still, of course. Kelly's warning is still ringing in my ears, to tell you the truth."

"Mine too," Clay agreed. "I just don't know any more what may or may not happen. I didn't think about things to this point or consider something like this happening at all. It changes everything. Even after all that's happened, all that we've been through, something like the plague has made that seem like a warmup."

"How's Lainie doing?" Greg changed the subject. "I haven't seen her in days."

"She's got her own projects," Clay replied. "I think, actually, she's with Abby right now, and her forestry class."

"She's doing a good job with that, too," Greg noted.

"She is, indeed," Clay agreed completely. "Good job convincing her to do it, man. She's perfect for the job."

"I told her that," Greg almost smirked. "This is also a good way to get her back to a point where she's involved with the rest of us again. She's been isolating herself for a while now."

"I know," Clay sighed yet again, scrubbing his face with his hands. "Part of that was on me, I guess. But at least it's improving now," he avoided rehashing old battles.

"So, what are we doing today?" Greg asked.

"We have a security meeting in about thirty minutes or so," Clay looked at his watch. "We need to take a look at our defensive measures."

"Sounds like fun!" Greg smiled.

-

Lainie Harper hung toward the back of the small group following along with Abigail Sanders' explanation of why careful management of forestry resources was necessary to ensure a steady supply of wood products for use by the farm's residents.

"But aren't there plenty of trees?" Roberto Sanchez asked hesitantly, raising his small hand about even with his shoulder.

"Well, it does look that way, doesn't it?" Abby smiled encouragingly. "And if we're only talking about right now, or in say the next year, then that's accurate. But what happens if we cut down all the trees, as fast as we can, and don't replenish them? Compare it to pancakes you have for breakfast. What if, instead of making as many pancakes as people wanted, we only made two for each person? Now, say we do that, and someone comes through the kitchen and instead of taking just two, they take three. The next person takes two, and maybe the third person only takes the two they were supposed to or maybe four if they're really hungry. If we don't keep an eye on what everyone takes, then what will happen when those near the end of the line start coming through, wanting pancakes for their breakfast?"

"There may not be any," Roberto replied thoughtfully, a lightbulb obviously going on somewhere in his thought process. A very intelligent boy, Lainie decided.

"That's exactly right," Abby complimented. "It's not the best comparison of course, since a new stack of pancakes could be ready in twenty minutes or so, right? But look at this tree," she pointed to a towering pine tree behind her. "This is a loblolly pine tree. They are ideal for areas where erosion is a problem because they grow quickly compared to other trees and have a decent root system to help hold the soil in place. Do you have any idea how old that tree is?" she asked the class.

"Ten years?" a female voice guessed. Lainie couldn't see who spoke.

"Anyone else?" Abby asked before answering. No one else spoke up.

EMBERS

"That tree is between thirty and forty years old," she told them gently, and Lainie could see a ripple of surprise run through the children, many of whom could not yet fathom how much time that was. "It was planted when my father was younger than I am now, as part of a reforestation project. If each of you planted a tree today, a tree like this one," she pointed, "then by the time it reached this size, you would all be older than your parents." 'Ohs' and 'Ahs' ran through the group as the information sank in.

"Now, this tree is only just now mature enough, old enough," she clarified, "to be used in building materials, and really needs another ten years to be used as more than a log. If we cut it today and used it, then it would take roughly thirty-five years, or older than your parents, to replace it."

"Wow," more than one little voice all but whispered as the enormity of what Abby was saying sank in.

"Wow, indeed," Abby nodded. "That's why it's so important for us to practice good conservation. Now, what is one of the ways you know of, and all of you should know this one, that we're already doing just that? Practicing conservation, I mean."

"We gather dead and downed trees for firewood," Jaqueline Sidell said at once, still studying the huge tree with open interest.

"Exactly right," Abby nodded firmly. "We had a storm last year that knocked down several trees. Over the past few months, we have collected all those trees to be used. Some, the harder woods good for building, we turned into lumber. Others we cut up for firewood. Remember the big fire we had? The one that scared us so bad?" Heads bobbed throughout the class.

"We had to cut a lot of trees down for that, too," she told them. "We've used all of them or at least have plans in place to use them soon. We're not wasting anything we've been given. We've also started replanting trees where we can. When spring gets here, each of you will be given a sapling and I'll help you plant them. After that, your tree will be your responsibility. I'll teach you how to check it for parasites or disease, and if we find any then I'll show you how to treat them, assuming we can." All of them looked excited at that prospect and Lainie mentally congratulated Abby for sparking that excitement in such a young crowd.

FIRE FROM THE SKY

"Okay," Abby clapped her hands once. "You've all got your folders, which have color photos of the trees we normally find here on the farm. Please remember to take good care of those folders because we may not be able to replace them. One day, when you're older and don't need them any longer, someone much younger will inherit that folder and learn the same things you are now. So, don't tear them or write on them, okay? Just study them and try to remember how to identify the bark, the leaves and the limbs of the trees we deal with every day. Okay?"

"Okay," the chorus of small voices replied. Abby smiled broadly at them.

"Then that's all for today," she told them. "Let's start heading back so we can all go inside and warm up. You've all been really good today, and I appreciate it!"

The children all started back for the warmth of Building Two under the watchful eye of Titus Terry and one of the Kangal pups, which was much larger than when he first came to live at the farm. Lainie hung back to wait for Abby.

"Nice work," she said as Abby slung her backpack and joined Lainie for the walk home.

"Thanks," Abby smiled. She was far and away different from just two weeks ago. She looked and acted the way Lainie imagined she had when she was still a teenager. It was as if a heavy weight had been lifted from her shoulders, allowing her to stand taller.

"I think you've won some fans in this crowd," Lainie nodded toward the children, hands stuffed deep into her jacket pockets. "They seemed really excited to be learning."

"They did, didn't they?" Abby nodded. "They're all smart. I think this new approach to teaching them is a good thing. Things we take for granted, growing up on a place like this, some of those kids never had the chance to learn. Might not have mattered before the sun went nuclear, but it definitely matters now."

"Exactly what Clay said," Lainie agreed. "It really hit him hard when Bobby died. He felt to blame even though there was not a single thing he could have done to prevent it."

"Nothing but keep them all inside forever," Abby nodded once. "He takes too much blame on himself for stuff. Sure, some stuff may be his fault, or at least his responsibility let's say, but not everything. No matter

9

how much he does, or can do, he's still just one man. Some of the rest of us have to step up and shoulder some of that."

"I've told him that very thing, and so have several others," Lainie assured her. "And to be fair, he is getting better. His little bout with exhaustion has, I think, shown him that there are limits to anything, and he has found his. He's finally starting to allow others to take care of things that they're good at while he just focuses on threat and crisis management."

"Which he is good at, there's no doubt," Abby commented. "The last thing we need is for him to end up down, or out altogether. There are days when I think he's all that keeps this place together."

"He said the same thing about Leon the Elder," Lainie sighed. "I think maybe that's part of his concern, to be honest. Leon always rode him hard to step in and take charge, to be prepared for when Leon was gone. Now, with Leon actually gone, I think Clay remembers all those warnings but instead of managing, like Leon did, Clay begins to get tied down doing things himself and then can't see his way clear of them."

"It's too much," Abby nodded slowly. "I get it. I do. He wants to make sure everyone is safe and provided for and feels like it's his responsibility to make sure that it happens. But damn. There's a farm full of folks around here anymore, and a lot of them are at least his age or older. There's no need or reason for him to be doing so much more than anyone else does."

"Exactly," Lainie said firmly.

-

"We know it's coming," Clay told the assembled group, deciding to tackle the eight-hundred-pound gorilla in the room right away.

"Do we?" Mitchell Nolan asked. "What's to say that Kelly guy didn't just make up a lot of that stuff to get what he needed? Oh, I know that old man Franklin is hating on Clay and the rest of us for sure, not to mention that crowd that wanted to seize the farm. But might be that's all there is."

"Could be," Greg allowed. "Tim Kelly used to be a straight guy, but a lot has happened and that changes people. Usually not for the better. We can't afford not to assume it's true, though."

"I haven't," Jose agreed, nodding. "We're at risk, to be certain, but not to the point of helplessness. We have the edge in weaponry, equipment, tactics and training, not to mention experience. It's one thing to threaten and posture. It's another thing entirely to be where the lead is flying."

"True that," Faron Gillis murmured. He tended to listen more than he spoke at these small meetings, which impressed Jose and the others. Usually, the younger officers were always trying to get their two cents worth into the conversation. This young man was not in the habit of doing so. He also didn't try to impress the others with his own exploits, another trait that most younger men, enlisted or officer, tended to have.

"So, what do you want to do?" Greg asked, looking at Jose.

"We, as usual, have a manpower problem," Jose admitted. "It's not nearly so bad as it has been in the past, thanks to Lieutenant Gillis and his men, but it's still an issue. We have three security mandates that must be met. Firstly, we must maintain our security patrols and posts here on the farm. Secondly, we have to maintain the new posts around the perimeter to guard against incursion. Finally, we must be prepared to meet an assault from Jordan. From either direction along the road, but likely it will be on the road to Jordan."

"We should have enough to handle that," Mitchell made a mild objection. "Between the Guard troops and the Amazons, we've gained a lot of manpower."

"We have," Jose agreed. "But you just said it yourself; we have enough to handle that. What we don't have is enough to handle all that and still meet all of our other obligations."

"Which obligations?" Greg asked. "I know the farm work has to be one of them, since our security people represent most of the young and physically fit."

"That is true," Jose nodded. "But there is also the matter of training. We have several people who are being trained to handle horses. While we could halt that until the crisis is over, experience has taught us that the crisis is never over around here," he snorted at his own dark humor. "We need to keep at it because those skills will be extremely important sooner rather than later."

"Added to that is our regular training regimen. We're able to do so much because our people are well trained, extremely fit, and highly motivated. Take away any of those three and we start to decline, which we can't afford. We are always outnumbered, and we must always remember that. And, finally, as you said, we have to think about the work here on the farm. All of us have other duties and responsibilities aside from security. If we start having to tie down more people on the watch, or on the response team, then we start losing those manhours elsewhere. Something else we simply can't afford."

"So, what can we do?" Nate Caudell spoke for the first time.

"I'm open to suggestions," Jose admitted. He had already gamed out this problem alone, but he was not happy with his findings. He was hoping to get ideas from the men around him.

When no one spoke for nearly a minute, Gillis cleared his throat.

"You have an idea, Lieutenant?" Jose asked, mildly surprised.

"We should dump the idea of a static defense," Gillis said, his voice low, but firm. "That eats away manpower for little to no return unless you happen to fool the enemy into hitting those prepared positions. While we may can do that, it's a gamble, and we can't afford to gamble."

"Go on," Jose nodded.

"We need more towers," Gillis started pointing to spots around the map before them. "Drop the idea of this ring of posts around the entire place. It takes too much in man hours and gives too little in return. Instead, we erect towers like the one behind the Sanders' residential area, and place two people on each with good glasses, or even a spotting scope if we have it. NVDs as well, in case someone tries sneaking around in the dark."

"We have a number of ATVs, as well as Humvees. Position them here, at Building Two, ready to go as soon as they get the word. Guns on the Hummers, and maybe even the ATVs if it's doable. Keep two full fire teams, if not a full squad, on watch here at all times, ready to respond to any problem. As soon as we get the word, the ready squad is out the door and gone, responding. The rest of us rally here, either to assist as needed, or respond elsewhere in case the first problem is a feint for an attack somewhere else."

"Rotate the ready squad and the tower personnel together, in teams, each with a shift commander. Let them get used to working together. We should be able to manage three teams, full teams, and have a few hands left over. Work a shift on watch, a half-shift on the farm, and then have some training and down time along with time to rest. The only problem I can see is there's no real way for us to give people a day off occasionally except in twos and threes at best. That will hurt morale if we have to keep it up for long. But, in the short run, it's workable and will fill our needs nicely."

12

Everyone in the room was looking at Gillis as if they had never seen him before. The silence was deafening and finally Gillis couldn't stand it anymore.

"What?" he looked from one face to the next.

"Damn," Mitchell Nolan was the first to break the silence. "That's a hell of an idea."

"I agree," Jose was nodding as he studied the map. "One I had not considered, because I was blinded by my desire to keep the already established patrols and posts and simply add another layer of defense over them. Any objections to this idea?" he looked at the rest. Heads shook around the table.

"Very good, then. Let's look at this and determine where we need to place our sentry posts."

CHAPTER TWO

Olivia Haley walked with only slight trepidation as she approached what had once been the home of Leon Sanders, known far and wide as The Old Man of Calhoun County. There were others older than he had been, but there was only one Old Man Sanders. Political power, thumb atop the criminal element, enforcer of his own moral code of ethics, and possibly the most charitable individual in a five-county area, though he would have denied that with his dying breath. He had been what her father, wherever he was now, called one hell of a man. A legend, literally, in his own time.

With the death of Leon, his grandson Clayton had become the mainstay of the farms, a place where so many now made their home since the night the sky had caught fire. Since the night her mother had died, leaving her alone with her two small sisters to fend for themselves and leaving their father who knows where with a truck load of no telling what. An over the road truck driver, her father had made a comfortable living for his family of five, but it required him to be gone a good deal of the time. He had been gone the night everything had turned off, somewhere far to the west, perhaps on his way home from a run to California. She had resigned herself to the fact that she would likely never know. Nor would she likely ever see him again.

She had buried her mother with her own hands in the backyard of their home, then spent the winter taking care of her sisters and worrying constantly over them. She had gone about as far as she was able when the most unlikely thing in the world had happened. Hiding in a fire station because it had gas heat, she had encountered a group that had come to take the small fire truck from the station, hoping it would run so they could use it to fight a huge wildfire. Among that group had been Gordy Sanders and Kade Ramsey, two schoolmates she had known all her life.

The two had convinced her to return to the Sanders' Farm with them, where she and her sisters would be safer and much better off than they were on their own. Having already nearly starved herself into illness to keep her sisters healthy, Olivia hadn't required much convincing.

She had known the Sanders her entire life, having attended the same church as Gordon and Angela Sanders, the current patriarch and

14

matriarch of the Sanders clan. Good people who were charitable to a fault, Angela had instantly taken Olivia and her sisters into her home without a second thought, treating them as well as she might her own grandchildren. Angela in particular had been a godsend to the teen girl, patient and understanding as Olivia had worked through the trauma of the months she had lived on her own with her sisters.

Nightmares, sleepless nights, stomach issues brought on by months of not nearly enough nutrition as she gave most of the food she could scrounge to her much younger sisters, Angela Sanders had been there through it all, her soft, firm voice and kind hands soothing her, holding her as she cried her eyes out.

Kade Ramsey had also been there for her, and she had gradually come to care deeply for the eternally happy teen who had made it his life's mission to make her smile, and then to laugh, going to great lengths to accomplish both. But then Kade had perished defending the farm from attackers disguised as soldiers, shot and killed in the street as he disabled one of the vehicles that was showering the farm with machinegun fire. And her heart had broken all over again.

Angela Sanders had once more been there for Olivia along with many others as Olivia Haley had yet again endured a devastating loss. Even now, months later, she felt his loss keenly.

She had worked hard since arriving at the farm, currently working to assist Angela with the seed garden, the plots and greenhouses that were home to the plants that were literally the lifeblood of their future. Every plant they were nurturing would produce new seeds, seeds that would reproduce after their own kind, allowing the farm to continue to feed not only themselves, but also many others. Something they had already been doing even at their own expense, though with little enough thanks for doing so.

She was also assisting Doctor Thatcher with the plants that would make the medicines needed for the farm residents in the future. Olivia had studied chemistry at a college level even while still in high school and had impressed the doctor with her knowledge. At present Olivia's work in that regard was much like her work in the seed garden; maintaining the plants and ensuring they remained healthy and viable. Soon enough, however, the plants would come to full maturity and when they did, the real chemistry would begin.

But now, she had been asked to visit Byron House, also known as Brick, at Leon Sanders' house, where the huge man made his home. Brick and a young woman around Olivia's age named Janice Hardy had come to the farm along with Clay Sanders' girlfriend, Lainie Harper, who had been taken under Leon's protection when she was still underage and on the run from an abusive mother and stepfather. Leon and Brick apparently went way back, as the saying went, and the big man had moved in with Leon once everyone had arrived at the farm. Janice had as well and had spent the remainder of Leon's life doing all she could to make life easier for the Old Man, the only true father figure she had ever known in her short life of fear and abuse.

Olivia hesitated for a moment at the foot of the steps leading up to Leon's house, her trepidation returning. Byron House was a dangerous man, and one who could seem to see right through a person. He had noted some of the things she had done to try and make the fire station safer for her and her sisters, noting that many of them were things that a girl her age would not normally know. She had admitted that her grandfather had taught her many things, and that she had learned others from books that he had. Nothing else had ever been said about it, but Olivia had a hunch that she was about to hear more from Brick on the subject now.

Deciding that hesitating would not help her, Olivia took a deep breath and started climbing.

-

Inside the house, standing at the window overlooking the steps, Brick stood beside former soldier Kandi Ledford as they watched the teen girl climbing toward them.

"Brave young woman," Brick noted, moving away from the window before Olivia could spot him.

"She is," Kandi agreed, moving to take a seat. "Her body language screams reluctance, but she's still coming."

"She could not have survived the winter, or kept her sisters alive, if she were not both strong and courageous," Brick said firmly.

"Why are you doing this, anyway?" Kandi asked.

"We have changed how we teach the youngsters," Brick shrugged. "She knows a great deal and is closer to their age. I want to see how much she knows, and if she is willing to share it with the others."

"Can't others teach that stuff?" she asked, curious.

16

"Of course," he replied easily. "But it will be better coming from someone their age who has used it to survive, proving that it will help them as well. It will help Olivia as well, I think. She still suffers from post-traumatic stress, though she is afraid to admit it. I think she fears that she will be separated from her sisters."

"As if Mrs. Sanders would let that happen," Kandi made a sound that might have been a very delicate snort of derision. Before either could speak again, there was a knock at the door.

Brick opened the door to find Olivia waiting, her face carefully neutral.

"Easy, now," Brick said gently. "Come in, please, and take a seat," he waved her inside. "I have asked Lieutenant Ledford to be with us so that you would perhaps feel less uncomfortable. I hope you do not object?"

"No, I don't mind," Olivia replied, her words coming out in a rush. She moved to the nearest chair and sat carefully, right on the edge of the cushion.

"Olivia, there's nothing wrong," Kandi assured her, recognizing her nervousness. "The fact is, we need your help. Brick needs to explain what's going on and then talk to you about how you can help. Okay?"

"How I can help?" Olivia's nervousness turned to confusion. "Help with what? What can I do?"

"You had booby-trapped the fire station to protect yourself and your sisters," Brick noted, no preamble of any kind.

"Yes," Olivia drew the word out, nervousness and confusion now warring with each other.

"You told me that you had learned from your grandfather, I believe?" Brick continued, ignoring her discomfort rather than continue to call attention to it.

"Yes," Olivia repeated, nodding slowly. "I did."

"I'd be very interested in knowing what else you learned at his feet," Brick smiled, and Kandi was surprised by the gentleness the smile revealed.

"Why?" Olivia asked. "What could I know that would interest you?" She didn't stress the word, but she clearly knew of Brick's reputation.

"We are teaching the youngsters a new set of skills, you know," he stated rather than ask. "While those lessons are going well, they are always expanding. A growing knowledge base for living in the world as we find it now. Tell me; would it be easier, more comfortable for them to learn these new things from someone like me? Or from someone such as yourself, closer to them in age, who has already used them to good effect while on your own?"

Olivia didn't reply at once, seeming to digest the words slowly, a look of disbelief slowly forming on her face.

"You want me to teach…what, exactly?" she temporized.

"I want you to share what your grandfather showed you with the others," he replied, watching her reaction. "But, as I said before, I'd first be very interested in knowing what else he taught you, or that you perhaps learned on your own. I walked around the fire station before we tried to load the fire truck, checking the area. There was a pile of small animal bones some twenty feet from the building, where they wouldn't be seen unless you walked right up on them. I assume you were using snares to trap small animals for food?"

"Yes," Olivia kept her answers short. "I was."

"Olivia, honey," Kandi broke in, "if you're nervous and want to leave, then go ahead and go. No one is trying to force you to do anything. You know what happened to little Bobby, yeah?"

"He got bitten by a copperhead," Olivia nodded, glancing at the door before looking back at the blonde.

"Because of that, we're now expanding the lessons that the smaller kids are being taught," Kandi explained. "I want you to think about something. If your sisters had been alone, could they have made it even a few days before someone found them? Assuming anyone was looking to start with?"

Olivia's heart seized at the thought. The two had barely made it with her there to help them. Alone?

"No," she admitted quietly. "No, they couldn't. They didn't…don't, know the things I do. My grandfather died before either was old enough to learn anything like that."

"The goal is to make sure that if something happened and any of the children were isolated or alone, then they would have the skills to take care of themselves until they could find their way back here, or we could find them," Kandi finished, sitting back in her chair. "How to build a shelter, safely build a fire, find clean water or clean it themselves and so on. We want all of them to be able to do those things and anything else we can manage to teach them."

18

FIRE FROM THE SKY

"That's a good idea," the teen admitted, her mind now racing as she began to recall everything she had learned, either from her grandfather or from the books he had left her.

"We would like for you to help teach them," Brick said again.

"Some of the rest of you have to know that stuff," she shook her head in mild disbelief. "I mean, some of you were soldiers! You were a soldier, Miss Ledford!" she looked at Kandi.

"Just Kandi, sweetie," the blonde smiled brightly. "And yes, I was. But you know what? After I went through basic, I ended up in what we called Sustainment Command. A supply clerk, to put it simply. I didn't continue into any combat specialty because of that. I knew a good bit about computers and tracking programs and the Army decided that meant I was needed in Supply. Which meant that was where I went, and where I stayed. I would imagine you know much more in terms of survival skills than I do. In fact, I'm learning a lot of those things myself, right now. Just in case."

"And please remember what I said earlier, Olivia," Brick said gently. "Would your sisters, for example, rather learn from someone like myself, or perhaps Clayton or one of his men, or from you, or else someone like you? Someone closer to their age, someone more familiar to them and less intimidating. Less threatening. Someone they can identify with as they learn from them. They can look at you and what you've achieved and believe that they can learn to do it as well, because you did the same thing when you were their age."

Olivia thought about that even as her mind balked at the idea of so much responsibility. She had avoided as much responsibility as possible sense arriving at the farm, having been responsible for her sisters throughout the winter before. She felt guilty about it at times, but not guilty enough to change it. Working in the seed garden and assisting Doctor Thatcher with the medicinal plants was plenty enough responsibility for her.

But this….

What if her grandfather had shirked that responsibility and never bothered to teach her anything at all? What would she have done without the knowledge he had given her? The skills to survive, and to take care of her much younger sisters?

"As I said, you don't have to do any of this if you don't want to," Brick injected into her thought process. "We are simply looking for

19

options, and for the best possible ways to teach the young how to survive."

"I...I don't know if I can do it," Olivia managed at last. "I really don't. I can try. That's all I can promise is that I can try. Maybe I can do it or maybe I can't. I won't know until I try it. But I need to have someone with me, or at least watching," she insisted. "Someone to catch a mistake I might make. I don't...I can't deal with thinking they might suffer because I made a mistake."

"Completely understandable," Brick nodded.

"Absolutely," Kandi agreed at once. "Tell ya what," she smiled again. "Why don't you settle back in that chair and get comfortable, then tell us what you can remember learning from your granddad? Give us an idea of what you can do. Would like something to drink?"

Olivia sat deeper into her chair, nodding as she did.

"Please."

-

"Not that way," Seth Webb said gently, catching Anthony Goodrum by his jacket.

"What? Why not?" the slightly older boy asked, almost angry. "It's clearly closer this way!"

"And it crosses this creek," Seth nodded, pointing to the slender blue line running along the map. "In this cold, if somebody fell in, they'd have hypothermy 'fore we could blink."

"'Hypothermy'?" Millie asked, eyebrow raised. "You mean hypothermia?"

"What I said," Seth nodded without looking her way. "Look here," he drew Anthony's attention back to the map. "Creek bends here and runs down and away from where we need to go. It's a little further along, but there's less risk. See what I mean?"

"Yeah, I do," Anthony nodded, anger gone as he studied what he was told. "I didn't think of that," he admitted.

"I hadn't fell into a creek in winter myself, I might not have neither," Seth chuckled.

"What did you do?" Millie asked. "When that happened, I mean," she clarified.

"My brother Matty was with me, or I was with him," Seth shrugged, the memory stinging a bit. "He built a fire and a shelter and got me inside, warmed me up. Not for that, I'd have died."

20

"Damn," Anthony said softly.

"Anyway, let's bear west a bit and avoid the water if we can," Seth abruptly got back to the present.

"Lead the way, Maestro," Millie grinned. "Seems like you're the one with the answers here, not us."

"Here, here, here and here," Gillis made pencil marks on the map in front of him. "I think that would cover the arc almost perfectly as well as give adequate time for the response team to spin up. The terrain actually favors us rather than the attacker, at least in this expected direction, since there's very little concealment for them to take advantage of."

"What about behind us," Jose pointed to the area west of the farm headquarters, down the country lane that divided the Sanders' land.

"Our detachment at the Plum House can catch a good deal of any movement behind us," Gillis mused. "But I agree it is a weakness. The only thing I can see to do is place a tower behind this house here," he pointed to where Leon's house was indicated on the map, "and another roughly here," he pointed to a field southwest of the cabins on the Hill.

"Between them and the Plum House, we should be able to see everything," he concluded.

"Six towers is twelve men," Mitch said at once. "Another eight to twelve on the response team...we don't have the personnel for that," he sighed. "And I wish we did. That was a hell of an idea, Lieutenant," he complimented the young officer, who blushed ever so slightly at such praise from a veteran commando.

"Let's don't be so hasty to write it off," Clay spoke for the first time in what seemed like hours, studying the map of the farm that was hanging on the wall. "The first thing we need to do is get a tower up in a spot we know we're going to use, and then see exactly how far we can effectively see from it. We might not need so many. Let's get Jody and Heath in here and ask-,"

"Heath's TDY for the next couple days, Boss," Mitch reminded him.

"Right," Clay remembered. "Call Jody then, and anyone else who has sat a tower on a regular basis. We might as well see how far they can see from what we already have. For that matter, let's start putting a team together to survey from the tower behind my parent's place. With the leaves off, it will do for a test run."

21

"Not bad for a test run, huh?" Corey Reynard all but whispered into his microphone as he watched the small group of teens struggle across the broken ground of a frozen corn field.

"Not really a fair test with Seth Webb along," Gordy mentioned. *"He's got more field savvy than most adults thanks to his brothers and his old man. If they listen to him, they'll make out fine."*

"True."

"Don't do that," Seth warned, taking hold of Millie's hand as she started to spread her ground sheet out. It was meant to keep her dry as she slept and had to go down on the ground first.

"What? Why?" she asked, looking at him. Seth had much more knowledge that she did, so she listened to him when her spoke.

"Check the ground, first off," he knelt, scraping the snow away with a small shovel he had brought along.

"Where did you get that?" she demanded.

"Out o' my bag," he replied without looking up. "Look here," he went on, pointing to his handiwork. "In weather like this, when we have to sleep out, we want to scrape the snow away from the ground, moving it toward the wind. Same time, you look for rocks and sticks and such that can tear your gear," he nodded at her ground sheet, "or make you miserable." He held up a large rock as an example before tossing it away.

"Bank the snow toward the wind," he showed her what he meant, constructing a small snowbank between her bed site and the west wind that was blowing. "Won't help much, but it will help some. Weather this bad, any help is good." He handed her the small folding shovel before moving on to help someone else.

Shaking her head with a rueful smile, she started crafting a snowbank. As she worked, she wondered what her Ace was doing, and why he wasn't out here with the rest of them.

"Will you settle down?" Gwen Paige demanded, tiring of watching Leon Sanders pace.

"What?" Leon looked at her. "What am I doing?"

"You're wearing a hole in the floor," Gwen said with a raised eyebrow. "You do know that your cousin and several of his friends are out there watching over them, don't you?" she reminded him.

"Yeah, I know," he nodded, taking his seat, a frown on his face. "I should be out there, too."

"Is there anything they're teaching those kids you don't already know?" she asked him, smirking.

"No, probably not," he admitted. "Even geeks who live on a farm learn to toughen up and deal. We know all that stuff and have since we were little kids," he waved a hand away. "Can do everything except drive."

"What's so hard about driving?"

"You tell me," He snorted. "Neither one of us can drive more than a golf cart. And we've wrecked it more than once."

"I've seen the dents in it," she sympathized. "Come summer, I'll try and help you learn to do better. In the meantime, you need to go and get some rest. I'm here for four hours and then I have to sleep before I go back and help Lainie with the sewing. You have to be back here in seven-and-a-half hours to relieve your sister. So, go. Shoo," she made a pushing motion with her hand.

"I'm going," Leon almost laughed, getting to his feet and grabbing his coat. "I'll have a radio on if-,"

"-if I need you. Yes, I know," she cut him off with a smile and another shooing motion. "Go, I said!"

"Going," he finally smiled as he departed, heading into the cold, leaving an amused Gwen behind him, shaking her head.

CHAPTER THREE

"This is so unfair," Corey Reynard complained once again. "They get to have a fire and we're freezing our ass off."

"Will you shut up, man?" Heath Kelly whispered. "One, they're gonna hear you and that whine of yours is distinctive. Two, I can't hear a damn thing with you bitchin' and moaning in my ear."

The two were back-to-back in a small thicket of scrub oak roughly fifty yards east of where the small group of trainees lay shivering in their bags, the exceptions being Seth and Lila Webb, who had without a word agreed to share their bedding for warmth. The others, having no family among the group, were alone, none willing to approach the others about sharing blankets to stay warm. They weren't to that point, yet.

Fifty yards west of the small fire, Gordy Sanders and Kurtis Montana sat a similar, albeit quieter watch.

"Reckon they did okay today," Kurtis mused softly.

"I do wonder how much of that was on Seth, though," Gordy agreed, mostly. "He's smart out here in the bush. Raised in it."

"Seems to know his business," Kurtis agreed. He shifted slightly atop his own bag, huddled atop it for the warmth it could provide.

"You're first for sleep, dude," Gordy whispered. "I'll wake you in four."

"Sounds like a plan," the lean cowhand agreed. Tucking his scarf into his coat a bit more firmly before anchoring it with his hat, Kurtis then leaned back slightly against the small pine tree the two had chosen to place between them as a brace.

In mere seconds he was asleep.

-

"I don't want to be out here no more," Anthony Goodrum said from deep inside his sleeping bag. "I want to go home."

"Dude, you need to cowboy up a little," Nathan Caudell told him quietly. "There's three girls out here and I don't hear them whinin' like a baby. Get some sleep. We made four markers today and that was all. Still got seven to go. We don't get 'em, we fail. I ain't gonna fail."

"I don't care if I fail," Anthony replied sharply.

"Then take off on home, man," Seth Webb spoke up. "It's yonder way, around four miles, I conjure," he pointed in the general direction of the farm, northeast of their own position.

"Let's all go," Anthony urged.

"No thanks, dude," Nathan replied. "I've come this far; I aim to go the distance." With that he settled deeper into the warmth of his sleeping gear and ignored the other teen.

"I'll pass, thanks," JJ Jackson spoke for the first time. "I'm not really a proper country boy, but I'm learning. If I fail, they won't teach me anything else, so I'm staying."

"Same here," Seth and Lila said together.

"I'm not getting out of this bag until daylight," Millie Long said simply. "Now shut up and let the rest of us get some sleep."

Janice Hardy was noticeably quiet, having already gone to sleep, untroubled it seemed by the cold and conditions. It didn't occur to any of the others that she had faced far worse in her young life than a fire and a warm bag to sleep in.

Defeated, Anthony Goodrum burrowed into his own bag and zipped it around him.

-

"Hear anything from Gordy and his crew?" Clay asked, leaning into the radio room.

"No, but we don't expect to unless they have trouble," Gwen shook her head. "They're on a talk-around channel so they can talk to one another. Just FRS stuff. Gordy has a tactical radio if they need to contact us."

"Okay," Clay nodded. "Sounds like they must have it covered. Night."

"Night, Clay."

-

Zach had drawn the short straw today, having to work the line during the morning and early afternoon, then return after six hours to work the response watch. He didn't mind it, really, and had never said anything about it. And it did give him a chance to visit Amanda Lowery.

"Evening, Mavis," he smirked as he strolled into the clinic. He was instantly met with a thrown spoon, an angry glare following the utensil to him.

"Wow," Zach said with faked shock. "Somebody's not getting enough to eat, looks like."

"I have asked you, repeatedly, *not* to call me that," Amanda all but growled. "And it's not funny, you jackass!" she added when Zach began to grin.

"It is, a little," he assured her. "So, how are you? Pain any better? Can you move any easier?"

"A bit," she nodded, frowning. "Not like I want to, though."

"Take a little while, I imagine," Zach shrugged. "Not that I'd know."

"You don't want to, either," Amanda promised. "What are you doing?"

"Got the response watch from six-to-midnight," Zach informed her. "Then got to be back in the morning for another round on the same job. At least it's warm," he shrugged again. "You need anything? I can make short trips away, so long as they're quick."

"No, I'm set," Amanda shook her head. "Even got a book to pass the time," she held up a worn paperback.

"Romance, huh?" Zach smirked and Amanda flushed.

"Nothing wrong with that," she defended. "A good read is still a good read."

"Guess so," he agreed, getting to his feet. "I'll leave you to it, then. Night, Sarge," he snickered, barely evading a butter knife that clattered against the wall as the door closed behind him.

"Jackass," Amanda muttered, wincing at the pain she was feeling from two throws. Doing her best to ignore that, she opened her book and returned to see how her favorite characters were doing. Safely hidden behind the book, she finally allowed a grin to cross her features.

-

Leaving the clinic, Zach stepped outside into the cold, the sun already gone for the day though the glow of sunset was still hanging in the sky. He looked to the horizon before him, facing south, and felt a slight itch at the back of his neck.

He didn't like that.

Stretching, he bent to touch his toes then stood and looked again, scanning every inch of what he could see. Unable to see anything out sorts, he stepped back inside to find Jose Juarez. Gathering his gear first, Zach went to the small office that Clay used, which had become the farm's security headquarters, in fact if not in name. Jose was standing inside, leaning on Clay's 'desk' staring at the map on the wall.

"You got a minute?" Zach asked from the door, startling the former commando.

"I'm gonna have to get you a bell, *cabrito*," Jose smiled. "C'mon in."

"There's someone watching us," Zach said without preamble, catching Jose by surprise for the second time in less than a minute.

"How do you know?" the older man asked him.

"My neck started itching when I went outside a few minutes ago," Zach shrugged. "I was looking around, and when I started scanning south, just looking, I got the feeling someone was looking back. We got no one over that way that I know about," he added.

"No, not really," Jose agreed. "Closest thing would be a Hummer we have about...here," he touched the map. "Your instincts are pretty good, according to Red," he looked back at Zach, considering.

"Just stuff I learned from you guys," Zach shrugged again. "I'm fine to creep out there once the light is gone and look around. Maybe I can find whoever it is and put an end to them."

Jose actually considered that for a moment but then shook his head in a negative response.

"No. No, I want you here, on your watch. I do need to warn Jody and Mister Meecham, though. Meecham is in the Hilltop Tower and Jody is upstairs. You, Virgil and Nate have response tonight, right?"

"Yes, sir," Zach nodded.

"Make sure and fill them in on what you think, okay?" Jose told him. "We'll do all this quietly so that maybe whoever might be watching or even listening doesn't realize we might be on to them. Good work, by the way," he complimented.

"Just my job," Zach shrugged again. "If you don't need me anymore, I'll go and talk to Nate and Virgil."

"That's fine," Jose nodded, reaching for the phone.

-

Kim Powers climbed slowly to her feet, dusting bits of dust from her clothing. She and Xavier Adair were preparing for a workout in the small 'dojo area in the back of Building One, now known as T1, for Troy Farm One.

With Amanda in the hospital and Zach on watch, it was only the two of them. She missed the presence of each, though for different reasons.

"Seems odd to be doing this without Zach and Amanda," she noted, taking the time to stretch her arm muscles.

"It does, yes," Xavier replied absently, nodding. "We shall have to be accustomed to Miss Lowery being absent, considering that she will be somewhat of an invalid for the foreseeable future. Zachary, however, should rejoin us tomorrow, or the next day." He spoke from the floor, where he sat in a meditation pose of some sort, his tone indicating that he was giving her only a small part of his attention.

"So how is this different from being in Special Forces?" she changed the subject. "I mean, not teaching me stuff, but how things are operating here on the farm," she clarified.

Xavier turned his full attention to her then, a flat-eyed, predatory look that made her want to take a step back even though she knew he wasn't a threat to her.

Probably. One could never be completely sure about Xavier Adair.

"I suspect you have a rather romanticized idea about what we did in the old days, so to speak," he said finally, uncoiling from a floor in a lithe motion that to Kim looked remarkably like a snake unwinding.

"In what way?" Kim was almost offended at the term 'romanticized'.

"There is a great deal of difference between what are called 'dark' or 'black' operations and the community within the military known as Special Forces," he explained, watching her closely.

"What kind of difference?" she asked, head laying over to one side as it was now her turn to study him.

"Special Forces is a tag normally applied to such elite units as Green Berets, Navy Seals, Marine Force Recon, and to a lesser extent ODD."

"ODD?" Kim's puzzlement at the term was clear.

"Often referred to in media as Delta Force," Xavier provided, a slight eye roll showing what he thought of the popular and multimedia's ability to trivialize and minimalize something important.

"Oh," Kim's eyes widened. "Them I'm heard of."

"No, you've heard of the movies and books and other rubbish that are built around the idea," Xavier corrected, though not unkindly. "That is understandable, as the very idea of the entire operation was supposed to be a secret. I believe it was Benjamin Franklin, however, who noted

28

that three people can keep a secret only if two are dead. Detachment Delta was conceived by a gentleman who was himself part of the Special Operations community after having been an observer attached to a Special Air Service unit while in operations. The Special Air Service, or SAS, is the British Special Forces, at least the land element. That is simplified, but still accurate."

"But as to your question," he got back on track. "We were not a part of that unique fraternity. We did not go into insurgent strongholds and train their troops to fight, nor, at least as a rule, rescue hostages. I say as a rule because we did, on rare occasions, do just that. The difference between the real Special Forces community and our own meager effort to world peace was that they are all, or were before the Storm, recognized as part of the United States Military. We were not."

"What?! Why not?" she demanded, shocked at the revelation.

"Because, dear girl, the United States and most other free nations would never admit to having units such as ours on the payroll," he replied simply. "To put it simply, we were hunters. We stalked terrorists, child traffickers, slavers and other contributors to polite society, and we killed them, though only after extracting as much information from them as we possibly could. We did that without the pomp, circumstance or recognition that the true Special Forces community rightly receives. Or did, before the lights went out."

"But didn't you deserve credit for doing all that?" she demanded, offended on their behalf. "That was a good thing! Right?"

"I suppose, at least in theory," he shrugged carelessly. "But none of us were interested in recognition or credit, quite honestly. If we had been we likely would not have been approached to participate in the program to begin with."

"Then what were you interested in?" she asked, stomping ahead into areas where angels feared to tread. "Why do it?"

"I can speak only for myself in answering that," he smiled slightly, though as usual it didn't reach his eyes. "Simply put, I enjoyed it."

-

Jose had decided to cancel the patrol circuit that would have taken one or two of the ground watch out across from the main buildings and into the area that Zach Willis had indicated as a possible spy or observation post. He had also added two more people to the ground watch around the buildings, just as a precaution.

Tomorrow, he would send a strong patrol into the area to reconnoiter the area. Until then, he would wait and watch. Or have others do it.

He had debated with himself over notifying Clay but had decided against it. No matter how good the boy's instincts were, it was still just a feeling, with no hard evidence of any kind to validate it. Clay had nearly killed himself with fatigue and worry, and they had been lucky that Thatcher had caught it in time. Jose and a few others had been trying extremely hard to take different parts of Clay's burden onto themselves, and Jose's area was security.

He had taken all the steps that could realistically be taken tonight and planned to investigate further in the light of day. That would be sufficient.

As he started home, he felt the snowflakes hitting his face. It seemed it was snowing all the time, nowadays.

-

Titus Terry sat in the enclosure that was part of the Hilltop water tower, using a night vision device with a low power magnification to scan the area around the cabins. Two other people would be patrolling on foot down below. Jose hadn't said why he had upped the alert factor, but Titus had learned that, one, he didn't need to know why in order to follow orders, and two, Jose Juarez didn't do anything without good reason. And that was good enough for one Mister Titus Terry.

A soft noise below him alerted Titus that someone was on the ladder. He eased to the trap door and pulled it open to find Marcy George climbing toward him. He waited for her in silence as she finished the climb, then closed the door.

"It's cold out there!" Marcy said, wrapping her arms around herself and shivering slightly.

"Snowing again too, I noticed," Titus nodded, taking his seat again after pulling up a stool for her. He added a blanket to the stool for her to wrap up in. Kissing his cheek in thanks, Marcy draped the blanket around her and took her seat.

"I don't know how you guys sit up here," she said quietly. "Not in this cold."

"You learn to ignore it, after a while," Titus shrugged, once more scanning the area around them.

"I notice the security is ratcheted up tonight," Marcy continued. "What's up?"

"Don't know," Titus replied simply. "I was just thinking about it when I heard you coming up the ladder. No one said anything, just doubled the watch and said be alert."

"I was at Troy House earlier, and there's two people patrolling there, and two more around the Sanders' homes and buildings. That ain't counting the people out on the line, neither."

"Like I said, got no word other than we were upping the ante, so to speak," Titus shrugged. That hurt his shoulder, which had taken a bullet a few weeks back, before the Plague had hit. It was healed, but still pained him on occasion.

"How's your arm?" Marcy had seen that wince despite the low light.

"Hurts," Titus admitted. "Not all the time, just when I make a quick move, or maybe use the arm too much at once. Still getting used to it."

"Long as you do what Thatcher tells you," She ordered. Titus suppressed a snort, wondering at how quickly and easily Marcy had slipped into the role of 'woman of the house', even though they didn't live together and there was no house.

"Yes, dear," he replied deadpan, to which she responded by sticking her tongue out at him.

-

"I meant to ask you earlier how it went with the girl?" Sienna Newell asked her roommate, Kandi Ledford.

"She's hesitant, but willing so long as someone is there to make sure she doesn't do something incorrectly," Kandi replied. "I think Brick is right though, after talking to her. She does have at least a slight problem with PTSD. She needs help, but I think she's afraid to ask for it, or take it if it's offered, worried we would separate her from her sisters."

"Can't see Angela Sanders letting that happen," Sienna was shaking her head before Kandi finished.

"I said the same thing, and Brick agrees, but Olivia, I don't think she understands," said Kandi. "I feel bad for her. There are others here that have had it just as bad, if not worse, but most of them have a lot stronger support system than Olivia does. And we haven't done a very good job of giving her one, either," she frowned.

"Well, in our defense, there has been a lot going on," Sienna pointed out, pulling the blanket around her shoulders a bit tighter. "All of it pretty important, too."

31

"I know," Kandi nodded. "Thing is, how many others here are suffering in some kind of way? I mean, Beverly is great and all, and she's always willing and ready to help, but some people might shy away from talking to a real therapist. That leaves them with whatever is around them. And Olivia is not trusting to start with. Losing Kaden didn't help that, either."

"He was a good kid," Sienna nodded. "Didn't know him well, but he was disciplined and focused. Would have been a good soldier. No," she corrected herself, "he *was* a good soldier. The fact that he wasn't on the Army rolls doesn't take away from that."

Kaden Ramsey had been a friend of Gordy Sanders, one of five that had come to live at the farm just after things had turned bad. The six of them had made a teenage 'squad' of soldiers, and the word 'soldier' was meant in every sense of the word. All six were trained far above standard and were a boon to the farm when they were struggling to find enough manpower to handle things on the farm.

He had been killed in an attack on the farm by a group of people pretending to be soldiers, trying to take one of their vehicles. The operation had succeeded, but Kaden had died of gunshot wounds, likely before he had hit the ground.

"We need to have a girl's group," Kandi decided suddenly, breaking Sienna from her memory of Kade, slim though they were.

"Huh?" she looked dumbly at her friend. "What kind of-, what are you talking about?"

"A social thing," Kandi told her, her hands moving now to emphasize her points. "Instead of doing it down yonder," her Texan came out as she pointed down the hill toward the Troy Farm, "we'll use the Mess up here! Make it our own thing, see? It will seem more distanced from the goings on down the hill and feel more like a private club or something."

"Make friends and influence people?" Sienna asked with a smirk.

"Especially the *friends* part," Kandi nodded enthusiastically. "We don't hardly know our neighbors up here, let alone anyone down below. If we knew each other better, then Olivia and others like her might open up some."

"It's a good idea," Sienna approved. "I'll help you however I can. I would suggest you talk to Bev about it, first. She might have some ideas of things we could look at doing that would help."

"Yeah," Kandi sat back, considering. "Yeah, I might just do that."

-

"Is something wrong?"

Brick turned from where he stood, looking out the window in darkness, to see Charley Wilmeth standing at her bedroom door, looking at him.

"I do not know," he admitted. "I have a strange feeling we are somehow being watched, but I cannot see anything out of the ordinary. Perhaps it is simply my imagination," he shrugged.

"Yeah, how often does that happen?" Charley snorted softly. Since her arrival on the farm, she had learned a great deal about the people, particularly her housemates.

"Almost never," Brick admitted.

"What are you going to do about it?" she asked, curious.

"Nothing unless I am asked," Brick turned away from the dark window and settled into a chair near the fireplace. "It is not my area of responsibility. If I try to intrude on others, I may create a worse problem interfering with their actions. I will watch. And wait."

"That takes more patience that I have to spare," Charley admitted, turning back toward her bed. "But if something happens, wake me up. Please?"

"Of course," Brick agreed with a nod. "Sleep well."

"If I was going to, then I shouldn't have asked what was wrong," she laughed lightly as she closed her door.

"Indeed."

CHAPTER FOUR

Weather forecasts were a thing of the past since the Storm, and Gordon missed them. He checked his own small weather station, noting there was two inches of new snow overnight. He also noted the humidity was high, and the temperature was below freezing, setting the stage for frozen precipitation of some sort, most likely.

Pulling on his Carhart insulated coveralls, Gordon ran over a mental list of things he needed to do as he laced his boots around a pair of battery powered heated socks. He'd miss them when they finally gave out. Getting to his feet he took a toboggan, a scarf and his hat and stepped out the back door of his house, headed for the barn.

Charley Wilmeth was standing nearby, waiting on him to emerge, and smiled when she saw him.

"Land sakes, young'un," Gordon exclaimed. "You should have come into the house instead of just standing out here in the cold!"

"I enjoy it," she shrugged easily. "This time of year, with snow on the ground, the early morning is always peaceful. I spend a few minutes just…being."

The morning was still dark, with only the barest hint of dawn showing to the east. Work started early on a place this huge.

"We'll take our time this morning and check shoes and hooves and straps and anything else we can think of before riding the horses out into this cold," Gordon told her as they stated toward the barn. "Do you know if Miss Knight will be joining us this morning?"

"No idea," Charley admitted. "I didn't see her last night to ask, and she may be assigned to security duty this morning. I guess we'll see."

"I imagine we will," he grunted as he slid the barn door open to admit the two inside and get their workday started.

-

"It snowed at least two inches of snow after we went to bed," Seth Webb noted as the gang of teens policed their small camp.

"Turned a bunch colder, too," his sister, Lila, added.

"We need to eat while it's still dark so we can get moving as soon as it's light," Nathan suggested. "We got a lot of ground to cover today, still."

"True enough," Millie sighed. "What is this stuff, anyway?" she sniffed of the bar she had opened, a frown marring her features.

"Meal replacement bar," Janice Hardy answered. "Twelve hundred carefully selected calories chosen for their nourishment value. There are twelve grams of-,"

"Janice," Millie held up a hand. "Janice, please. Don't throw numbers at me like that this early in the morning. I haven't even had any coffee. I'll just take your word for it that they're good for me. Okay?"

"Of course," Janice smiled, dimples breaking out on her face, already red from the cold wind.

"They may be good for you, but they don't taste good," Anthony Goodrum complained. Most ignored him completely and those who didn't failed to grace him with a reply. Sullen, he continued to eat in silence, for which the rest of the group was thankful.

"We didn't make great time, yesterday," Seth told them as he squatted by the fire, eating his own energy bar and drinking a cup of water that came from melted snow. "We got to make up for that today, assuming we can. We need at least four more points today out of the seven points we still have to hit on the way back to the Terminator." It had been an almost automatic nickname when the 'T2' designation had been placed on Building Two.

"Seth, be honest with us," Millie spoke from across the fire. "Can we do this? Because if we can't get it done, and pass, then there's no reason for us to be out in this weather. If we can, then I'm in, all the way. I'm just saying that if we can't do it, then let's cut our losses and go get warm. They will let us try again, I'm sure."

"It'll be rough," Seth admitted. "I know most of the terrain, and while it ain't all flat, there's no major hills or other obstacles between us and the prize. That said, the soil is rocky and kind o' uneven here and there, which means even walking will be trouble, even at best."

"The sticker is time," he continued. "We have to reach the finish line by around noon tomorrow. The ground won't stop us, but it may be slow going at times, and this weather won't be helping. Wind's probably blowing eight to ten miles an hour, and it's got to be below freezing right now. Hopefully it warms up above that once the sun comes up, but there's no guarantee of that. And it's still snowing. So, we'll be dealing with windchill, covered rock formations and rough ground, and every one of 'em will slow us down. If everyone is determined and can keep moving, then we can do it. We can pass this and be done with it."

"And if everyone isn't and doesn't?" Millie pressed, glancing at Anthony Goodrum and then back to Seth.

"Then we ain't got a prayer," he shrugged.

"I say we give it a shot," Nathan said at once. He was already packed, sitting on his bag to eat his delicious and nutritious meal replacement bar.

"Same," JJ Jackson spoke for the first time. He was not accustomed to cold like this and was having a rough time adjusting. He had set his cup near the fire to warm it and was now cradling the metal dish in both hands.

"Me too," Lila Webb said simply.

"I'd like to finish," Janice stated hesitantly.

"Well, we've already froze our asses off for one night," Millie sighed. "Might as well make it pay if we can." Everyone looked at Anthony Goodrum.

"What?" he asked, looking from one face to the next. "I don't want to be here, but it's not like I'm going to slow us down on purpose! I just want to be home, where I can get warm. That's all."

"That mean you're gonna shut up, step up, and keep up?" Millie asked him, eyebrow raised.

"Fine," he muttered something else under his breath, but so long as he got with the program, everyone would ignore that. More than one member of the group had thought about how like his father, Darrell, Anthony was behaving. Millie went so far as to wonder how long it might be before someone had to deal with Anthony the way X had dealt with Darrell.

-

"Wake up stupid," Heath elbowed Corey in the ribs, startling him from a sound sleep. Instantly alert, he grabbed his rifle from his lap and sat up straight.

"Relax," Heath told him. "Just waking you. I can hear them talking at their camp. Sounds like they're going to keep on going."

"Great," Corey's voice was laced with sarcasm as he rubbed the sleep from his face. "Damn, it's cold," he shivered, getting to his feet.

"Temperature's been dropping all night, feels like," Heath agreed with a nod. He reached for his radio, but it spoke before he could key up.

"*You guys awake and aware over there?*" Gordy's voice came through softly.

"Getting that way right now, Lil Boss," Heath replied, knowing it would wind Gordy up some. He hated the nickname for some reason, but the rest had decided it fit him better than 'Chip'.

"*Thanks for that,*" Kurtis Montana's voice was just as heavy with sarcasm and Corey's had been. Muttered cursing could be heard in the background.

"Anytime, brother. Anytime," Heath smiled in the dark. He climbed to his feet and went to empty his bladder. He figured the kids in camp would be moving as soon as it was light enough to see.

-

Clay had almost crept down from his cabin to stand in the trees near Building One, or T1 as it was now known, so that he could examine the southern horizon without being observed himself.

The feeling that something was wrong had not gone away. Clay was restless and wary, but there was nothing he could put a finger to right now. All he had was a hunch. It was never wise to ignore a hunch, especially as one gained experience in such things, but you couldn't make a plan based solely on a hunch or a gut feeling. You could wait, watch, and increase your awareness, but that was about it. The ranch had done all that.

Now it was a waiting game.

-

Corey Reynard had slipped around to take the point position in the four-point diamond used to surround the struggling youngsters as they began their trek across the snow. Despite his complaining and 'whining', most of which was designed to just be funny, Corey took his job seriously when working. Knowing roughly the direction Seth Webb would go, it was easy enough for Corey to get ahead of the small group and stay to one side, in this case the east side, so that his tracks would not be visible.

Concealed movement was in no way easy. Movement draws the eye, and noise draws attention. Concealing signs of your passage was just as important as preventing someone seeing you move at all. If your trail was found and led to you, or worse, to your base, then an enemy might be able to use that to attack.

All the boys had been hunters, and knew the basics of concealment, and the use of camouflage, but their training under Jose and the others had taken that to an entirely new level. Even Jody, universally acknowledged as the best tracker in the unit, had difficulty finding and following their trail. This was especially true of Kurtis, who had not needed the training but had taken it anyway. He was long accustomed to moving without being seen.

Corey moved a few steps at a time, always a random number, working to stay on ground that would not reveal that he had passed that way. He would then stop and kneel, taking a long and slow look around, studying the area around him for hints of any dangers, man-made or not.

He couldn't afford to linger long, as the small group behind him might catch up, or even spot him if he was careless. This meant that he had to be quick, but not careless. Carelessness killed you.

Having seen nothing to alarm him, Corey rose from his hiding spot and began to move yet again.

Jose looked at the group before him, his face grim.

"We think someone is watching us, over that way," he nodded south. "No idea who, or why, though we can guess the why."

"You will be divided into two fire teams, one lead by Mitch, the other by Zach." Jose was watching Zach carefully as he announced that, but if the teen was surprised, he hid it well.

"After reaching the edge of our AO, you will separate, one team going east, the other west," Jose continued. "This will be a blackout operation, so no coms except in an emergency. If nothing else, today will be good training."

Lieutenant Gillis, at Jose's request, had placed his men along the defensive line facing Jordan while leaving Sgt. Gleason behind with his command as a ready reserve should an attack occur. Mitchell Nolan's team would consist of Savannah Hale, Freda Fletcher, Danica Bennet, and Stacey Pryor. On Zach's team would be Jena Waller, Carrie Jarrett, Eunice Maynard, and Greg Holloway. Jose had asked Greg to observe Zach but not to interfere unless the teen was about to make a major mistake.

"You have your orders," Jose finished. "Move out."

FIRE FROM THE SKY

In silence, the two teams turned for the southern border of the farm, adjusting equipment as they went and settling rifles into position. They were gone from his view in less than a minute, disappearing into the snow.

As he headed inside, Jose noted idly that the snowfall was heavier now. He had taken two steps into T2 when Clay's voice stopped him.

"Happy?"

"Not in the slightest," Jose admitted. "I agree with Zach. Something is wrong, somewhere. I just don't know where."

"I'm also in agreement," Clay nodded firmly. "Spent most of the morning before dawn searching the tree line, but between the snow and the bush, I couldn't see anything."

"If someone is out there, then this will either find them, or else force them to withdraw," Jose stated, though it lacked conviction.

"We'll see," was Clay's reply.

-

One minute, Corey saw nothing out of the ordinary. The next, he caught a flash of movement to the east of their position. His binocular rangefinder told him it was just over two hundred meters away. He scanned back and forth looking for more movement.

And then he found it.

Never letting his eyes leave what he was seeing, Corey raised his radio carefully to his lips and called Gordy.

"Ah, Lil Boss, we got a major problem up here," he said softly. "I've got eleven possible hostiles, moving with cover toward the farm. All are armed and trying to stay unnoticed."

"*Roger that*," Gordy's voice came back at once, though it did show his surprise and maybe a bit of tension. "*Stay there and wait for us, we'll rally on you. Whisper, get to the kids, get them stopped, and then rally on Raygun.*"

"*Copy that*," Heath almost whispered back. "*Moving.*"

"*Cowboy, you go ahead and move up to support Ray. I'm on my way as well.*"

"*Cowboy copies*," Kurtis replied, already headed that way.

Behind the group, riding 'trail' as it was known, Gordy raised his unit radio and broke radio silence.

"Operations, this is Chip with emergency traffic. How copy?"

After a minute of waiting with no reply, Gordy tried again.

"Operations, this is Chip with emergency traffic. Repeat, with emergency traffic. How copy?"

Another minute of silence. Worried now, Gordy tried once more.

"Operations, this is Chip. Please respond." When he got no answer this time, Gordy stopped trying to communicate. Either his radio was out or the weather, crappy as it was, interfered with the small radio with its limited range. He refused to believe for a minute that the radio room was unmanned. Muttering under his breath, he picked up his pace, moving toward Corey's position.

"*Boss, the count's up to fifteen, now,*" Corey told his softly. "*All armed, most with AK rifles it looks like. I also see a good bit of milspec gear in there, too.*"

"Probably from Jordan," Gordy said aloud, though without keying his radio. Instead, he clicked the microphone twice to let Corey know he'd been heard. Then he tried his tactical radio again.

"Operations this is Chip with emergency traffic, please respond."

Nothing.

One minute later he was kneeling behind Corey's position, looking through his own binoculars.

"Count is now seventeen, Boss," Kurtis noted, prone on the ground and tracking the intruders with the powerful scope on his rifle.

"They're headed straight to the farm, too," Corey noted, holding a photocopied map of the farm and the surrounding area. "Not that it was in doubt," he shrugged, putting the map away.

"*Kids are still and quiet,*" Heath literally whispered across the radio.

"Move up on us, Whisper, and tell them all to stay put," Gordy ordered.

"*Copy that.*"

-

One minute they had been trudging along, heads down against the wind for the most part, the next they were looking at an apparition that had appeared from nowhere in front of them.

"Easy, now," the apparition soothed. "Easy does it."

It took a few seconds for it to dawn on the small party that the apparition was Heath Kelly.

"What are you doing here?" Millie asked, surprised.

"You didn't really think they abandoned you out here, did you?" Heath smirked. "We've been shadowing you since you left the truck, making sure you were safe. But now, there's a problem. School's out for today. I need all of you to go to ground, right here, and stay put. Oh, and stay quiet, no matter what you hear. Understand?"

"What's going on?" Anthony Goodrum demanded, stepping forward.

"That is not you saying you understand," Heath almost growled, his voice low and soft. "It's also not you being quiet."

Anthony tried to outstare Heath, but that was a non-starter. The teen sniper was not going to be intimidated by many, and certainly not someone like young Mister Goodrum.

"We got it," Seth Webb's voice was soft, and serious. "We'll hide in that brush, yonder," he pointed to a small stand of scrub pine and oak about fifty yards to the west.

"Good deal," Heath nodded his approval. "Get over there and hide. Don't say anything unless someone calls out to you, and then only if you know who it is." With that, Heath was moving, heading east.

"He could have at least told us what was happening," Anthony grumbled.

"Will you shut the hell up and get moving?" Nathan Caudell almost hissed. "Save it for when we get home, okay?"

Frowning, Anthony began moving, though he muttered under his breath the entire way.

-

"Twenty-one, no, twenty-two, now," Kurtis observed, calling it out softly for Gordy as he tracked the line of armed men and women making their way to the farm.

"Whoever is doing this, they know not only how the farm lays, but also where our defenses end," Corey noted, studying the group.

"Operations, this is Chip, please respond," Gordy tried his radio again. "Operations, this is Chip with emergency traffic, please respond." The radio was deafening in its silence.

"Looks like we do this on our own," Kurtis looked up for a second, then returned his eye to the scope.

"We got to get them kids out o' here, man," Corey said softly. "Ain't none of 'em trained for this kind of thing."

"I know," Gordy nodded as Heath appeared over his shoulder.

"Kids are squared away in a little thicket about fifty yards west of their trail," he said softly.

EMBERS

"Jesus!" Gordy just barely kept himself from screeching in a far less than manly fashion. "Make a little noise once in a while!"

"That would defeat the purpose," Heath replied as he took to the ground near Kurtis and began to scope the intruders for himself.

"I got an idea," Corey said finally. "One that will get the kids out of the line of fire, and maybe get some help on the horn."

"What is it?" Gordy asked with no little trepidation.

"Well…."

-

"Surprised Jose put you in charge?" Greg asked as he and Zach lead the way for their team.

"Putting it mildly," Zach admitted, reaching down to pet the head of the massive Kangal hound that had decided to follow them. The woven collar around the dog's neck sported a tag that said 'Jayne'. *Stupid name for a male dog*, Zach thought.

"You guys have done really well, so it was just a matter of time before you began moving into positions of greater responsibility," Greg pointed out.

"I just don't care anything about it," Zach shrugged, his gaze on the trees ahead. "But I don't care anything about most stuff and that never kept me from doing what I was supposed to."

"What bothers you about being in command?" Greg asked, careful to use the phrase 'in command' rather than 'in charge'.

"It's not that it bothers me," Zach replied. "I just don't want to do it. I like being on my own. I work better that way."

"You mean you kill better that way," Greg corrected him, and Zach shrugged but made no further reply.

"There's more to it than that, Zach," Greg said carefully.

"You say so," the teen shrugged yet again, eyes still roaming the approaching tree line. "But regardless of what I like or don't, putting me in charge of anything just seems like a damn stupid idea."

-

"That is a damn stupid idea," Gordy stated, waiting only for Corey to finish.

"What?" Corey managed to look both offended and scandalized. "That is not a stupid idea! That's a damn *fine* idea, even if I am forced to be the one to say it."

"I hate to agree," Heath sighed, "but it's a solid plan. The guys at Plum house will be less likely to give you any lip. Kurtis and I can cut the odds, while Corey watches our backs. The main thing is that it gets those kids out o' harm's way while getting a warning to the farm."

"Anybody else feel silly calling them kids?" Corey chimed in again. "I mean, at least two of them are roughly our age. Man, whose idea was it to put us out here to watch over them?"

"Much as I hate to interrupt this little show, we got some issues here that need seeing to," Kurtis reminded the three lifelong friends. "Without radio contact, our options are limited, and our time is short here, fellas."

"Fine," Gordy almost spat in disgust. "It pains me to say it, but this seems like the best idea we can come up with. I'll get the…party," he settled for in lieu of 'kids', "and head for the Plum House. You guys," he looked from one to the other, covering all three, "do not get dead."

"Now there's an order I can get behind," Kurtis chuckled. "Let's move about fifty meters to the north. There's some brush along that little ridge that we can hide in, and we can move faster than they do. Remember to stay well to the west of them. We don't want to catch any friendly fire. I put the range at about two hundred and fifty meters?"

"Right on the money," Corey nodded, laser range finder in hand. "Lased the middle figure at two hundred and forty-nine. I love this thing," he added, putting the precious instrument away.

"Let's go," Heath said, folding his bipod up and ensuring his rifle's camouflage was not disturbed. "We're about to have a warmer morning."

"Nah," Kurtis chuckled, following. "They are."

-

"Any word from anyone at all?" Clay asked, stopping by operations.

"No, but there is a lot of interference on every band," Leon replied without looking up. "I suppose it's the storm, except normally it wouldn't be that big a deal. All I can figure is that this wet snow is covering everything. Our radios aren't really meant to be long range, other than our gear here, the gear went used to establish outposts, and the stuff in the vehicles, which is all a lot stronger than handheld stuff. I doubt we could hear Gordy even if he did call, to be honest. I'm trying to tune out as much of it as I can, but I'm not having the best luck. What is it that's going on, Uncle Clay?"

"Just a lot of people with a bad feeling, Leon," Clay admitted. "Started last night and hasn't let up."

"Well, that's just great," Leon sounded disgusted, his mind no doubt on the fact that Millie Long was out in the weather in roughly the same direction as the 'bad feelings'.

"She'll be fine, kid," Clay promised, a firm, reassuring hand on his nephew's shoulder. "Got two of the best shots and two of the best brawlers on the place out there guarding them. Try not to worry, okay?"

"Should I call Gordy?" Leon asked. "Warn them?" Clay considered that a minute before nodding his head.

"Go ahead," he ordered. "If they know we might have trouble coming they can up their own security." Leon immediately turned to the radio.

"Lil Boss, this is Operations, please respond."

"'Lil Boss'?" Clay asked, grinning.

"Corey and Titus came up with it," Leon chuckled. "He hates it, so we all try to use it."

"I guess it's not a bad name, all things considered," Clay mused. "What about the others?"

"Lil Boss, this is Operations, please respond," Leon repeated the call before replying.

"What about them?"

"Does everyone get a new name?" Clay clarified.

"I dunno," Leon admitted. "I just sorta work here. Why aren't they answering?"

"*Operations, this is Unit 50,*" Greg Holloway's voice was scratchy and barely readable. "*Any problems?*"

"Trying to reach the training op, Unit 50," Leon replied. "Be advised you are three by three, at best. How are you receiving?"

"*We have you four by four, Operations,*" Greg answered. "*Need us to divert up that way?*"

"Negative," Clay shook his head. "Too far and takes them off the patrol route Pancho set up. Charley Mike."

"Negative, Unit 50," Leon replied. "Charley Mike at this time. Lil Boss, this is Operations, please respond."

"I'll see about getting a Hummer out that way," Clay decided.

"Be a rough ride for anything," Leon noted. "Even a Hummer."

"Sometimes that's just how it is."

FIRE FROM THE SKY

Clay hadn't made two steps outside before the shooting started.

CHAPTER FIVE

Zach froze on a dime, raising a gloved fist into the air. Down the line, Mitch did the same. Zach waited for five seconds, then turned to make sure his team was watching him before opening his fist with his fingers spread as wide as possible. He then flattened his hand and pushed down toward the ground. Everyone nodded and began to move.

Following that hand signals, the team spread out, roughly five meters from each other. As soon as they made it, everyone hit the ground, flat on their stomachs, with Greg Holloway on the far west flank, his rifle pointing in that direction rather than front.

Zach looked to his left and saw that Mitch had given about the same orders, his own team now also spread out and on the ground. There was still a lot of open ground between them and the tree line.

Not knowing what was happening, they would hold in place for the moment. Zach knelt as he saw Mitch do the same, the older man's hand going to his radio.

"Operations, this is Thug. Be advised we have gunfire to our front and a bit to the west. Slow but steady. Likely marksmen. Please advise."

"I heard it," Clay radioed before anyone could speak again. "Hold position for now. If attacked, fall back and advise."

"*Thug copies. Roger that.*"

"*Gunner copies all.*"

"Get a Hummer and a two-man crew and try to get around to the other side and see can you figure out what's happening," Clay ordered Jose when the security manager came running up. "Gleason, rally your men at T2 for now until we have orders."

"*Moving now,*" the tough NCO replied.

"Gordy and the others?" Jose asked.

"Probably," Clay nodded. "They wouldn't break training like that for nothing, either. Looks like all those hunches might just have been right."

"Imagine that," Jose snorted, grabbing his radio even as he headed for Building Three.

"Doc, Archer, Petra, meet me at T3. Mission up!"

46

It barely registered on Clay that the three people had answered, or that Jose was taking three rather than two. That was fine. He might need the extra rifle, after all.

Having done what could be done, Clay settled in to wait for information. As he continued to hear gunfire from where his nephew and others were escorting a training mission, he really wished he could get Gordy on the radio.

-

It took Gordy announcing himself for him to be able to find the seven teens he had been escorting. He nodded in admiration as they stood up, having been hidden by the skills and cunning of Seth Webb.

"Nice work," Gordy slapped Seth on the shoulder lightly in approval. "Anyone hurt or unable to relocate?" he asked the group. Seeing head shakes from everyone, he nodded in silence.

"What's going on?" Millie asked, presuming on her position working in Operations as well as her closeness to the Sanders family. The shooting was steady behind Gordy.

"Looks like someone moving on the farm, and we can't raise operations," he slapped his unit radio with a grimace. "Heath and Kurtis are trying to cut the odds, plus the shooting will at least get the farm moving. Meanwhile, we're heading toward the Plum Farm. You guys will be safer there, and their radio should be able to reach the farm, plus I think they have a phone, now."

"They do," Millie nodded.

"Good deal," Gordy sounded relieved. "Probably three miles or so to Plum House, so let's get moving. Buddy up so that everyone has a partner. Seth, you lead off, I'll take the drag. Millie, you're with me," he winked, and the girl grinned. Her relationship with her, Ace, and Leon, had made her family to most of the Sanders clan. There was no denying the pleasure it gave her to have that sense of belonging.

"We should be in the clear, here, but eyes open and heads on a swivel just in case, okay?" he told everyone. All seven nodded, fear flickering across more than one face at the thought that they might encounter enemies on their way out.

"Let's move, then," Gordy ordered, already walking. "We have a lot of ground to cover and need to do it as quickly and quietly as possible."

Quietly but as quickly as possible, the small group started moving.

-

"They ain't figured it out yet," Kurtis drawled softly as he slowly moved his rifle to a new target.

"Don't seem like it," Heath agreed before taking another shot.

Three hundred meters and a bit more downrange, blood flew from the back of one of the enemy combatants before he hit the ground, never to move again.

"Nice shot," Kurtis noted.

"Thank you, good sir," Heath replied quietly, knowing that Kurtis' electronic hearing protectors would pick up his voice even while filtering out the louder report of his rifle.

"Y'all shouldn't really be enjoying this so much," Corey said from behind them, listening to their chatter. "It's creepy as hell, too," He was ignored as the two continued to target the combatants whose only reason for being where they were was an attempt to attack the farm.

Both young riflemen had been 'gifted' new rifles before Christmas. The entire teen contingent had, in fact, received new and improved hardware of different kinds, a reward for the good work they had done so far. It would also enhance their combat capability, a happy and added plus all around.

Kurtis and Heath had each received an M2010 ESR, or Enhanced Sniper Rifle, chambered for .300 Winchester Magnum. The rifles were equipped with a tremendous Leupold Scope and accompanied by a clip-on SNS, or Sniper Night Sight. Essentially, the rifles were good for both day and night use with a simple attachment that was easily carried with them wherever they went.

The pair were making exceptionally effective use of the new rifles. With the extreme engagement range of their current position, it would be difficult at best for their enemy to get the smallest hint of where their attackers were located. Attached noise suppressors would add to that, disguising any sound that might give the attackers even a direction to look for their enemy.

Each young man was a superb rifleman and equipped with an equally superb and highly accurate rifle platform.

It wasn't fair, really.

-

"That has to be Heath and Kurtis," Zach said softly, his voice carrying to Greg. The older man nodded slowly so as not to attract any attention with his movements.

"They wouldn't be shooting at anything if they didn't have to," Zach continued, his face a mask of concentration as he ran down his options.

"No, they wouldn't," Greg agreed.

"We're coming under attack, or were about to, and they caught it," Zach said suddenly. "We need to deploy for that if we intend to engage them here. I doubt even those two can get them all."

"How do you know there will be a bunch of them?" Carrie Jarrett demanded softly.

"I don't know it, but those two are really good shots," Zach explained. "They rarely miss, or even shoot when they aren't sure of hitting their target, so that means there are several targets out there. Plus, no one would attack this place with just a few people. It's suicide, and everyone knows it, nowadays. Even if this is a feint, there would have to be enough of them to draw us away from the actual point of attack. All that adds up to there being a solid number of folks sneaking up on us. Or trying to," he added with a chuckle. "They're failing, but that doesn't mean their attack won't reach us."

"I agree," Mitchell Nolan had low walked over to Zach's position in time to hear the end of Zach's explanation. "Suggestions?"

"We need to pull back to a better defensible position," Zach told the former soldier. "Somewhere with at least some concealment if not actual cover. We probably don't have the numbers for a standup fight, and I still worry that this is all just intended to draw all of us off, away from the farm."

"That ditch we had to cross on the way here?" Greg suggested. "Sixty-five meters or so back?"

"That would be a decent place," Zach agreed. "With only ten rifles, that would give us a good edge in defense and allow us to move east or west under at least some cover."

"Then let's do that," Mitch agreed with a nod. "Fall back by teams. Your team first. Ten-meter spread. I'll let Operations know." He reached for his radio mike even as he moved back to his own team.

"You heard the man," Zach told his group. Pull back ten meters, maintain our own five-meter spread, wait for the signal to continue withdrawal. Let's go."

-

"Operations, this is Thug, how copy?"

"Thug, be advised we have you three-by-four at the moment," Leon replied, watching a meter on the radio rack. "Say traffic."

"*Believe a major attack, or else a major feint is under way,*" Mitch reported. "*We are withdrawing about sixty-five meters from current posit to take up defensive positions in a drainage and irrigation trench running east-to-west. Will advise when in position.*"

"Roger that, Thug. Standing by." Leon turned to Clay, who was nodding.

"Best move they can make at the moment," he sighed. "We need to know more about what's going on before we can do much else. Everyone on alert posts?"

"Everyone is where they should be," Gwen Paige nodded, looking at her clipboard. "Shelters all confirm their rollcall is full."

"Then all we can do now is wait and see."

-

"That's five," Kurtis spoke gently, replacing the magazine in his rifle.

"Four for me," Heath replied before taking another shot. "Five, now," he almost smiled. "All tied."

"Will y'all stop doing that Hannibal Lecter type shit, please?" Corey asked, almost whining. "I'm going to have nightmares for weeks."

"Not afraid of a little blood and violence, are you?" Kurtis asked.

"I don't care about the blood, or the violence," Corey snorted. "Y'all doing this Freddy Kruger slasher-movie type shit, though? That's weirding me out." Throughout their banter, Corey's eyes had never stopped scanning the area around them for threats.

"Take it easy, Whiner," Heath snorted. "It's all good."

"And, we go again," Kurtis noted as his let the bolt slam home on a new round.

"Right behind you."

"I hate you," Corey sighed. "Both of you."

"Don't be a hater, man," Kurtis chuckled.

-

When the alert sounded, Samantha Walters had grabbed her rifle and ran for the tower behind the Sanders' homes, her assigned position in case of trouble. She was among the best long-distance shooters on the farm, and Jody Thompson's training had made her even more formidable. At the end of her training with Jody, he had given her a

50

Springfield M1A rifle with a heavy, threaded barrel and the best Zeiss scope she had ever seen. Considering some of the rifles her father owned, that was saying something.

The sight of seeing such a small woman with such a large and heavy rifle might have made some laugh, but Samantha Walters was much stronger than her slight figure would indicate. Muscles already well defined by sports and ranch work, the training regimen she had been through since arriving at the farm had made her a truly formidable power, considering her size. Weight training with Ellen Kargay had made her stronger still. As a result, pulling herself up the tower's ladder with her gear wasn't difficult at all. She wasn't even breathing hard when she reached the platform to find Vicki Tully already there.

"Hey there," Vicki said as she used the scope on the tower to scan the area around them.

"Hey," Sam smiled as she closed the trapdoor to the tower and readied her rifle. "Anything?"

"Just the shooting over that way," Vicki pointed south-west without taking her eye from the scope. Sam nodded and made her way to the phone.

"Operations, this is Gwen," she heard after one ring.

"Gwen, this is Samantha," Sam told her. "In position on Tower One with Vicki. All clear so far."

"Thank you," Gwen said before hanging up abruptly. Sam smiled at that, knowing how busy she and Leon must be with an alert on.

"I had checked in by radio," Vicki admitted. "Forgot all about the stupid phone. I was too busy trying to look around."

"Easy to do," Sam nodded. "Now it's hurry and wait."

"Ain't it though?"

Marcy George had joined Titus Terry on Tower Two once more, but this time Gary Meecham was there as well. Both me were busy scanning the area for threats when she arrived, so Marcy reported herself on post and began to assist.

"Marcy, if you would scan the cabins and the surrounding area while we try to sweep the area further out, that would help us cover more ground," Gary told the teen.

"On it," Marcy nodded, taking a pair of binoculars and beginning a careful inspection of the area around the tower and the cabins it protected.

"Do we need to go topside?" Titus asked without looking away from his own scanning.

"Not yet, I think," Gary replied after a minute. "We'll clear the area first, and then you can go up and take a better look. I'll stay here and set up the M240 in case we need it. Marcy, you can go with him up top and help him watch. Remember that you don't have a phone up there, so listen to your radio."

"Gotcha!"

-

Kim Powers settled into the bunker in front of T2 and checked her gear as Nate Caudell reported her as on post. She took the opening facing east, toward Jordan, before asking what was happening.

"So far all we know is that there is shooting coming from the direction of the training operation to the south-west," Nate informed her, Sienna Newell, and Mikki Reeves, who had arrived first. "Several people had a strong hunch about the southern approaches, and two fire-teams were sent that way at dawn. They're currently holding position about seven-hundred meters or so to the south, in a ditch that runs across the fields from west to east. We assume that the firing we're hearing is Heath and Kurtis, neither of which would be shooting if they didn't have a damn good reason for it. All we can do now is wait and see what happens."

"What do you think is happening?" Petra asked the former commando. He was the experienced hand here, after all.

"It's either an attack that the boys busted up, or it's a feint to draw us off the farm while they attack from the highway, or maybe from the north," Nate exhaled. "There are just too many options for them, if they're smart and patient."

"That doesn't describe too many in that bunch from Jordan," Kim noted with a raised eyebrow.

"Not everyone who has survived lives in Jordan."

-

It seemed like forever and yet no time at all before Gordy was looking at the Plum House in the distance. Seth had stopped, waiting for

52

Gordy and the others to catch up. Gordy gave the younger teen a firm slap on the back.

"Nice work, man," he nodded, reaching for his radio once more.

"Plum House watch, this is Chip. Please respond."

"*Go ahead Chip*," the answer was immediate. "*Plum House copies five-by.*"

"Thank God," Gordy almost sighed rather than spoke. "Plum House, be advised I am behind you with seven others. We need shelter for them, and I need to let Operations know that there is an attack headed for the farm."

"*Roger that, Chip. Plum House copies all. You're clear to approach. I'll raise Operations while you're on the way. Standing by.*"

"We're on the way in," Gordy replied. "Let's go, gang."

-

Faron Gillis was watching the highway from the hatch of the M-RAP that sat on the road, blocking access to the farm from behind the log trailer wedged across the road between the trees that lined each side of the road. His binoculars swept over the visible area to his front every few seconds, straining for any sign of a possible intruder or attack.

"Sir, we have movement across the highway," Corporal Raven Elliot said softly from within the vehicle. Gillis didn't look down.

"Where away, Corporal?"

"One hundred yards north of the interchange, sir," she replied at once. "At least twelve so far."

"Are they advancing?" Gillis asked.

"Not at this time, sir," Elliot shook her head, though the Lieutenant couldn't see it. "They seem to be marshalling in the tree line."

"Very well," Gillis sighed. "Make sure all stations are aware of that tactic and are looking for it. Inform Operations of that as well."

"Roger that," Elliot nodded, ducking back inside to where her radio was sitting. Gillis returned to scanning the area before him, wondering if this was the feint, or if it was the real attack.

But then, any attack was real when bullets started flying, wasn't it?

-

Clay listened to the radio traffic as he moved markers on the map that showed where all their people were as well as where they knew possible enemies were.

"This is a major move," he said finally as the phone rang yet again. "I wish we could hear from Gordy."

"Ask and ye shall receive," Gwen Paige said, holding out the phone. "Gordy, for you. He's reporting from the Plum Farm." Clay had already taken the receiver by the time she finished.

"Gordy, what's going on up there?" Clay demanded without preamble.

"Numerous hostiles working their way across the countryside toward the farm," Gordy replied at once. "At least twenty-seven at the last count before I left. Heath and Kurtis are trying to cut the odds as well as evaluate their actual number. Corey is covering them while I brought the kids here for safety and to contact you. My radio wouldn't reach."

"We had assumed that once the shooting started," Clay confirmed. "Look, this is just part of what may be a major development. I need you to get back and help the others. If the enemy tries to keep moving, I need you to shadow them. Get a radio from the Plum House as well. It may just be your radio. I'll order the men at Plum House to set up a man between you and them as a radio relay if nothing else." He paused, conflicted over what he was about to say.

"You'll have to do it alone, Gordy, the four of you," Clay said finally. "I can't weaken that outpost any more than I already have with the radio relay. I need the rest of them on alert and on post."

"Got it," Gordy said firmly. "I have to go."

"Be careful, kid," Clay told his nephew even as Sergeant Lowell Martinson came on the line asking for instructions.

Trying to forget that he was once again sending teenagers into harm's way, Clay started telling Martinson what was going on, something that his hindsight told him he should already have done.

-

Zach stood with Greg Holloway as they watched everyone settle into the ditch they had chosen as a defensive position. They should have been in there as well but waited for the rest to get set.

"Eunice, you're too far out," Zach said softly. "Move to your left a bit. Yeah, right there," he added as the young woman complied.

"Settle in, I guess," Zach told Greg, who nodded and made his way to the far right of their position. Zach had the left. The idea was to keep

54

the trained but unbloodied troops between them, hopefully steadying them and maybe preventing one or more from being injured.

"Operations, this is Thug," Mitchell Nolan whispered from Zach's left. "In position."

"*Roger that, Thug. Operations copies four-by-four.*"

"Now we wait," Mitchell said just loud enough for the rest to hear.

-

"I think they figured it out," Kurtis drawled, adjusting his rifle as a group of armed combatants made their way toward the small rise where the three teens lay hidden.

"Looks as if," Heath replied, changing his own point of aim. Behind them, Corey shifted in place, his safety snapping off making a louder sound than it should have.

"Okay, there are seven, no…eight to our front," Kurtis noted.

"Concur," Heath agreed softly.

"Ah, I think we got other troubles, guys," Corey said gently, moving to Heath's right. "I got six moving in the tree line to the south. No, seven now…wait…damn," he finally said.

"What is it?" Kurtis didn't move his eyes from his own target.

"Guys, I think the people you've been taking on were just a skirmish line or something," Corey sounded concerned for the first time since the shooting had started. "There's at least a dozen coming through the woods behind us."

"Did they bring the entire town?" Kurtis' consternation was understandable at this point.

"How many are left in town?" Heath asked rhetorically.

"Good question," Corey nodded. "Between the plague and starvation, how many are left?"

"What if these people aren't even from Jordan?" Kurtis voiced a sudden thought. "I hadn't even considered that until this very minute."

"Me neither," Corey and Heath muttered in unison. As the three of them considered that, Corey noted that the snow was getting harder.

"This is just turning into a doozy of a day, officer," Corey sighed, using an old movie line that was a favorite.

"Ain't it though?" Heath snorted. "Time to get back to work."

"We're working for ourselves, now," Kurtis agreed just before pulling the trigger, sending a hard-hitting round downrange.

"I guess that means I can't complain about the pay, huh?" Corey grunted as he tried to get closer to the ground, waiting until he could effectively engage the approaching enemy with his M4.

"Pay?" Heath asked in mock incredulity. "You get paid? I'm filing a grievance."

-

"Call Gleason in," Clay told Leon. The teen nodded and quietly called for the NCO on the radio. Thirty seconds later the old soldier trotted into T2.

"Sir," he reported, not quite at attention.

"I wanted you to see what we know right now," Clay said. He leaned over the map, Gleason joining him.

"We have known combatants here, and here," he indicated the borders of the farm to the south and along the interstate to the east. "We suspect there are others here," he indicated the southern border again, but east of the first spot by over a mile.

"This is a major attack, sir," Gleason said at once, studying the map. "If I may, sir, what do we have watching the north?" He gestured to that area of the map as he spoke.

"We're thin there," Clay admitted. "Covered and reinforced foxholes here, here and here," Clay indicated. "Each has two people in them at present. They were meant for three, but we're spread thin right this minute."

"Would you like us to reinforce that area?" Gleason asked, looking up from the map. Clay was shaking his head before the question was finished.

"Negative. We need your men standing by as a reaction force. Between what's in the field and what we have on defensive positions around the farm, your squad is all that's left. I've got Jose and two others in a Hummer trying to get around the back way and see what the hell is going on. They should be getting close by now. Hopefully it will be good news."

-

"Well, that can't be good news," Kevin Bodee said softly from the back seat as the Hummer carrying him, Jose, Tandi and Petra Shannon crested a small to find a ragged collection of ragged vehicles, horse drawn wagons and saddle horses on pickets. It hinted at a large number of people.

"Damn," Jose sighed. "Stop here," he ordered Petra. She nodded and eased the big vehicle slightly off the road, partly concealing it.

"Doc, on the gun," Jose ordered after a minute of planning. "Arrow, you're on me. We'll move up enough to see if there's anyone still around. If you guys come under attack, bug out and head back to the barn. We'll make our own way home. Copy?"

"Got it," Tandi was already scrambling into the turret.

"Keep a lookout for the kids, and for Gordy and his crew," Jose reminded them. "This is near where they were set out, isn't it?" As if to punctuate Jose's statement, the sound of two rifle shots cut the cold, still air.

"About a mile further along, yeah," Kevin nodded, his head tilted as he tried to decide where the shots had come from. "They're surely long gone by now," he added, frowning.

"Still out there, somewhere," Jose shrugged. "Let's go."

"Want us to try and raise Gordy on the radio from here?" Tandi asked. Jose had told them about the inability to contact Gordy earlier.

"Not yet," Jose shook his head. "We'll stay quiet until we know the lay of the land, or until we hear them calling for help." With a jerk of his head, he motioned Kevin to follow and eased into the woods, heading for the gaggle of vehicles and horses. He removed a suppressor from a pouch on his belt and attached it to his rifle. Kevin did the same, but then readied his bow.

It was much quieter and just as deadly at short ranges in his expert hands. They'd be quiet for as long as possible.

They had made it perhaps fifty yards when the sound of an M4 rattling off three-round bursts joined the two heavier rifles in the distance.

-

"Well, this is just getting better all the time, ain't it?" Corey muttered as he changed magazines. Cold hands made it more difficult than usual. Now taking fire from three squad sized groups, they were effectively pinned in place.

"How many of these guys are there, man?" Kurtis grumbled as he changed his own magazine.

"Definitely more of them than there are of us," Heath replied before taking another shot. "How are you guys fixed for ammo?" he asked after shooting.

"I've got fifty rounds, counting the mag in the rifle," Kurtis reported at once. It was nearly automatic for him to count his rounds as he fired.

"I got a hundred and twenty-five rounds in five magazines, counting this one," Corey tapped the newly inserted magazine in his M4. "I got three mags for my pistol, too."

"Yeah, I got that too," Kurtis nodded. "Forgot about that. Ain't used to having one," he actually chuckled a bit.

"Well, I've got forty-two rounds left, and that counts the mag I'm using, too," Heath told them. "I've also got five total mags for my pistol, so there's another forty, but I hate to let them get that close."

"I don't think we're 'letting' them do a damned thing," Kurtis observed. "I wonder if Gordy managed to get us some help?"

"Yeah, that's a great question," Corey agreed.

"I'm sure Gordy's doing all he can, knowing him," Heath told them, just before taking another shot at an exposed attacker.

"Forty-one rounds," he added following the shot.

-

"Pancho reports multiple vehicles and horses along Baxter Road, south of us and slightly east of where the training mission started," Leon told his uncle. "He can also hear what sounds like an M4 added to the heavier rifles, now."

"I heard it as well," he told his nephew. "Sounds like problems are increasing. Get me Pancho on the horn, okay?"

"Right here," Leon held a mike up and Clay took it.

"Pancho, this is Bossman. Any estimate on numbers based on what you see?"

"*Could be anywhere from fifty on up,*" Pancho replied at once. "*Got eight trucks, including one box truck and two pickups pulling trailers. Probably two dozen saddle horses, and at least five horse-drawn wagons that I can see. I can see at least one car, as well, and a tractor pulling a four-wheel trailer. There is no way to know how many people rode here in those rigs, Boss.*"

Too many for four people and a Hummer, Clay decided. And they weren't all, he reminded himself.

"Copy all, Pancho. Be advised the training group is safe at Plum outpost. Abandon your scout and see if you can find our wayward chicks. Take a deceptive course and leave them at the Plum outpost to bolster their numbers. Then get back here. Note we also have a threat along the interstate."

"*Roger that*," Pancho sounded as if he were running while responding.

"Bossman, clear," Clay returned the mike to his nephew, then scrubbed his face with his hands.

"Hell of a morning, ain't it, Boss?" Leon said quietly, with none of the mirth he would normally have used.

"Ain't it just?" his uncle gave a single, short chuckle at that. "Ain't it just."

-

"Who the hell are these people?" Kevin Bodee wanted to know as he and Jose clambered back into the Hummer.

"Good question," Jose nodded once. "I think that box truck is the one Jordan got when that bunch down south attacked us. The other vehicles I don't recognize, but none of them really stand out. I can't even begin to identify the horses."

"Must be the whole town attacking us, then," Kevin muttered.

"Or else someone already kicked their ass and took that truck," Jose replied. "Got no way to know any of that. Petra, we're going to look for Gordy's crew. Kevin will take you to where they let the kids out and we'll start looking there. You up for this?" he asked the young woman who had never really been under fire like this.

"Eat it with a spoon," she replied at once. "Seriously, I got this," she added when Pancho didn't immediately say anything.

"Good deal then. Let's get it on."

-

"Sir," Faron Gillis heard from below. He looked down at Raven Elliot, once more standing at the step to the turret.

"What'cha got, Raven?" he asked her. It was terribly unprofessional, but they were probably going to be in combat soon anyway.

"Corporal Tanner reports armed men and women emerging from the tree line across from his position. Sir, he is north of the interchange," she added, for information. Gillis knew where everyone he was commanding this morning was, but held his tongue, anyway.

"Very well," he nodded. "Nothing on the south side?"

"Not as yet, sir," she shook her head.

"Radio," he ordered, holding his hand out to her. She immediately placed the microphone in his hand.

"Tanner, you copy?" Again, it was sloppy, but he didn't have time to do it 'Army', considering the mess he was sitting in.

"*Yes, sir,*" Tanner replied immediately.

"Let them get on to the highway and then light 'em up," Gillis ordered without even a twinge of conscience. These people were attacking the only place he had to lay his head or feed his hunger. The only home he and the people under his command had left.

"*Roger that, sir.*" Tanner didn't seem to have any problems with it, either.

"All line units, be advised we're about to be engaged on our northern flank and front," Gillis announced to the others. "Be prepared in case more come rushing at us, and we are weapons free at this point onward. All units acknowledge." He handed the radio back to Elliot, trusting that she would ensure that everyone checked in.

He was certain now that they were about to be engaged. The question was, how many enemies there would be, and how well armed and trained were they? He knew he and his people would find that out soon enough.

The hard way.

60

CHAPTER SIX

It was bound to happen. There was too much lead flying in the air and too few targets for it. Corey was the first.

"New line coming from behi-," his warning was cut off by a heavy grunt as the teen soldier fell forward, suddenly gasping for air.

"Corey?" Heath looked around to see his friend looking right at him, blood seeping from the corner of his mouth.

"Corey!" Heath shouted, moving to check on his friend.

"Th-third t-t-time cha-arm, huh?" Corey gave him a bloody toothed smile before losing consciousness. Heath frantically grabbed his friend's trauma bandage even as he looked for the wound.

"Heath don't profile yourself-" Kurtis warned, but no sooner had he got the words out than Heath slumped away from Corey and onto the ground. A dark scoring had appeared on his helmet and blood was flowing from his left arm.

"Damn it!" Kurtis exclaimed, crawling along the ground to Corey's rifle, dropped from hands that had stopped responding to their owner. He grabbed the M4 and dialed the selector to 'auto'. Holding the trigger down, he allowed the weapon to spray the closest group to his position before fumbling a new magazine from Corey's bloody gear. Letting the bolt slam on a new round, he took the time to key his small radio in hopes someone was listening.

"This is Cowboy! Ray and Whisper are down! Repeat, Ray and Whisper are down! We're on a small ridge roughly three miles due east of the Plum House with hostiles on three sides in unknown numbers!"

His one Hail Mary thrown, he pulled his own rifle closer before turning Corey's M4 on the next group, giving them a reason to keep their heads down.

-

Gordy tried to push his fear for Corey and Heath down to a manageable level as he ran. He had to use some caution running in the icy, unfamiliar woods, but he tossed as much of it to the wind as he could risk.

As he ran, his subconscious cursed and flailed at all the things that were going wrong, starting with their radio problems. That made him remember that he had taken a new radio from the Plum House, which he now grabbed.

"This is Chip. I'm on my way back from the Plum House. Cowboy says that Ray and Whisper are both down. Our position was about one mile from White Oak Pond in Pasture Eleven, on a small ridge overlooking the hay field there. We need medical and transport ASAP. Be advised their position is still under attack. Anyone read me?"

"Chip, this is Pancho. We're cutting across the fields trying to get to your position. Your location intel helps. We're moving as fast as we can. Doc is with us. Copy?"

"Copy," was Gordy's one word reply. He relief at hearing Pancho's voice was palpable. Hearing that Doc was along was even better news. Knowing that his friends had help coming, Gordy returned his attention to trying to reach them as quickly as possible.

-

"Where the hell is White Oak Pond?" Petra Shannon demanded, her foot easing off the accelerator as she looked around her.

"Turn left, toward that clump of trees," Kevin Bodee pointed over her shoulder. "Pasture Eleven is that way, maybe a mile-and-a-half. Should be able to see it from there." With that he clambered into the turret and began to ready the M240 machine gun atop their ride.

"We need to get there as quick as we can," Doc said as he inspected his bag. Pancho thought that was a needless observation but knew that his friend was already considering what he might find and how to deal with it, so let it pass.

"Fast as you can, Petra," he urged his driver instead. She nodded, flooring the big vehicle now that she knew at least roughly where she was going.

-

"Uh, Clay?" Leon said softly once the radio had gone silent again.
"Yeah?"

"I know we're all busy and stuff, but...maybe somebody needs to tell Leanne what's happening? I mean, before she hears it some other way?"

Clay froze at that. He was already concerned at the news that two of his young men were wounded, but the jolting reminder that one was his niece's boyfriend ratcheted that up to a new level.

"We should wait until we know something other than he's down," Clay finally replied, his voice soft. "Until then, we don't know anything good or bad."

"Okay," Leon acquiesced at once, though his tone told Clay all he needed to know about his nephew's opinion of his decision.

It wasn't that Clay didn't agree, because he mostly did. But what if they warned her Heath was hurt and his injury was minor? Worse, what if they assured her that he was fine, but he wasn't? No, this was better. Not preferable, maybe, but better.

Meantime, he had to put it out of his mind and work the problem in front of him. Gordy was on his way back and Pancho would be there soon with help, including Doc. That would have to do.

"*Operations, this is Gunner*," Clay heard in the background and closed his eyes for just a few seconds, praying his decision was the best one.

-

"I heard Gordy for just a second," Greg mentioned as Zach moved down their small line.

"Me, too," Zach nodded. "Sounds like Corey and Heath are in trouble, maybe."

"You hear Pancho?" Greg asked, getting a nod in return. "Well, Doc is with him, and they're in a Hummer. They'll be there soon."

"Yeah," Zach nodded slowly, looking at the woods before them. "Where did all these people come from, I wonder?"

"No idea," Greg shrugged. "Sounds too organized for Jordan, doesn't it?"

"Not if the surviving soldiers are on their side, it doesn't," Zach caught Greg by surprise.

"I honestly hadn't thought of that," Greg admitted. "That might just swing things in their favor, sure enough."

"Makes me wonder what kind of gear they'll be carrying," Zach speculated. "They could have-," He stopped abruptly, lowering his head. Greg followed his gaze and saw immediately what had gotten his attention.

"Damn," Greg muttered even as he started counting. Zach was counting too, and when he reached thirty, he stopped, reaching for his radio.

"Operations, this is Gunner."

63

"*Operations, go,*" Leon's tone was clipped.

"Be advised we're looking at thirty, that is three-zero hostiles emerging from the woods to our front. Count is now three-three and rising. Estimated range roughly one hundred fifty meters."

"*Roger that, Gunner,*" Clay's voice came back this time. "*Be advised I'm spinning up some help for you. Engage at your discretion. Further, know that we're looking at a similar attack along the interstate, and dealing with the initial contact back to the west.*"

"Trying to spread us out," Zach nodded as he replied. "Roger that. Gunner clear."

"*Operations clear. Standing by.*"

-

"Red, I need you at Operations, on the double," Clay spoke into his own radio as he stepped outside.

"*On my way,*" Xavier's cultured voice replied. Clay looked to where Gleason was standing, listening to the battle.

"Sarge, I need three of your men to go with X," he told the NCO. "I want them to take the M-RAP six-wheel in T3 and reinforce our southern position where Mitch and Greg are."

"Roger that, sir," Gleason nodded at once. "Howard! Brigham! Hathoway! Building Three, right now! Ready the Cougar there for action! Mister Adair will be in command!"

The trio replied at once, moving at a jog toward their destination before Gleason was done speaking. Before they could make it all the way, Xavier was standing beside Clay.

"You heard?" Clay asked.

"Indeed," Xavier nodded calmly. "Orders?"

"Reinforce the position and hold it, if possible," Clay said simply. "If not, get everyone aboard and back to a defensible position and try again. I doubt we can send anyone else without leaving us weak elsewhere."

"Then we shall just have to be sufficient," Xavier acknowledged, already on his way. Clay wished he could go himself, but then he'd want to go check on Gordy, and then he'd want to see the interstate, and then there's be something else he'd feel the need to check. He had to trust the people he'd placed in charge. They were trained, experienced, and knew their business.

64

FIRE FROM THE SKY

He didn't like it, but there were a great many things he didn't like, and there were few of them he could change.

-

Gordy's breathing was slightly labored as he approached the last known position of his friends. Gunfire was popping in the distance, usually three-round bursts or full-auto fire, punctuated on occasion by the booming of a heavy rifle. He hoped that one of those was Kurtis, or maybe even Heath.

Topping the small rise, Gordy observed at least a dozen people moving against the small ridge, none of them even bothering to look his way. Going to ground, Gordy brought his rifle up and sent a three-round burst at the nearest figure. Seeing that one fall, he automatically moved to the next, and then the next.

Behind him, he could vaguely hear an approaching vehicle bouncing across the fields and hoped it was Pancho and the others. If it wasn't, then this was going to be a short fight.

-

The Hummer was bouncing alright, literally lifting off the ground every few feet as Petra Shannon kept the big vehicle hammering flat out, attempting to get to the others before they were beyond help.

"I hope this thing had the reinforced chassis," Tandi's voice sounded as if it were speaking through a fan.

"No kidding," Petra agreed, her own voice bouncing along with the Hummer. "I know it's rough, but this plowed ground is hard to cross, even frozen."

"I don't care how rough it is, so long as we-" Jose began, but was interrupted as the Hummer topped a very small rise and Kevin Bodee immediately opened fire with the machine gun atop the vehicle. Jose swore as he noted the numerous figures visible through the windscreen.

"There they are!" Doc said, pointing over Petra's shoulder to a small clump of brush. Petra immediately steered in that direction. She veered suddenly, throwing Tandi to the opposite side of the compartment as she dodged Gordy Sanders, laying on the ground.

"Shit!" she shrieked. "I almost hit him!"

"You didn't, and that's all that matters," Jose told her at once. "Put us tail first to our guys if you can. Doc, egress through the rear. Petra, you follow and assist. Archer and I will provide cover and try to get Chip over here as well."

65

"Roger that," Tandi replied, clambering into the rear.

"Yes, sir," Petra said at the same time, turning the big vehicle even as the M240 continued to hammer away above her head.

-

Gordy had assumed he was going to die when the Hummer came screaming over the rise behind him, but somehow the driver, whoever it was, had managed not only to miss him entirely, but continue moving on course without pause. That was intense driving. The Hummer going past him meant he was still alone, however, and the passing vehicle had drawn attention to his location. He was now taking significant fire and knew he needed to relocate. He began to low crawl his way toward the Hummer. He would move twenty or thirty yards on his belly, then get to his feet and run for the vehicle, exposing himself as little as possible.

That sounded like a good plan.

-

"Are we sure this is a good plan?" Stacey Pryor asked gently, his voice carrying to Mitchell Nolan.

"Best of any I can come up with," Mitchell shrugged, not taking his eyes from the advancing enemy. "We have to hold somewhere, and short of a prior fixed position, this is the most ideal location."

"That is true," Stacey acknowledged. The ditch was more like a trench, over four feet deep and at least five feet wide. There was no water now, though there was plenty of snow. Still, it provided cover and concealment in the face of a far superior number of personnel. About all you could ask for in their situation.

There was a three-round burst of gunfire to his right, and the battle was joined.

-

Zach itched to be moving. He didn't like this. Didn't like being stuck in one place, didn't like being responsible for so many people, didn't like giving the enemy any advantage he didn't have to. He should be moving behind the approaching enemy right now, following them and killing them silently, one after another. He knew some might find that distasteful or dishonorable, but that didn't bother him. These people were his enemies, intent on taking the only home he had left from him.

There was no getting out of it, however. The older men in the group, the more experienced men in other words, refused to make decisions, looking to him for orders. He was reasonably sure that if he screwed up, one of them would point it out or even take over. He had been tempted for a few seconds to test that theory but discarded the idea almost as soon as it formed. Xavier would never approve of such a thing, and Xavier's approval was one of the few things Zach found to be important to him.

Thus, here he was, tracking a target with his M4. Almost sighing his breath part way out, he squeezed the trigger gently.

And then there was nothing but shooting.

-

"Sounds like Greg and his group are engaged," Clay murmured, mostly to himself. He was surprised when Gleason answered.

"Sounds like," the NCO agreed. "I don't hear anything other than rifles, so far, sir," he added, head cocked to one side. "Either their attackers lack heavy weapons, or they haven't brought them into play as yet."

"If we're being attacked by what's left in Jordan, we have to assume they have heavy weapons," Clay nodded slowly, running things over in his mind. "They would have not only the gear we left them, but whatever was left from the detachment you had there. For all we know, the survivors of your group are with them, which would levy them with experience as well as whatever heavy weapons they may still have. No offense," he added as he turned to look at the old soldier.

"None taken," Gleason assured him. "Thought of it myself. Cut off, leadership gone, no source of command or resupply, no mission orders going forward, the list just keeps piling up. There comes a point you stop fighting for Uncle Sam and start fighting for yourself. The way things sit now, I won't hold it against any man or woman to be doing what's best for them, absent any other information."

"Makes sense," Clay took a deep breath and released it, watching his breath to vapor in the cold morning air. "Truthfully, if they weren't attacking us, I'd feel the same way. I think now, after the plague, it's going to be strictly dog eats dog. What little we had saved and had rebuilt since the Storm is all gone now. The fire is truly out and all we'll have are a few embers scattered around the world. I plan for this place to be one of those embers," he told Gleason flatly.

"So do I, Lieutenant," Gleason nodded. "This is home, now. All most of us have. We got nowhere to go from here."

"You've got a home here so long as you want it, Sarge," Clay promised, turning for the door to T2. "I need to get back."

-

"Left. Left, LEFT!" Zach's call was louder and louder as he tried to call attention to a group of people moving behind the enemy's front line, crossing left behind the confusion to try and flank the defender's position.

"Got it!" Mitchell Nolan acknowledged.

"More coming from the woods," Jena Waller called from Zach's left. Zach saw them and swore softly to himself.

"Operations, Gunner," he spoke into his radio. "Enemy count now fifty plus, say again fifty plus. Continuing to emerge from the wood at this time. If you're sending help, now would be the time."

"Hold tight, Gunner," Xavier Adair's voice replied instead of Leon Tillman. *"We shall be there momentarily and have brought a lovely surprise for our unannounced visitors."*

"Roger that, X," Zach nearly grinned. Business was about to pick up.

-

"Heath, can you hear me?" Tandi asked, huddling over Heath Kelly.

"Yufm," the younger man grunted. His voice was slightly slurred, his eyes looking unfocused.

"Heath, look at me," Tandi ordered, penlight moving. "Heath. Heath!" Tandi shook the young man by his good shoulder. "That's it, bud. Look here for me. Looks like you took a round on the Kevlar pot, Heath. Must have just grazed you and bounced over. Left a gash in the helmet and a knot on your head. Okay, arm wound…pretty sure your left arm is broken, buddy." He quickly secured the trauma bandage from Heath's gear around the arm and strapped it to his chest to keep it immobile, then moved to Heath's left leg.

"Through and through here, looks like," Tandi spoke more to himself, then produced a second trauma pad for that wound.

"Okay, you're good for the moment," he promised. "Lay still until we can maybe suppress this shit enough to get you loaded. Read?"

Unable to speak effectively, Heath nodded, but then reached for his rifle. Tandi stopped him, grabbing the outstretched hand and moving it back down.

"No, no, bud. You're done for today. Now sit still while I check on Corey." The little medic didn't wait for Heath to nod again but instead went straight to work on the next patient.

Tandi tore open Corey's collar and pressed fingers against the young soldier's neck, first on the right side, then the left. Next was an ear to the chest, followed by the penlight to the eyes again. His movements had become increasingly frantic, but now slowed to a crawl as he lowered his forehead to Corey's chest.

"What is it?" Petra was watching, splitting her time between watching Doc and being there to help him and watching the enemy as Kevin Bodee continued to hammer at the approaching enemy with the machine gun. Supported by rifle fire from both sides of the Hummer courtesy of Heath, Jose and Gordy, the enemy advance on the small position had been halted for the time being.

"I'm sorry, kid," he said too softly for anyone else to hear. "I am so very sorry."

-

Gordy had waited until everyone at the Hummer was firing before erupting from the ground and running flat out for the vehicle. He could almost feel rounds kicking the ground and buzzing through the air around him, but he ignored those in favor of going faster. He never slowed down, instead diving for the ground and sliding part way beneath the big vehicle on the ice.

"What do you need me to do?" he shouted to Jose from the rear passenger door.

"Help Doc!" Jose replied. "We need to get loaded and get the hell out o' Dodge! There's too many to hold here!"

"Got it!" Gordy slipped and slithered his way behind the Hummer, stopping short as he saw Tandi Maseo lower his head to Corey's chest. He could see Tandi's lips moving but not hear what he was saying. Behind him, Heath sat on the ground, blood-soaked bandages on his arm and leg, his face blank. Kurtis was prone, still shooting. Petra Shannon was there as well, standing guard over Doc while the medic worked.

"Doc?"

Tandi's head jerked up at the word, his gaze finding Gordy immediately.

"Help me get them loaded," Tandi ordered, pointing to Heath first. Gordy nodded and moved to Heath's side, careful to keep the bulk of the Hummer between him and the incoming fire.

"C'mon, buddy," he told Heath softly, putting an arm beneath Heath's undamaged shoulder and levering his friend off the ground. "Let's get you guys the hell out of here."

"Hmfh," Heath's voice sounded hollow. He was able, barely, to place some weight on his injured leg and help Gordy assist him.

As Gordy helped Heath into the rear of the Hummer, Doc looked at Petra and jerked his head toward Corey Reynard.

"Give me a hand with him," he ordered. The young woman nodded, slinging her rifle and moving to help get Corey off the ground and into the vehicle. They moved to the back of the vehicle, where Gordy was waiting to help with Corey, Heath bundled up and leaning against the seat wall.

"Get behind the wheel and be ready," Doc told Petra and she nodded jerkily, clambering over and through to the front seat, careful to keep down.

"Doc," Gordy frowned as he placed Corey next to Heath.

"I'm sorry, Gordy," Doc gripped Gordy's shoulder lightly and squeezed. "He was gone when we arrived."

With that, Doc was back outside, grabbing equipment and telling Kurtis it was time to get loaded. The hunter grabbed his gear and rolled in behind the Hummer before clambering to his feet and jumping inside.

"Go ahead and get in the back seat," Gordy told him absently, still looking at the body of his friend. "I'll get this back here."

"I'm sorry," Kurtis said before doing as Gordy instructed. Gordy nodded slowly as he closed the door, preparing it to allow him to fire out the rear window behind the Hummer.

"Me too."

In the back seat, Doc was yelling at Jose.

"Pancho! Let's go!"

Jose didn't need to be told twice. He crawled into the passenger seat and closed the door, looking to Petra Shannon.

"Punch it!"

Kevin Bodee turned the turret as the Hummer moved, continuing to hammer at their approaching enemy with the machine gun even as the group was forced to withdraw. In the front seat, Jose considered their

70

options before pointing out a path for Petra to follow. One that would leave a false trail to follow if any of the attacking force decided to try.

Once they hit the roadway, they turned for the Plum House. Kurtis and Gordy could stay there to bolster that flank while Jose returned to the clinic with Heath and Corey.

Corey.

Tandi's stone faced look told Jose all he needed to know about Corey.

There would be yet another empty chair on the farm.

CHAPTER SEVEN

People continued to pour out of the woods to the front of Zach's position and the teen wondered how many could still be coming. This was a massive, coordinated attack on the farm.

A sharp grunt from his right made Zach look in that direction in time to see Jena Waller fall back into the ditch, blood flowing from both the front and back of her shoulder. Carrie Jarrett knelt quickly at her side, pulling her pack off as she did. In seconds she was evaluating Jena's wound exactly as Tandi had taught her, bandaging it tight to prevent further blood loss.

Zach turned his attention back to the fight in front of him. He couldn't spare any time to check on Jena's condition. Not with two rifles now out of the fight for the time being.

"Medic!"

That call came from his left, further down the ditch. Savannah Hale was leaning over a prone Stacey Pryor, probably looking for injuries. Even as Zach looked, blood flew from Savannah's right thigh, and she grabbed her leg and went down.

Carrie Jarrett was moving their way before Zach could tell her to, her medical bag in one hand and rifle in the other. Zach once more returned his focus to the battle. They were quickly losing this one, and it was too late to withdraw. They would be cut to pieces trying to escape over open ground with so many people shooting at them.

Whatever X was doing, Zach hoped he did it quick.

-

"Our comrades have taken refuge in a large ditch," Xavier told his crew. "We will position the vehicle as close to the center of their line as possible," he instructed Elijah Brigham, "nose on the enemy. You," he pointed at Specialist Brannon Howard. "Are you capable of manning the Deuce?"

"I am," the man nodded firmly.

"Outstanding. Do so and use the fifty to cover us and them. We shall work to get any wounded aboard and then examine whether we can hold or not. I suspect not, based on the reports of increasing enemy numbers, but we shall see. You will join me on the ground," he told Vince

Hathoway. "Let's have the gun up now, just in case," he added to Howard. The other man nodded and scrambled for the turret.

"And now, my friends, unto the breach we go," Xavier said aloud, though to no one in particular.

-

Faron Gillis sighed as the opening shots of his own battle drowned out the battle to his rear. Tanner and his team had opened fire, which meant that the aggressors they faced had reached the interstate. The sounds of multiple rifles as well as the hammering of a SAW came to him now from his own left.

"Report to Operations that we are engaged, Corporal," he ordered his medic and temporary radio operator.

"Yes sir!" Raven Elliot called from below.

Gillis chewed on his lower lip for a moment, considering his options. He currently had a total of eleven people on the line facing the interstate, including Corporal Elliot and his driver, PFC Dezi Martin. The remaining nine were spread across the front. Four of his own men, two more of Gleason's troops, and three of the young female troopers trained by the farm. Some might question their presence, or their ability, but Gillis wasn't in that number. He had seen these women in training and was certain they knew their business. To him, that was all that mattered.

"Operations is aware of our situation, sir," Elliot called from inside.

"Very well. Have all other posts report status, please," he called down. She acknowledged and continued to work the radio.

Three people out of nine that were on the line were now engaged, probably against high odds. The SAW would help, but if the numbers were very great, he would have to shuttle help to Tanner from elsewhere. That would leave his line even weaker than it was now.

He briefly considered ordering Tanner to withdraw and take up a position near the M-RAP behind him. Let their enemy come through the woods and into the open where the heavy weapons mounted on Cougar could be brought to bear and make a greater impact.

After a few seconds he decided against it, at least for the present. If Tanner felt he couldn't hold then he would report that, and Gillis could decide what to do.

Meanwhile, he listened.

-

Zach heard a heavy machine gun start hammering somewhere to his left and feared the worst; that the enemy had somehow brought up a BMG and gotten it operational. That would make a desperate situation much worse.

Even as he began to doubt their ability to save themselves, let alone to hold their position, he heard a heavy engine. Risking a look behind him, he saw the six-wheel Cougar named *Phantom* bouncing across the rough, frozen ground, a fifty-caliber machinegun cutting through the enemy and forcing them to go to ground.

"Hell yeah," he nodded to himself, his confidence restored for the moment. He watched as the big rig pulled right up to the ditch, placing itself at the center of the small defensive line. The back doors opened and Xavier and a soldier whose name Zach couldn't remember hearing, hit the ground and began crawling toward the ditch.

"Medic!" Greg Holloway called just then, and Zach whipped around to see the former Marine kneeling over Eunice Maynard. After a few seconds of effort, Greg looked up at Zach and shook his head slowly. Maynard was gone.

"Damn it!" Zach swore to himself. They were losing people left and right. A glance back to the left saw yet another person down, this one Freda Fletcher, her face covered in blood as Jena tried to check on her.

"Seems you've a bit of a situation, Zachary," Xavier's voice was calm as ever as he dropped into the ditch, the other man right behind him.

"Ain't we though?" Zach nodded. "We're in a bad way, even with you and that fifty helping. We've lost five people so far. I hate to give them the field, but we can't hold them here, even with the Cougar. And if they have an RPG somewhere, then that's that."

"What do you intend to do, then?" Xavier inquired, shooting two people who tried to dash for the ditch right in front of him.

"We need to load up in that M-RAP and pull back to a better position. There are two bunkers on this side of the road in front of the Troy House, one across from the Sanders' homes, and one more on the slope to the Hill. We need to spread out to those bunkers and try to cut away at their numbers with heavy weapons."

"An excellent idea," Xavier approved. "Bossman ordered us to hold if possible and withdraw if not. I concur we cannot hold in the face of such overwhelming numbers. We should detail two men to loading our casualties while the rest of us provide cover."

"See to that if you will," Zach nodded. "I'm going to start shrinking the line down as we do, until we're concentrated in front of the Cougar."

"Excellent idea," Xavier nodded before turning to the man beside him and issuing orders. Waving at the driver to join them, Xavier pointed to the far end of the ditch and sent the two scrambling that way with orders to stay low and to move beneath the Cougar in order to return to the rear door.

"We can run a line beneath the vehicle and use it to pull the wounded to the rear using the Cougar as cover," Xavier noted. "I will get that set up. Don't get dead," he grinned, patting Zach's shoulder.

"Do my best," Zach promised with a nod.

-

Mitch Nolan had received a 'cut', a graze that drew blood, on his right arm at some point. He had tied it off with a handkerchief he carried in his pocket, judging the wound nowhere near bad enough to waste a trauma bandage on it. He also had a stinger on his temple, probably from a ricochet of some kind from somewhere. He had let it bleed so far, but it would need bandaging soon to stop the bleeding.

Mitch ducked below the lip of the ditch to change his magazine and observed two Guard troopers carrying a bundle that looked familiar. When the two passed by him, Mitch realized the bundle was Stacy Pryor.

Stunned for a few seconds, Mitch watched the two carrying him to the front of the M-RAP, at which point he stopped watching and returned to the line, his mind racing.

Edge was dead. He had known Stacey for a long time, Mitch had. Years. Years spent in combat and in some truly spectacular drunken exploits around the seediest bars in Southeast Asia, Africa and the Philippines, not to mention South America.

That was all done now, Mitch realized. Stacey was going to meet Bear and wait for the rest.

Pushing that from his mind, Mitch began to target the approaching enemy more carefully. He needed to kill as many as he could. For Edge.

-

Greg Holloway began working his way toward the center of the line, firing as he went. A glance down the ditch line was all it took to realize that this engagement had already cost the farm more than most of the others combined.

Carrie and one of the troopers that had accompanied Xavier, Brigham his name tag said, had crawled beneath the M-RAP to the rear of the vehicle. From there, they began pulling wounded beneath the vehicle the same way, using it for whatever cover it could provide. Jena Waller and Savannah Hale were both loaded first, as they were wounded. The bodies of Stacey Pryor, Eunice Maynard and Freda Fletcher, who had died even as Carrie had worked on her wounds, were next. Bundled together, they were dragged beneath the vehicle by Brigham, Hathoway and Carrie Jarrett as a team.

Then it was time for the living to go. Mitch and Danica Bennet went first, Danica's motion almost frantic as she crawled underneath the M-RAP. Once they were at the rear, the two joined Brigham and Hathoway on each side of the vehicle, adding their rifle fire to the machinegun to cover the rest of the line as they withdrew.

This left Greg, Zach and Xavier still in the ditch. They wasted no time in making their way to the rear door, where the others were already boarding. Vince Hathoway had made his way to the driver's seat and waited for the last members of the group to be loaded. All the while Brannon Howard continued to sweep the field before them with the BMG, the big rounds killing many and horrifically wounding those 'lucky' enough not to be killed outright.

"That's it!" Zach called from the rear hatch, having been the last one aboard as 'commander' of the patrol. "Let's move!"

Hathoway eased the vehicle back and away from the ditch, which gave Howard time to slew the turret around so that he could keep the gun on the target. Xavier, who had taken the passenger seat back, nodded to Hathoway.

"Let us be away from here," his cultured voice in no way sounded like a man under fire. Hathoway warned Howard before hitting the gas, the big vehicle moving at once.

"*Operations, this is Gunner,*" Xavier heard over his earpiece. "*Be advised we are Oscar Mike. Our casualties are such that we are unable to hold this position any longer. With Bossman's approval, I plan to spread our able bodies among the fixed positions along the south side of the road. Please advise.*"

There was a pause, Zach imagining that Clay was looking at a map and considering what Zach had told him. After a minute, he had his answer.

"*Gunner, Operations. Move is approved. Five-Oh is to report to Sentry Four to reinforce that position. Other dispositions are at your discretion. Have everyone advise when in position along with location.*"

"*Gunner acknowledges. Clear.*"

"*Operations, standing by.*"

Conferring with Xavier and Mitch for less than a minute, the three had divided their remaining people between the available positions. The M-RAP stopped long enough to let those going to new positions out. Greg Holloway and Vince Hathoway would stay aboard until they reached T2, where they would snag transportation to their new positions, Greg on the Hill and Hathoway in the small bunker fronting the Sanders' homes, which was empty now.

"This is very thin," Mitch noted before he, Danica and Elijah Brigham started for the empty bunker south of Troy House.

"I'm afraid so," Xavier agreed. He and Zach were moving to the next position, west of Mitch's destination and covering the gap between the Troy and Sanders' farms, enabling them to cover both.

The M-RAP continued to the clinic with the wounded, Carrie staying with them and Howard at the wheel. He would join Hathoway once he was no longer needed behind the wheel or helping unload wounded.

-

Clay agreed with his men's assessment; things were very thin.

He studied his map, unconsciously sucking on his teeth as he noted where his troops were. The message from Zach was a sobering one, informing him that several of his people were either dead or wounded. How many of them? Which ones? He had to put that aside. He could only concentrate on the combat power he had lost and how to adjust his forces to fix it.

"I let the clinic know they have casualties incoming," Gwen Paige said quietly. Clay nodded his thanks but didn't turn away from the map. He still didn't know how many enemy troops there were, or where they were coming from. Such information might not make a difference in the outcome, but knowing those things would be helpful, nevertheless.

77

Until he could figure it out, however, he had to continue to defend the farm and the people who called it home.

"Ask Sergeant Gleason to report to Operations, please," he told Leon. "And bring four men with him to help carry the wounded."

"Got it."

The big M-RAP stopped before T2, the door already open as Carrie Jarrett jumped down, setting her bag and rifle aside. Patricia Sanders and Jaylyn Thatcher were both waiting for her and listened intently as the medic ran down the list of injuries and what she had done to treat them. Clay had stepped outside as well, though careful to stay out of the way. When the stretcher bearers returned, the next one out was Stacey Pryor. Clay felt a jolt as he realized that Stacey, the Straight Edge, was gone.

"Ah, Stace," he murmured, watching the body be carried inside. "Damn."

"Friend?" Gleason asked softly.

"Brother," Clay replied, sounding lost.

"Sorry, sir," the NCO offered.

Clay didn't reply but watched as Freda Fletcher and Eunice Maynard were both offloaded. Two of the young women they had trained, at their request, to fight against the people who were trying to take over everything. They had been trained to the best standards and had passed them. But no standards made you bulletproof. The body of Stacey Pryor proved that.

"War doesn't discriminate, sir," Gleason seemed to be reading Clay's mind. Almost like Big John Barnes had once done.

"No, Sergeant, it doesn't," Clay sighed. "Thanks for your help, by the way," he added.

"Sir, you're in command," Gleason replied. "You give orders, and I follow them. We all do and will. If I may, Lieutenant, you're doing just fine. Keep on doing what you're doing."

"Thank you again, Sergeant," Clay managed to smile. "Remind me after this to tell you about a man named John." He looked up the road at the sound of an approaching vehicle and saw a Hummer racing their way.

"Will do, sir," Gleason promised, using a hand gesture to order his men to stand by.

FIRE FROM THE SKY

The Hummer slid to a stop, Petra Shannon at the wheel. Clay decided she was an excellent driver and promised to use her more in that role, assuming they all lived through the day.

The rear hatch popped out and Doc bailed out, waving for help. Two of Gleason's men stepped forward and took Heath Kelly in hand, easing him out on a stretcher and moving at once to the clinic. The next two stepped forward and carefully removed the body of Corey Reynard. Tandi spoke quietly to them and the two nodded before moving inside. Clay felt another stab in his heart as he realized Corey was dead.

"It was too much," Tandi reported as he leaned against the Hummer. "The round took him under the arm, around his vest, and went straight through him. Like what happened to Shane a while back, but Shane's was across the back. Corey's was through the chest cavity."

"Damn these people," Clay said through gritted teeth. "Damn them to hell and gone. I want them all dead."

"Works for me," Tandi nodded easily. "What next?"

"We left Gordy and Kurtis at Plum House," Jose reported as he made it to the rear of the vehicle. "They were not overly happy with that but understood the need. Kevin and I are ready to go anywhere you need us, but you may want to keep Tandi to respond to other wounded. What do you want us to do?"

"Wait here for the moment," Clay told him. "I want to let the others settle into their new positions and see what happens. In the meantime, I want you to pull a pair of M240s and another pair of M249s. I want a 240 in each of the center emplacements across the road, and a 249 at the flanks, including on the hill. I sent Greg up there and he knows how to handle one. We're outnumbered, so we're going to have to depend on firepower rather than manpower."

"We're on it," Jose nodded, waving at Kevin Bodee to follow him. The two took off to gather the equipment their boss wanted.

"Carrie is inside," Clay told Tandi. "She apparently did very good. Had two wounded and three dead. You may want to check on her."

"Got it," the little medic nodded, heading inside at a trot.

"You got good people, sir," Gleason waited until they were alone to speak. "You ain't so bad yourself," he added with a chuckle.

"Thank you, Mister Gleason. I sincerely appreciate that."

"What sergeants is for, Lieutenant," the older man assured him. "What sergeants is for."

79

-

Patricia Sanders looked down at the bloody face of Corey Reynard, the blood in sharp contrast to the peaceful look on the teen's face. She had known him since he was born and watched him grow alongside her own son. Grow into a fine young man with a heart bigger than he was. But he wouldn't be growing anymore.

"Pat," Jaylyn Thatcher said gently. "We've got people who are still with us, including Heath."

"Right," Patricia nodded, turning to where Heath Kelly was being placed on a table. "I'll get him."

"No," Jaylyn placed a hand on Patricia's arm. "He's too close to you, Pat. You look at Jena. Her wounds are a bit worse than Savannah's, and Kate is already checking her out. You take Jena and let me handle Heath."

"Okay," Patricia didn't argue. She knew Jaylyn was right. But that didn't make it better.

-

Leanne Tillman had been trapped into shelter duty at the start of the alert by virtue of being in the right place at the wrong time. School children flowing into the underground shelter with Dixie Jerrolds and Terri Hartwell and no one else. She had remained until Amy Mitchell, breath coming in gasps, had arrived with her rifle and gear, the shelter her assignment when the alert sounded. Leanne waited at the entrance until she was certain things were in order and then started for Operations. Once there, she decided to check on things in the clinic before checking in at Operations. The first thing she saw upon opening the door was the body of Corey Reynard laid out on the floor, hands folded over his chest.

"Wha-" she tried to speak, but her throat closed on her. As she searched for her Aunt Patricia to ask what had happened to Corey, she saw Heath Kelly lying on a gurney, Jaylyn Thatcher cutting his uniform off him.

"Heath?" she said aloud, stunned to see her boyfriend lying there. "Heath!"

"Leanne," Patricia tried to intercept her, but missed, the smaller Leanne evading her and moving to Heath's side. Jaylyn was quicker and caught Leanne by the shoulders.

"Leanne," the doctor said softly. "Let us-"

80

"What happened to him!" Leanne yelled, tears flowing down her face.

"Leanne, calm down," Patricia told her sternly. "Heath was shot, more than once. He needs immediate care, and you being here, doing this, is preventing that care. Now, I need you to go back outside, and I'm sure that Clay needs you wherever it is you're supposed to be."

"I'm staying right-" Leanne began, but Patricia cut her off.

"No, sweetie, you aren't," Patricia's voice was kind, but iron firm. "We are under a major attack and need everyone doing their job! That includes you, Leanne. Now, Heath is getting the best of care we can provide, or was until you barged in. Let Jaylyn and I get back to work, and you do the same! Someone will need you sooner or later, and if you aren't there then we might see even more people in here. Understand?"

"Please, Leanne," Thatcher's voice was soft, out of character really for the tough Army surgeon. "We've lost too much already. Let me take care of him for you. I know how important he is to you, and I swear to you I will give him the best care that I possibly can. Okay? I swear."

Looking up at the doctor, Leanne slowly nodded. She reached out and took Heath's hand, squeezing it once, then turned without another word and departed, leaving the clinic behind.

CHAPTER EIGHT

"Sir, Corporal Tanner reports he has a casualty," Raven Elliot called from within the Cougar. Gillis closed his eyes for a mere moment before snapping them back open.

"Get going, then," he ordered Elliot. "I'll contact Operations and tell them we need an evac, and probably some help. Be careful," he added as the medic grabbed her gear.

"You got it, sir," she flashed him a thumbs up before hitting the ground, running. Gillis picked up his radio. He could hear sounds of firing from his right, now, signaling that his other units were engaged. Only the center, where he sat blocking the road with his M-RAP, had avoided contact so far.

"Operations, this is Gillis. Be advised we have at least one casualty and are engaged all along the line. Request evac for the wounded and, if possible, an extra fire team as a QRF. The numbers are heavily against us right now."

"*Operations copies all, LT. Stand by one.*"

"One might be all we got," Gillis murmured to himself, raising his binoculars to check his front. It was just him and Martin, now.

-

"Gillis can't give any ground," Clay said aloud, looking once more at the map of the farm. "That line has to hold where it is."

"Send Kevin to help, with two of Sergeant Gleason's men," Jose suggested. "Doc can take Howard in the Hummer for the evac. And have Kev carry some heavier weapons. Maybe Mark 48s," he shrugged. "We need more force multipliers."

"See to it, Jose," Clay ordered with only a few seconds consideration. "Sergeant, pick a couple of guys to go with Kevin?" he asked kindly.

"Of course, Lieutenant," Gleason nodded at once. "We're yours to command." The NCO followed Jose out, leaving Clay staring at the map.

"Where in the hell are these people coming from?" he wondered. He desperately wanted to know that. Where would there have been so many people as this, all eager to run into gunfire to attack the farm? It was almost unreal.

The still forms of Corey Reynard and Stacey Pryor reminded him it was very real, indeed.

-

Thane Tanner had been under fire before, but never without the support he was trained to work with. He was accustomed to having armor and artillery to call on, and even air assets when the situation was bleak enough. What he had right now was a woman whose only claim to usefulness was good training and some experience as a constable. His teammate, Parnell Plank, was lying on the ground behind them, slowly bleeding out despite the best efforts of Raven Elliot, who Tanner firmly believed to be one of the best medics in his old regiment.

"Thane, I don't think he's gonna make it," Raven told him quietly during a lull in the shooting. "It's too much damage. And the round to his helmet penetrated, even if it doesn't look like it did."

"Just do what you can, Raven," Tanner told her as he seated a new magazine in his rifle. "We're supposed to have help on the way, including evac. Maybe the docs can help him." With that he raised his rifle and began firing yet again. Beside him, Talia Gray was firing her Mini-14, picking off the front-line people moving against them. There was no doubt she could shoot, Tanner admitted. But things were about to get more than slightly real, and he had to wonder how she would deal with that.

"I hear a vehicle," Raven told him as she prepared Plank to move. Before Tanner could comment, several figures eased into the woods around them. One immediately knelt to check on Plank, while another set up a stretcher and prepared it for Plank to be rolled on to it.

"You're in charge, right?" a man that Tanner recognized as Bodee asked.

"I am," Tanner nodded. "Better get down, sir. Their shooting ain't bad."

"Bullet will find me wherever I am if my name is on it," Bodee shrugged. "Kenny, Samuels, fall back to that tree we saw coming in and set up the next line. You got about one minute so make it fast. I need you ready to lay down suppressing fire after that."

"Sir!" the two replied in unison, disappearing into the brush.

"Doc?" Kevin asked, looking at his friend.

"He's had it," Doc shook his head. "You did a good job," he told Raven Elliot. "It was just too much to treat in the field. Not your fault.

Let's get him out of here." Howard took one end of the stretcher and Tandi the other, carrying the fallen trooper out of the combat zone and back to the Hummer they had come in. Raven followed, waiting for someone else to call her. Kevin turned back to examine the battlefield before them.

"Okay, gang. We can't hold this spot. Too many in that swarm. We're going to fall back about twelve to fifteen yards into the woods, where my associates will have set up a M48 along with some other surprises. One surprise I got with me, right here," he grinned, pulling an M18 Claymore from a pouch and setting it in the open area before Tanner's position. Arming the radio detonator, Kevin nodded to himself before looking at the other two.

"Always leave a lovely parting gift," his grin was almost evil. "Alright, fall back firing, but don't shoot each other, or me. Especially me," he added with a chuckle. "Let's go."

Tanner nodded, tapping Gray on the shoulder. She began to squirm back away from the open area they were in, then turned and hunkered down as she ran to the next position.

"You're next," Kevin ordered Tanner. "Get clear." The young NCO nodded and repeated Gray's moves, moving quickly back. Once they were all gone, Kevin settled back into the edge of the wood and waited.

He didn't have to wait long as the enemy across the way realized that the lack of fire meant that they had an opening. Erupting from the woods on the east side of the highway, a mass of people, some dressed in little more than rags, charged down the hill onto the interstate and across. Kevin waited, judging their progress and holding the detonator in his hand.

He allowed the rampaging mob to sense victory before tripping his parting gift.

The Claymore mine has at times been referred to as the ultimate equalizer for small units. A pound of C4 explosive propelling 600 steel ball bearings in a near one hundred-eighty-degree arc tends to have a scything effect on a charging horde of humans, and this time was no different.

Kevin didn't bother to wait for the smoke to clear in order to see the damage. He had seen the effects before. He withdrew immediately to a chorus of screams and groans behind him, enemies who were discovering why it was better not to attack the farm and her defenders. It was a hard lesson, but then life was hard.

It was harder if you were stupid.

-

Gillis heard the Claymore go, followed by a sharp drop off in the gunfire from his left. That would ease some pressure on the line, though they were now at least one man down. Even as he had that thought, Raven Elliot came hotfooting it out of the woods toward the M-RAP. Behind her, Gillis could see a Hummer moving back toward the farm, too slow to be carrying a badly wounded soldier to see a doctor.

Which meant one of his men was gone.

"Plank's gone, sir," Raven declared as she piled into the M-RAP, immediately restocking her medic's bag with supplies she had positioned inside. "It looked like he caught a three-round burst, probably of steel core ammo."

"Very well," Gillis replied. Steel core ammunition was cheap and made good target ammunition. It also made for a heavily penetrating round.

"Bodee and two more are over there with Tanner now," she continued. "Bodee was the one who set off the M18. Bought some time, at least."

"Good deal," Gillis responded. She didn't really need to hear him, but he knew it was expected.

Heavy gunfire erupted from the right before she could say more as their attackers began pushing at another place in line. Gillis had six people on his right, spread across two positions. It would not be enough against a determined push.

Fortunately for him, Clay knew it too. Even as Gillis watched, an ATV skirted his position, Kevin Bodee at the wheel along with another trooper Gillis recognized as Matt Kenny.

-

Corporal Lynden Witherspoon held the position to the immediate right of Lieutenant Gillis' M-RAP, along with Private Richie Millard and Carol Kennard. They had not been so heavily engaged as Tanner's position yet, but the traffic to their front was starting to pick up. Witherspoon was starting to sweat a bit, and the only reason he hadn't called for help was because he knew there was none to send.

EMBERS

The sound of an ATV behind them was a welcome relief to the young NCO. Either they were being reinforced, or else they were being pulled. There were other possibilities of course, but he didn't want to think of those.

"That's Kevin Bodee," Carol told him quietly. "Don't know who that is with him."

"Matt Kenny," Richie Millard said. "Hey, they're bringing equipment with them."

They were indeed bringing equipment with them. Bodee was carrying a Mark 48 machine gun while Kenny was carrying extra ammunition for same. Bodee also had the satchel for another M18 strung over his shoulder.

"Things are tight and getting worse," Bodee didn't mince words or waste time on small talk. "We're being hit all along the line, seems like. Maybe to try and find a weak spot or else maybe they're just that stupid, I don't know. You qualified on the Light Weight?" he asked Witherspoon, wanting to know if the trooper was trained on the machine gun.

"Yeah," Witherspoon nodded.

"Me, too," Millard volunteered.

"Great," Bodee nodded. "You shouldn't need any coaching, then. I'm going to set this," he pulled the M18 over his shoulder, "and rig it with a remote detonator. If you need it, wait until you'll get the most possible damage from it before you pull the plug. Me and Matt are going to go and deliver this same setup to Gates at the far end, then we'll be back to fix you a fallback position. We're doing that for everyone. Keep in mind that we can't let this line go. There's nothing behind it in any strength until the farm, and if they get that far then we failed. Got it?"

"Got it," all three replied.

"The fallback spots are meant to be a new, more solid position, so when you get there, be prepared to stay, no matter what. I doubt I need to say it, but make sure that 48 makes the trip. We're not exactly flush with heavy equipment and can't afford to lose one, let alone get it turned around on us. Okay, we're gone, but we'll be back." With that he set the mine, left the detonator with Witherspoon, and then he and Kenny were moving.

"In and out like a whirlwind," Millard noted.

FIRE FROM THE SKY

"That's how all of them move," Carol noted. "Fast, hard and unyielding. Training under them was a cast iron bitch."

"I imagine," Witherspoon nodded. "Well, we can-, never mind," whatever he was about to say was left behind. "We got incoming. Get settled in. I think they're going to try us now that they maybe failed on the other side. Looks like no one wants to try the fifty on that Cougar."

"I can't say I blame 'em for that," Millard shrugged as he tried to mold himself to the ground. "I sure wouldn't want to."

-

"Sounds like Kev got the line positions fixed up," Jose noted as multiple machine guns began firing to the east.

"We're eventually going to have to send them some help," Clay noted. "Gleason has four left, plus himself, and I really want to keep them as a reaction force. See if we can pull anyone from somewhere else to lend a hand on that line."

"We can't weaken our rear areas any further," Jose swept the positions in questions with one hand. "None of them have more than two people. We need to leave the strength we have to the south, since that's seems like a major push. That line was pushed back once already. Heavier weapons and better fixed positions should hopefully fix that, but not if we weaken those posts further." He paused, studying the map yet again.

"We can retrieve Gordy and Kurtis from Plum House," Jose suggested after a brief pause. "We may can pull one more from there, since there's no current action in their area. We can't pull anyone from the hill since we expect them to be hit, assuming we can't finish this off down here. We can pull Vic from Tower One," he indicated the tower behind the Sanders' homes, "which will leave Sam alone, but she's definitely the better shot. We can take one of the girls from the bunker out front to replace Vic. Really need two people up there, even if they're just spotters. Anyway, Gordy, Vic and Kurtis will make a good fireteam. Vic on a SAW or maybe a Mark 48, Kurtis on overwatch and Gordy for close-in action. It's not perfect, I guess, but it's close. And it will still leave Gleason and his few men left in reserve." Having a reserve in a battle like this was of grave importance and could swing the battle their way at a crucial juncture.

87

"See to it, then," Clay ordered, his voice firm. He had to make decisive decisions and do it without hesitation when the time came. He couldn't afford to waffle. Too much depended on it.

"Right away," Jose nodded and started posting orders that would move people around the board.

-

Ten minutes later, Mikki Reeves was in Tower One with Samantha Walters while Vicki Tully, Gordy Sanders and Kurtis Montana were gathered at T2, the latter two quickly filling ammunition pouches left empty by their earlier actions. Vicki was hurriedly checking out a Mark 48 machine gun while Moses Brown shuttled ammo cans to the trio to carry with them. Kurtis Montana also picked up HK MP5 a stubby 9mm submachine gun that would give him a short-range alternative he had lacked in his earlier fight, without weighing him down or getting in the way. He didn't want to get caught in an up close and personal environment again with just his sniper rifle. As they finished, Kevin Bodee and Matt Kenny pulled up in front of the building in a large ATV.

"Okay, gang, gather round," Jose ordered. "Kevin has been up to the line and set them up as well as we can. Beefed up their firepower and left a man to replace a KIA. You five," he swept the group with one hand, "are going up there as a reserve force. Arrow is in command. That line has to hold, people. There is nothing between it and the farm except air and opportunity. If we lose even a small part of it, then the farm is wide open. Make sure it holds. Any questions?"

There were none. Everyone knew their business.

"Then get loaded and get moving."

-

It was like a chess game, and yet not. Clay looked at pieces on a map, moving them from place to place, either in response to a move by his opponent, or else for reasons of his own. It was far too easy to forget that each piece on this board represented a real, live human being. He glanced at a small pile of markers to the side at that thought. Not all of them were alive anymore, he reflected sadly.

But in a chess game, he would be able to look at his opponent. Be able to see his opponent's eyes as they studied the same board he did. In an actual chess game, if Clay made a mistake, no one would die because of it. While he might lose, it would still be just a game.

If he lost here, now, then everyone on the farm would pay for it. Not just those fighting but the women, children and infirm now hiding in the shelters.

So, he had to win. Using everyone to the best of their own abilities, no matter who they were, or how close to him they had become. He could grieve after it was over, provided he won. If he lost, then he wouldn't need to grieve at all.

-

Jose returned to Operations to find Clay still studying the map showing where all their people and fortifications were.

"Kevin and the rest are on their way back," he reported. Clay nodded without speaking, still looking. Jose waited, mostly patiently. He knew that Clay would speak when he was ready and likely not before.

"Pull the Plum House detachment," Clay said suddenly, his finger landing on the small square that represented the Plum farmhouse. "Have them shut it down completely. Bring their Cougar to the Hill to bolster the defenses there. The kids can go to the shelter unless they have a normal duty station like Millie and Janice. Martinson will take command of their defenses and place his men as he sees best. If he thinks he can spare someone to join Hathaway in the bunker in front of my folk's house, I'd appreciate it, but that's not a demand. Just if he can spare them." After the 'rescue' mission that had brought Mitch and the others back to their new defensive lines, Hathaway had been assigned to the empty position in front of the Sanders' homes. Brannon Howard had been meant to join him but had remained with Tandi instead to help with moving the wounded.

"I'll be sure he knows," Jose nodded, heading for the phone. "Anything else?"

"Do we know where my father is?"

-

"Mister Sanders, you really need to let me get you to a shelter, sir," Gail Knight said for possibly the tenth time since the shooting started.

"Missy, no offense, but I am not going to be herded, shepherded or guarded by a young woman, no matter how skilled, who is no older than my grandchildren. Well," he amended, "some of my grandchildren, anyway."

"Yes, sir," Gail sighed in defeat. She had expected it but would keep trying anyway. If Gordon Sanders were killed, she dreaded the result. And Clay would not be happy with her, either.

"Might as well give up, Gail," Charley Wilmeth told her, a dry chuckle punctuating her words. "Wasting your breath."

"I know," Gail gave another sigh, this one a very longsuffering one.

"Are you two calling me stubborn?" Gordon demanded.

"Yes," they replied in unison.

"Hmph."

"Too stubborn to even reply to us," Charley snickered, and Gail had to cough to keep from laughing outright. Gordon feigned outrage at that, fighting a laugh of his own.

"I blame this lack of respect for your elders on today's lax moral standards and the lack of discipline in the home and school," he told the two of them. Now, both of them were fighting a laugh, trying to keep the noise down.

The three had been far back into the pasture areas when the shooting had started. Gail had been able to pick up some information on the radio, but contact was spotty at best. The three had decided to keep quiet for now and work their way cautiously back toward the farm, watching for trouble among the herds. They were approximately half-way home when Gordon had stopped.

"What's wrong, sir?" Charley asked, looking around them.

"Nothing that I can see," Gordon admitted. "But it has occurred to me just now that whoever is causing all this may well be after these very cows and horses. If that is the case, then the three of us and a few hounds are all that are standing in their way. Maybe instead of heading back, we ought to be staying put?"

Neither woman wanted to admit it, but both though he was right. Two of the farm's Kangal hounds were with them, both waiting to see what the humans of their pack were going to do. Dogs in general were very intuitive, and livestock dogs even more so. They could easily feel the unrest the three humans before them were feeling.

"Operations, this is Gail, please respond," Gail tried to raise the radio room. "Operations, this is Gail in Pasture Four, please respond." There was no reply.

"Nothing," Gail shook her head. "If we stay out here, then it will just be us I'm afraid."

"We need to find a decent place to hole up, then," Gordon noted. "One with room for the horses and us. Just so happens, I know of one such place. It's not comfortable by any mean, but it has the room for the horses and can give us a high point to see from."

"I'm for it," Charley said at once. "Anything beats sitting out here in the open. Did that once already."

"Let's go, then," Gordon heeled his horse lightly. "Ain't but a little piece."

The three rode in silence for perhaps five minutes before Gordon drew up before a huge clump of....

"A dozer pile?" Charley asked, bewildered.

"A what?" Gail looked at her, speaking before Gordon could answer.

"A dozer pile," Gordon chuckled, climbing down from the saddle. "When you clear land, land with trees and brush I mean, you end up pushing it all together, like so," he indicated the brush pile. "Dozer pile just became the name for it since it was brush piled up by a dozer. Anyway, three generations of kids have used this place for everything from drinking underage to hunting to just…hiding out. C'mon. I'll show you." With that he disappeared into the brush, leading his horse. One of the hounds went before him, the second following.

The two young women followed him with not a little trepidation, but neither had a better idea and it would at least provide cover and concealment, something hammered into Gail until it was second nature.

Once through the outer brush, the two women stopped short, amazed at what they were seeing. The interior of the 'pile' was a rough circle of ground about thirty feet in diameter, mostly devoid of snow due to the cover above it. Around the center were dirt and wood ledges with rough steps leading upwards to the top. A large ring in the middle of the circle showed evidence of fires from the past, indicating that at some point people had used this place to camp, or at least for a bonfire.

"Not a Holiday Inn, I admit, but then there aren't any Holiday Inns left," Gordon chuckled. "That plastic can over there should have a bit of sweet feed in it for the horses. There are treats in my saddlebags for the hounds. From here we can see most of the land around us and stay hidden at the same time. What do you think?"

"I think it's amazing that Clayton hasn't thought of this place as a defensive post," Gail admitted.

"Well, he's got a lot on him," Gordon shrugged. "And I could have reminded him about it, as could any of the rest of us. We're just so used to it being here that none of us really think on it. But in our case at least, it's about perfect. We can get comfortable and set up a watch around us. Let's get to work."

CHAPTER NINE

Things were quiet for a time as the survivors of the battles so far took time to get reorganized. No one complained about that, using the time to strengthen their own positions and to resupply after the earlier actions.

But now it seemed that quiet was at an end. The pressure against the line along the interstate had never really stopped, merely shifted from flank to flank. Clay had been surprised that no one had tried to go around, but Jose reminded him that the line was itself flanked by deep and thick briars and thickets that would make passage difficult at best, not to mention make enough noise for anyone to hear it.

"Operations, this is Thug. We're seeing Tangoes advancing on our position," Clay heard over the radio.

"Operations, this is Gunner. We are seeing the same, all along our line of sight."

"Thug, Gunner, roger that. Received." Leon replied, looking at Clay to see if he had heard. Before Clay could even nod, the radio was speaking again.

"Operations, this is Rattler. We're seeing action as well. I count a minimum of twenty-five to our front. Hunting rifles, AKs, even a few shotguns, over."

"Operations this is Five-Oh," Greg sounded grim. *"We have a large group moving on us as well. Count is already at thirty and still rising."*

"Where are all these people coming from?" Clay exclaimed. "Acknowledge. Weapons free. Engage at their discretion," he added to Leon. The teen nodded and turned to the radio to relay orders.

"We can find that out later, Clay," Jose said softly. "Right now, we need to get rid of them. Either kill them all or kill enough of them that they withdraw."

"I know that," Clay fought not to snap. Jose was just trying to help. "What can we do that we haven't already done? We have a small reserve of four men and a medic. We need them everywhere, and we also need them in case somewhere fails. I don't see a way to put them in action that doesn't leave us hanging."

"The only thing I can think of is a flank attack," Jose admitted. "Get someone in behind them and start working their way down the opposition line. If we play it right, we could be a quarter of the way or more through their formation before they even notice."

"And who do we send to do that?" Clay asked. "I like Gleason, and he says his men are solid, but I doubt they are up to that kind of combat. It's just not their thing is all."

"Give me X, Rat, Thug and Zach. I'll pick up Nate from the big bunker and swap Isaacson, Gleason's medic, for Doc. We'll take a pair of Hummers up the hill, maybe to the Plum House, and come in behind their left flank. I'll give Zach a 240 to lug around, or maybe a 48. We'll have all the firepower we need, right there."

"That's a lot of gun to be 'lugging', Jose," Clay noted softly.

"He's young," Jose shrugged. "He can handle it. If not, Mitch can help him. Besides, anyone who can manhandle a Ma Deuce like he does can handle a Bravo with no trouble, let alone a 48. We'll make it work."

Clay thought for mere seconds, though it seemed like days. Suddenly, he nodded once.

"Go for it," he ordered. "Make sure our southern front isn't too weak to stand."

"Will do," Jose promised. "I'll send Gleason to you to take my spot. He's rock solid."

"Do it," Clay agreed. "Go."

-

It took ten long minutes to get everyone situated, and even then, Shane Golden's replacement had to be dropped off as the small procession went up the hill. Once Shane was on board, they continued on, stopping less than a mile past the Hill community. Jose had decided at the last minute to use electric carts rather than Hummers. While slower, the carts were quiet and easily hidden. And the loss of three golf carts, while annoying, would be nothing compared to the loss of two Hummers.

The seven of them assembled alongside the road, Zach showing an easy familiarity with the light machine gun he was carrying, including an ammunition box beneath it. Jose had gone with the Mark 48 and Zach carried it easily. Everyone else was carrying rifles, in this instance the military grade M1A/M14 used by special operations groups. A solid rifle that fired the heavier 7.62mm cartridge rather than the standard 5.56mm of the M4. It was the weapon of choice for the group when they could justify using them.

"We have a simple plan," Jose told the assembled group. "We move east until we find their flank, then we roll it up and kill them all. Any questions?"

"Do we have any idea who these people are?" Nate wanted to know.

"None, and we can worry about that when we're done," Jose's reply was fast. "Anything else? If not, we're moving. Zach, take center with that machine gun. If it gets to be too much, sing out and let someone else handle it a while."

"I'm good," Zach promised. "Let's go."

With that, the seven of them started off at a brisk walk, looking for their enemy's left.

-

"Sir, this line is paper thin," Gleason said quietly. "I'm sure you know that, but it bears repeating."

"I do know," Clay assured him. "I'm trying to keep a few people here and there in reserve that I can use to plug a break in our defenses. I have sharpshooters here, here and here," he indicated the cupola and towers, "with orders not to engage until ordered or until there is a direct threat to them or those below. Another sharpshooter is here," he indicated Leon's old house, "but he does as he deems best. He's an excellent shot and has a tremendous rifle, so his impact will be felt when he does choose to open fire. I have three in this bunker here I can pull if I absolutely have to," he indicated the large bunker in front of the pad, "but I'd prefer to leave them there if possible."

"I notice the line to the east is a bit stronger," Gleason pulled a finger along that particular area of the map. "I assume it's been hit harder?"

"Until now, yes. It's possible they were trying to get us to pull men away from our southern line to reinforce the east, but we've managed not to do that. That has led us to strip our reserves bare, however," Clay admitted with a frown.

"You just sent seven top quality men off on a mission, sir," Gleason reminded him. "They would have made a handy QRF."

"But they wouldn't have been able to do as much damage as they might with this," Clay shook his head. "Those men in particular have an excellent chance of getting behind our enemy and chewing them up. It's what they do."

"Sounds good to me, sir."

-

EMBERS

"This is Gates. I have a man down and we're still under fire."

"Sir," Elliot called, and Gillis nodded.

"I heard," he promised. "You should go and team up with the other medic running wounded, Raven. They might need you, and you're worth far more as a medic than being stuck here running a radio."

"Thank you, sir," the young woman smiled slightly at the compliment. "I'm gone." She slipped out the rear door and into the still falling snow.

"Mister Gates, we have help coming to you, so hold tight," a new voice came over the air. Bodee, Gillis thought. Whatever help he could send, Gillis would gladly take it.

"This is Witherspoon, Mister Bodee. Millard is down hard. He needs help right away, and we're in a hell of a fight." The report was punctuated with near constant gunfire.

"Got it, Witherspoon. Be there shortly," Bodee promised.

"I'll get Millard," he heard Raven say, obviously running. *"Will need transport, though, and help moving him."*

"We can get that for you, and thanks," Bodee replied at once. "Get that, Isaacson?"

"Roger that, sir."

Gillis was starting to feel like a fifth wheel.

-

Gordy Sanders arrived right after Raven Elliot, sliding into position with a smoothness that belied his age.

Raven worked feverishly on the young man before her but feared her work would be for naught. Richie Millard had been hit with something large and likely steel-tipped, as it had torn through his vest and kept going. She warned those around her about that even as she tried to stem the bleeding and assess the damage.

Meanwhile, Matt Kenny dropped into the far-right position, where he passed the still form of Keely Irvine. Damn. Keely was good people. He could spare no more time for such reflection as the position was under heavy fire and needed his full attention. Behind them all, Kevin Bodee stood with Kurtis Montana and Vicki Tully.

"And then there were three," Kevin noted. "We need to set up a backdrop position back here, I think. What we really need to do is close up and consolidate this line, but I don't think we can hold the entire line if we do that. If we could get another Cougar up here with a fifty, we

96

might could use it to anchor one end and Lieutenant Gillis' to anchor the other. I am open to suggestions, by the way," he looked at the two.

"A consolidated line is definitely the way to go in my book," Vicki said at once. "We don't have to be crammed together to make it work, just all sharing the same line of sight. If we use the Cougar on the road as a center piece, then it adds strength to the line."

"Also lets people go right around us," Kurtis said softly. "Kinda off my range, here, but I'd say we're better off having a line of positions with two or three people each, spread out across here," he motioned from north to south of their location. "One automatic weapon," he nodded to Vicki's machinegun, "and at least one rifle for security. Let the heavy lifters do the work. Back that Cougar down a ways and get that fifty engaged. Something like that might just break 'em."

Kevin debated that for a moment, weighing both options. While Vic's idea was appealing, it was also hamstrung with one fatal flaw, that being the one that Kurtis had pointed out. They couldn't afford to allow people off behind them, even in small numbers.

Kurtis' idea wasn't perfect, either, but it did have the advantage of being simple, quick to implement, and easily supported. That and getting the heavy machine gun involved in the fight. So far, their enemy had avoided the big gun. If the line were moved back some, and the Cougar with them, then Gillis would be able to get the Deuce in play. Kurtis was right about the psychological aspect of it as well. Watching your comrades chewed apart by a fifty-caliber weapon was a giant morale killer.

"Honestly, both ideas have merit," he said at last, looking toward where their people were engaged. "Kurtis' plan does have the advantage of being spread out more and allowing us to cover most if not all of the area we need to. Not to mention, the chance to get the fifty in action. We'll back off say…fifty to seventy-five yards. We'll scratch out four spots as quick as we can. Logs, rocks, anything we can use to protect as well as conceal. Whatever we can manage in ten minutes or so. After that, we withdraw. I'll go tell Gillis. He can go ahead and pull back so he can support the rest when they run for it."

-

"Sounds like a plan," Gillis nodded. "Let me know when you want us to pull back. It'll feel good to let this thing speak after sitting here all morning just listening."

"We're shooting for no more than ten minutes," Bodee promised. With that he jumped down from the hatch and took off to assist his two minions.

They weren't hard to spot as they were currently using the winch on the front of the ATV to haul a large tree into place for a new defensive position. The snowblade quickly pushed as much of the frozen soil as the smaller vehicle could manage beneath the tree to help stop incoming fire from getting through. Heavy rocks finished the work, all done within five minutes.

The two went straight to the next spot without pause, this one an uprooted tree that had left a deep wallow where the root system had been torn loose from the soil. Dirt was pushed into a berm around the wallow, along with whatever large rocks were available, making a passably strong 'hasty fighting position'. A small cedar and two small pines were torn from the ground and placed in front of the position to help give it some minimal concealment.

For twenty minutes this scene replayed itself all along the line, albeit with Kevin joining in. Hurried decisions on where to best place the next position, then hurried and frantic work to get them constructed before moving on to do it again. Finally, the three stopped to survey their work, all of them breathing a bit hard from the exertion but satisfied with their efforts.

"Okay, time to start pulling back," Kevin noted. During the time they had spent preparing emplacements, two more people on the line had been wounded. Talia Gray high in her left arm, Ellis Gates across the top of his right shoulder. Both were bleeders but had been swiftly and expertly treated in the field by Elliot and Isaacson.

"You two find a place to set up shop to help cover their withdrawal," Kevin ordered. "I'll let Gillis know, and he can give the order once he's in place to cover them. This will be about as far as we can go, so we have to hold here. At least with this line we can support one another. That should make it stronger."

"We'll be ready," Vicki promised. "Let's go, Cowboy." The two headed for a position they had already prepared for themselves, having left their gear and supplies there earlier while they were working.

"Reckon this'll work?" Kurtis asked as they settled into their own hole, checking their weapons and gear. Vicki had taken a page from Kurtis' book and snagged herself an MP5 for close-in work, just in case.

"Got to," she shrugged. "We got nowhere else to go. We either hold here, or we die here. There are no other options."

Agreeing, Kurtis merely nodded. There wasn't anything to add to that.

-

"Okay gang, we're about to pull back," Gillis said over the radio. "The Cougar has pulled back about fifty yards, which will let us cover your retreat. We haven't been able to use the BMG to this point since they're avoiding it. This move will change that."

"Don't waste any time getting to your assigned spot. Remember, this is it. We hold here, because there's nowhere else to go. So, dig in and be prepared to stay. Team leaders check in when you're ready."

"Tanner, good to go."

"Witherspoon, good to go."

"Gates, ready."

Gillis waited for a lull in the action before giving the simple order; "All units, go!"

-

In a perfect world, everyone would have withdrawn without a problem, settled into their new positions, and held their enemy off with nothing but grit and determination.

Unfortunately, this was not a perfect world.

It might have been skill on the part of whoever was leading the attack on the farm. It could have been that something the defenders did tipped their enemy off and gave them a perfect opening to attack. It might have just been plain bad luck.

Whatever the reason, the wood line on the east side the highway erupted with screaming men and women, all charging for the west side, supported by still others who were targeting the areas where defenders were known to be. For the first time the people attacking this area had done something smart and coordinated their attack.

Talia Gray, already lightly wounded, took a round in the thigh just as they set off. Samuels and Tanner each caught an arm before she could fall and literally dragged her to their next post.

Lyndon Witherspoon's group was more fortunate. Having already lost Richie Millard, they managed to withdraw with their only injury being a bullet burn across Carol Kennard's upper left arm. Bloody and painful to be sure, but not life threatening or even enough to pull the young woman out of combat.

Ellis Gates' group, on the far right, were hit the hardest, with Gates himself being caught dead center in profile, where his armor didn't provide complete coverage. The steel round went through him like a battering ram, tearing at everything it touched. Matt Kenny grabbed the rescue strap, sometimes darkly referred to as the 'tag and drag handle', located just below the neck of his vest and began dragging Gates with him. Heather Patton followed, using their Mark 48 to hose down anyone near them. She grunted as a round smashed into her left arm but kept firing, firing in short bursts so she could keep control of the weapon she was barely familiar with.

Luck was with them at least partially as Brannon Howard saw them struggling. Telling Carly Isaacson and Raven Elliot to hold tight, he drove their ATV right into the fire, spinning to present their tailgate to the fleeing soldiers. The two medics yanked Gates' body on board, followed by Kenny, who fell face down across Gates as a large caliber round smashed into his vest.

Heather Patton was the last one aboard, being pulled up by the medics even as she continued firing.

"Go, go, go!" Raven shouted, already trying to see how badly Kenny was injured while Carly worked to get to Gates. Brannon needed no encouragement, flooring the machine and weaving away from the area. Behind him, Heather rummaged through Gates' pockets even as Carly tried to stop her. Ignoring the medic, Heather kept looking until she found what she was after. Arming the detonator immediately, she triggered the M18 mine left behind by Kevin Bodee, just as Gates had shown her. An echoing boom to their north signaled Gordy Sanders doing the same thing.

"Don't waste it!" Heather told Brannon. "Get us somewhere we can fight!"

"On it!" he nodded, having never stopped moving. The ATV tore across the frozen ground toward the nearest spot from which this Amazon behind him could keep shooting.

-

Faron Gillis grit his teeth as he watched his troops being caught in such withering fire. All this time he had sat blocking the road, unable to help them at all. Now, things had changed. Hard charging assailants were coming through the woods in three places, the three places his people had just withdrawn from. His face grim from the losses he had seen so far, Gillis lowered the Ma Deuce and depressed the butterfly firing mechanism.

If you've never seen a BMG in action, it can be difficult to picture just how destructive a fifty-caliber round could be. The damage inflicted is beyond the imagination of most people who have never encountered the kind of violence that generally would involve such weaponry.

The word horrific is not an exaggeration.

People who had just moments before been screaming in victory for having driven the defenders back now screamed in agony as they lost limbs or watched their comrades be torn apart. Gillis swept the big gun back and forth, turning the turret so that he could cover the entire front. Deep in his subconscious it occurred to him that he should be horrified at the damage he was inflicting, at the carnage he wrought over and over.

But his conscious mind was running the show, and all it could see was that the people he was targeting had hurt and killed soldiers under his command. And for that, there could be no forgiveness.

-

"Damn," Kevin Bodee muttered as he watched Gillis expertly break up the oncoming attack all by his lonesome, literally chewing it apart with the big machine gun. His attention turned to the ATV carrying the medics as is slid to a halt nearly on top of him. Heather scrambled off the rear of the vehicle, shouldering a rifle and then grabbing the Mark 48 Kevin himself had left for her group.

"Gates is gone," Carly Isaacson told him. "Kenny is alive, but I think busted up inside. He took a high caliber round to the back of his vest. Didn't penetrate, but it did do some damage. We're taking him to get checked out."

"Stop at the left flank on your way out," Kevin ordered. "They've got a casualty over there. Need one of you to stay here since we've got walking wounded. Once they're dressed you can get back to making runs."

"I got it," Raven Elliot nodded, grabbing her bag and jumping to the ground. "Better look at that arm, first," she told Heather Patton, climbing down into the hole with her.

"Just a scratch," Heather told her. "I'm good."

EMBERS

"That 'scratch' looks like it might have broken your arm," Raven snorted. "Let me see it while there's time."

"We're gone then," Howard told Kevin. "Be back as soon as we can." With that the ATV roared away, leaving things surprisingly quiet for once. Kevin realized that the heavy machine gun had stopped and immediately feared something had happened to the Cougar or to Gillis, but a hurried look found Gillis sweeping the area looking for more targets.

There were none at present. Kevin surveyed the area, including the bodies, and pieces of bodies that littered the area, and had a stray thought; had they won?

Heavy gunfire erupting behind him to the west answered the question before it was fully formed.

CHAPTER TEN

Nate stopped the group with a fist held in the air, his own movements stopped in mid-stride. Slowly kneeling to the ground, he signaled for the others to do likewise and then join him. Jose was the first to reach him, and immediately saw what had prompted Nate's actions.

"Twenty, maybe?" Jose asked as Nate looked through binoculars.

"I count twenty-two, but they disappear into the trees," Nate noted, lowering his glasses. "I'd say this is the far left of whatever line they have. And they aren't far from the Hill, here, either."

"No, they aren't," Jose agreed. "Well, this is what we came for, so let's be about it. Zach, you stand by with the 48. The rest of us will open the ball with suppressors until we're spotted. Zach will provide cover for us until then, and after that he can start hammering at any groups we find. Questions? Then we go in one minute."

Everyone took their position, Zach remaining in the center. Jose's first shot was the signal for the rest and then everyone was shooting.

-

"Sounds as if your men are engaged, Lieutenant," Gleason noted, his head cocked to one side as he tried to pin down the exact bearing. He was fairly sure it was southwest of their location.

"Sounds that way," Clay agreed. "That probably means we'll be hearing-," He was interrupted by the sounds of gunfire to the south.

"And now they're all in," Gleason nodded once. Before he could say anything else, an ATV came roaring through the yard to slide to a stop in front of T2. Moses Brown and Devon Knowles were already outside, stretchers in hand to assist with moving the wounded. Kaitlin Caudell was also there, doing triage.

"Two wounded and one KIA," Carly Isaacson reported, her voice professionally precise. "One male, heavy round to the back of his vest. No penetration, but definite bruising to the center of the torso and likely some internal damage, almost certainly cracked or broken ribs. One female, hit high on the thigh, and it's a bleeder. Possible that it hit the femoral artery. The KIA caught a round on the side where his armor didn't close. I doubt he knew what hit him. The enemy is using steel core ammo in some spots and it's devastating when it hits."

"Alright, get the bleeder in first," Kaitlin nodded to her stretcher bearers, who moved to Talia Gray. Brannon Howard jumped down from the wheel to help with getting Matt Kenny inside and unloading Ellis Gates' body.

"Rusty Gates was a good man," Gleason said, his voice all but toneless. "Solid NCO."

Clay said nothing. He didn't have anything to add. Within three minutes the medic and driver were back outside, guzzling water from canteens before climbing aboard the ATV and heading back out.

Clay silently wished them well and said a prayer for their safety. There was likely no more dangerous job on a battlefield than a medic.

-

Zayne Parris divided his time between watching for the enemy and watching Carrie Jarrett. He didn't know the young woman well and had no idea how she would react under fire. For that matter, he wasn't at all sure how he would react under fire. He wiped his hands on his pants as he peered out the slot in front of him.

"Stop that," Beau Abramson said, smacking Parris' hands lightly. Parris, as a corporal, actually outranked PFC Abramson, but the two had been together since boot camp. He gave Abramson a mock glare and muttered something that might have sounded like 'respect'.

"You two are a real laugh riot, aren't you?" Carrie snorted, her eyes constantly moving. "You better start paying attention before something bites you. Some of this bunch can really shoot."

"I ain't even seen any of 'em, yet," Parris declared loudly. "If I do see one then we'll see who can shoo-,"

Zayne Parris' statement would remain forever unfinished as a jacketed hollow point from a hunting rifle slammed into his forehead and blew his brains into the helmet strapped to his head.

"Shit!" Abramson turned while as a sheet, trying to grab his friend and help him.

"Forget him, he's gone," Carrie told him, her voice flat and dull. "Get back on your window or we'll be with him sooner rather than later. And keep your head down," she added. Normally that would not have needed to be said, but considering what had just happened, she decided to throw it in.

"How can you be like that?" Abramson demanded, standing fully erect in the bunker, hands balled tightly into fists. "You're a medic, aren't you? Do something!"

"He took a round to the head, big man," Carrie shook her head slowly, never looking around. "There's nothing I can do about that. Don't take that helmet off!" she warned, but Abramson did so anyway, immediately turning to puke his guts out after seeing what was left of his friend. Carrie sighed and picked up the field phone, ringing the switchboard.

"Operations, this is Janice. How can I assist you?"

"Janice, for God's sake, don't you know there's a war on?" Carrie Jarrett almost laughed despite her situation.

"Oh, yes. Of course, I do!" Janice replied. "How's that going, by the way?"

"Can't say how it's going for the others, but I got one man KIA and another who is puking up everything he's eaten in the last two days, looks like. I need help out here, and I need it pretty quick. But tell whoever comes that we're taking sniper fire, so be extra cautious."

"Got it!" Janice assured her, writing the message down. "I'll let Mister Clayton know right away!"

"You know, Janice, there are times when I swear you can't be real," Carrie chuckled drily.

"Really? Why?" Janice asked, but Carrie was already gone. Shrugging, the blonde got to her feet and carried the note to Clay, returning immediately to the switchboard to take another call. With the addition of Millie, Janice and Leanne, the center was becoming crowded, but the team had divided up the work with everyone taking one area of responsibility. Janice had the switchboard, Millie was monitoring the FRS bands, Leon the tactical channel, Gwen the military bands, and Leanne was more or less pinch hitting and supervising. Everyone knew by now that Heath Kelly was in the clinic, in dangerous condition. They did their best to give Leanne room.

As Clay read the message, Janice was on the phone again.

"Yes, he's here, but he's very…okay, I can ask…oh, well, hold on then," she finally said. "Mister Clayton? Miss Newell is on the phone and says she needs to talk to you right away, sir!"

"So does everyone else," Clay muttered. Even still he turned toward the switchboard. Sienna Newell was rock solid. If she said she needed to talk to him, then she did. "See if you can find someone to send out to this bunker," he ordered Gleason as he pointed to where Carrie Jarrett was.

"Yes, sir," the older man nodded, going to work right away. Meanwhile, Clay picked up the phone from Janice.

"Cece, I'm really in a bind, here. What's going on?"

"You do know that we have a perfectly working Stryker ambulance sitting behind T3 don't you?" the former Lieutenant didn't waste any words.

"I know we have one, but last I heard the transmission on it was shot," Clay replied, his mind already thinking ahead.

"Jake and I rebuilt it," Sienna said proudly. "Purrs like a Singer sewing machine, she does. Already set up to take wounded. And armored a lot better than a Hummer or even a Cougar, and damn sure better than an ATV. It doesn't have a gun, but that's the only downside."

"It sure is," Clay almost hummed. "And we can fix that. Get your ass over to Operations right now. And don't get it shot, or Jake will crush me."

"Yes, sir!" The line went dead at once. Clay turned to Gleason.

"We may just have a trump card, Sergeant."

-

"Advance," Jose said calmly. The entire line walked forward, still shooting. Zach held back roughly one step, Keeping an eye behind them as well as on their flanks.

The enemy, whoever they were, had not yet noticed they were being clipped from the west flank and continued forward. They began to come under fire from people defending the Hill, and at that point they noticed that they were losing people at a high rate.

"Down," Jose issued another one-word order and all seven men hit the ground prone. Zach no longer held back, instead bringing the light machine gun into play against the survivors. Keeping to short, controlled bursts, he swept the area to their front, the Mark 48 demoralizing the enemy as much as it damaged them physically. Their adversary was now pinned between two fields of fire and could not stand that kind of heat for long.

Perhaps two minutes after being engaged from two directions, the surviving aggressors seemed to come to a unanimous and unified decision to jump to their feet and run for their lives. Normally the defenders might have stopped shooting, but not this time. Too much farm blood had been spilled, too many friends were dead.

"Pursuit," Jose ordered, getting to his feet. "Cautiously. Take no chances. Or prisoners."

The line moved forward without a word.

-

Carrie Jarrett heard a powerful engine behind her but couldn't spare the time to check it out. Hopefully it was a Cougar with some help. Parris was absolutely dead, and Abramson was not dealing with that fact well at all. He was essentially useless, leaving her to defend the position alone. She was confident of her ability, but she also knew her limitations, something mercilessly drilled into her psyche during her initial training. Those limitations included holding this position alone for any length of time. She could hear firing to her right and left, which meant she was not completely alone and isolated, but having someone dozens of yards away was not nearly as comforting as having competent help right beside her.

As the noise got louder, she finally risked a glance behind her and found a large, armored vehicle backing over her position, covering the entrance. As the hatch opened, a Guardsman named Howard and a Guardswoman she knew as Isaacson, rushed inside. The woman guided Abramson to the safety of the vehicle while Howard grabbed Parris' body and dragged it in the same direction. Devon Knowles passed the two as she stepped down into the bunker.

"Pest control," Devon snarked. "Clay heard you needed a squad to help and sent me. Figured I'd be enough."

"You definitely talk enough shit for a whole squad," Carrie gave her friend as good as she got. "I am glad to see you, girl."

"Pleasure to be here," Devon said sarcastically. "Now, let's kick some ass."

-

Despite Devon's apparent desire to 'kick some ass', within five minutes of her arrival, it became obvious that their enemy was breaking off their attack. A few parting shots from much further back toward the tree line than just a minute before were the last efforts of a defeated enemy.

All along the southern line, people continued to watch from their sunken defenses, hoping it really was over.

-

Faron Gillis scanned ahead of him with binoculars, trying to see through the trees and onto the highway as he looked for any sign of the next attack. He knew that the last attack had taken a great deal of damage, but so far that hadn't seemed to discourage them. While he wanted to hope that the battle was over, he knew better than to take it for granted. The people attacking them had fought with a fervor usually attributed only to the truly desperate or else the true fanatics.

Both were extraordinarily dangerous.

There were ten people left on the eastern line, and he and Dezi Martin, his driver, were two of them. Several of the others were wounded and all of them were tired. Another massed attack just might be enough to get by them, and that could spell doom for the farm. The area behind them was only lightly defended, a hollow shell with very few actual guns. That meant that his people, regardless of their condition, had to fight and hold, right here.

His eye was drawn to movement to his front, and he turned the binoculars to look in that direction. Movement continued, though he was unable to clearly make out what it might be. He was about to call out a warning to the line when the sound of a powerful vehicle, punctuated by the hammering of a machine gun, came roaring through the woods from the direction of the interstate.

"What the hell?" Gillis leaned forward, ducking almost instinctively, until he realized that none of that fire was reaching him. Or kicking up dirt around the rest of his group. The firing continued for over a minute before going quiet. The silence was almost deafening.

He tensed as the front end of a Hummer came into view, having obviously driven around the log trailer blocking the road. The gun atop the Hummer was unmanned and pointing skyward.

"Who in the hell is that?" he wondered aloud.

-

"Enough," Jose ordered finally as the final dregs of their enemy escaped through the heavier woods to the south. He had to repeat the order as he roughly patted Zach's shoulder. The teen nodded and ceased firing at once. He simply hadn't heard the first time, Jose realized.

"We need to sanitize this area," Jose noted, removing his pistol and screwing a suppressor on the end of the barrel. Others followed suit, or else reached for their knives.

"I don't want anyone left alive out here," Jose ordered flatly. "Nobody to kill one of ours as we try and investigate and glean the field. Make sure of it."

-

"Operations, this is Gillis, over."

"Go for Operations, Lieutenant," Leon replied.

"Please advise Bossman that we are clear up here, and that he may want to take a ride up this way. We have some visitors he'll be interested in."

"Who is it, Faron?" Clay took the radio. "I'm a little busy here."

"Someone we thought was long gone, sir," Gillis said carefully. *"Rather not say more than that, even on our own channel. Maybe especially on our own channel."*

Clay pondered that for a few seconds. There were only a few reasons for Gillis to be less than forthcoming with his radio traffic. He obviously felt someone might be listening in, and that the news he had was sensitive at least for now. It wasn't bad news, well probably not, anyway, since all they'd had this morning was bad news. Thus, it was likely to be good news, or at least neutral. At this point, he'd take neutral, to be honest. Suddenly the quiet broke through his ruminations.

"Do you hear that?" he asked the room in general.

"I don't hear anything," Janice was the first to respond, sounding apologetic.

"I don't hear any shooting," Millie noted. "I…I don't hear any shooting at all!" she added with more enthusiasm.

"Neither do I," Leon nodded slowly. He reached for the phone and called Jody Thompson, then Samantha Walters.

"Jody and Sam both report no fire from any direction at this time," he informed his uncle.

"I'll be up there in a few, Faron," Clay told Gillis suddenly. "Soon as I can secure everything here."

"Roger that, Bossman," Gillis sounded happy. *"We'll be here."*

-

"Rat, Scope, get the rides and bring 'em this way," Jose ordered. "Rest of you, spread out and look for anyone we may have missed. I'd prefer none of them escape, and certainly none to hide and wait. Move it."

The two commandos began running back to where their electric carts had been left while the other five began beating the metaphorical bushes for any enemies that remained. By the time the carts caught up to them, Jose was satisfied that no one was left of the force that had attacked the farm from their current direction.

"Load up, back to base," Jose ordered. "Sounds like we're in a lull, at least. Maybe it's over. We can comb this area later. Right now, security of the farm is the highest priority."

Without a word, the seven men loaded onto the carts and started down the road for home, leaving nothing but carnage behind them. A fit calling card if ever there was one.

-

"What is that?" Clay leaned forward in the passenger seat of the Hummer he was riding in.

"That would be a Hummer," Greg Holloway couldn't contain his sarcasm even in the face of an attack. "It's a military vehicle."

Clay had sent for Greg before going forward to see what Faron Gillis wanted.

"He's right," Gleason, behind the wheel, added with a straight face. "Army uses them sometimes."

"Aren't you two a pair of comedians," Clay all but snarled. "A regular Laurel and Hardy."

"Dude, no need to get testy," Greg chuckled. "You would have figured that out without our help." He paused before adding: "Eventually."

The Hummer pulled to a halt behind Gillis' Cougar before Clay could summon a response to that dig, so he didn't bother to try. Gleason was the one who leaned forward this time, muttering under his breath.

"What is it?" Clay asked, looking the same way.

"That is Lieutenant Flores," Gleason said flatly. "Sir," he added as an afterthought. Seemed that Gleason really didn't think any more of Flores than Clay did. How 'bout that?

"Well, shit," Clay sighed. "Just when you thought things couldn't get any worse." Shaking his head, Clay dismounted, the other two following suit. Gillis saw them and jogged their way.

"Mist-, Clay," the young man caught himself, "they showed up during the final attack. Smeared the biggest attack so far across the highway from the rear. Probably saved us some casualties. Then Flores came through with a single Hummer and driver, no one on the gun. The rest of her folks are waiting on the highway."

"How many 'folks' are we talking about?" Clay asked, his stomach beginning to boil.

"Gordy and Bodee have gone to check on that," Gillis informed him.

"What does she want?" Clay demanded.

"All she asked for was to talk to you, Clay," Gillis shrugged. "And she asked, not demanded. Whatever she has been through seems to have changed her quite a bit."

"Uh huh," Clay grunted. "Well, we may as well get this over with," he sighed. "Let's go see what she wants."

Snow crunched beneath them as the four men walked to where Lieutenant Flores stood waiting. Clay had to admit she didn't look like the arrogant little diva he had met before. She looked haggard and worn, tired even.

"Mister Sanders," Flores said softly, nodding her head. "Sergeant Gleason," she smiled faintly at the NCO. "I'm glad to see you well."

"What can we do for you, Lieutenant?" Clay all but demanded. He hadn't missed the fact that she apparently wasn't happy to see him doing well.

"I'm glad you seem to have made it through the virus, Mister Sanders," Flores shocked him to his core. "I honestly had my doubts, though I had hoped that you were okay. I figured if anyone could escape the plague and the uprisings, it was you."

"Uprisings?" Clay asked, frowning.

"After the plague, things turned into a free-for-all," Flores nodded. "Most of the surviving soldiers have left, trying to get home to their families, or where they hope their families are. Some lost the family members they had with us and…well, they lost more than that, I'm afraid. Some seemed to have wandered away in the dark while others simply packed up and left, unable or unwilling to stay behind where children or spouses had died. Same for survivors of our people who died. Disappeared into the night without a word. I…I wouldn't have tried to stop them, other than talking to them, but maybe they thought that I would." She shook her head slowly.

"I wouldn't try to make anyone do anything now," she said softly after a brief pause. "There are horrors out there, Mister Sanders. Things you couldn't imagine-,"

"I don't have to imagine," Clay cut her off, though not harshly. "I've seen them before. So, your men ran away, and you don't care? That it?"

"It's not that I don't care," she continued shaking her head slowly. "If I could have, I'd probably have joined them."

"Why didn't you?" Greg asked, speaking for the first time.

"With the major, and probably the captain gone, I was the senior officer," Flores shrugged, looking up at them all. "If I just…ran off, then someone else would have had to shoulder that burden. I may not be the best officer ever, but even I know that's a chickenshit move."

Clay's non-existent respect for Flores went up a notch at that.

"So, I stayed," she continued. "I stayed until there was nothing left that we could do. No one left to protect except ourselves. Everyone else decided to fend for themselves, melting into the woodwork. Like I said, I don't blame them, and I hope they do well."

"How many are left?" Clay asked. He had a sudden inkling of what Flores might want.

"Fifteen, counting me," she told him flatly. "Fifteen," she repeated in a whisper. "Just fifteen."

"And what brings you here?" Clay asked, his tone softening. Flores was in bad shape, he suddenly realized. Exhaustion for sure, and maybe more. "As I recall, I promised I'd have you shot if I saw you on my land again."

"I'm looking for a home for the people I have left," she admitted. "We brought everything we could from the park, everything we could fit into a truck. Everyone driving a vehicle, alone. Five tractor trailers and six 939's. All stuffed to the rafters with supplies, including the cab areas. One Hummer and one six-wheel Cougar to make it look as if we had at least some kind of escort. Both of them are full up, as well."

"What kind of supplies?" Clay asked. "And what do you plan on doing with them?"

"Giving them to you if we can join your farm," Flores said openly. "Like I said, we're looking for a home. There is a little of everything, really. MREs, medical gear, tools, all our remaining weapons and ammunition and other munitions, what clothing, boots and gear we had left, the list is long. I've got it all catalogued for your supply group, assuming you agree," she held up a thick sheaf of papers.

"What is the breakdown of your personnel?" Clay asked her.

"Most are officially listed as non-combatants, but that hasn't really worked out for any of them," Flores snorted. "Besides me, there is one Physician's Assistant, one Registered Nurse, two combat medics, one supply specialist, three MPs, an armorer, a mechanic, a firefighter, a combat engineer and a carpentry and masonry specialist. We were running a small hospital at the park, but we don't have an actual doctor. We do have the gear and remaining supplies of a field medical unit that we grabbed from Medical Command in Smyrna; we just didn't have a doctor. The two medics were there assisting the PA, the park was the official duty station for the supply troops and the others. The MPs were part of our security."

"A lot we don't have, gear wise and skill wise," Greg whispered behind Clay's head, and he nodded fractionally.

"Is this some place to winter to you, Flores, or are you looking to stay here permanently?" Clay asked, keeping his voice carefully neutral.

"We're looking for somewhere permanent," Flores told him without hesitation. "Those here with me are all without attachments and have no one to look for or go to. We're all each other has. I brought us here because I'd been here, and I knew that if you were willing to let us in, we could make a good addition to your place. I know I didn't make the best impression on you, Mister Sanders, but…you were right. I was still looking at things as if this were temporary and that things would return to normal, or at least some version of it. I'm sorry for the way I approached you before. The long and short of it was that I listened to the wrong Captain."

"There was a Captain in the Headquarters unit that…well, to be honest, she fed me a load of bullshit, as Major Whitten called it, and I ate it up. Told me that martial law changed things, made us the ultimate authority in the land. Convinced me that people in positions like yours had to be put 'into check', as she called it. I suppose she saw me as fertile ground to sow her line of crap in. It didn't help me any that I had let my position go to my head and my attitude get the better of me. They try to teach us not to do that, but most of us do it at least once, anyway.

Mine was more than once, I'm sorry to say, but it's a weakness I no longer possess. I'm responsible for too much, even now."

"What I *should* have done was stick to Captain Adcock like glue," she finished. "Course, if I had, I'd probably be dead now. Damned if you do, and if you don't."

Clay was at a loss for words. Was this the same woman he had met...how long ago? It seemed like years, now. Humble, worn, tired, she looked almost but not quite defeated.

Clay liked that. She was still going despite it all.

"I'm impressed, Lieutenant," Clay used her rank as a courtesy. "Not just with your actions, but also your determination, and your attitude. Owning up to past mistakes, even pointing out the cause without shifting the blame. I almost don't know who I'm speaking to." Flores snorted at that.

"Major Whitten said the same thing," she chuckled. "Before he died," she added, her humor fleeing at that.

"Might interest you to know that Captain Adcock had a high opinion of you when you all first got here. Bragged on your professional development a good bit," Clay's voice was gentle. "I assume you're all clean? Health wise I mean?" he changed gears suddenly, trying to avoid embarrassing Flores any more than she was already.

"We are, but I have blood samples already drawn from all of us if you want to look them over," Flores nodded, back to business, the emotional part of their discussion behind them for now.

"Let Mister Gillis collect those samples and take them in, then," Clay ordered, nodding at Gillis. "You and I can continue our discussion in the meanwhile. You mentioned uprisings earlier. What did you mean by that?"

"They're in the back floorboard, in a sealed box, Faron," Flores told Gillis.

"Roger that," Gillis nodded, hurrying to the Hummer. She turned back to Clay as Gillis departed.

"Hunger, plague, loss, it all adds up after a while, I suppose," Flores told him. "I don't know what it was, Mister Sanders-,"

"Okay, how about you just call me Clay from here on?" Clay cut her off, but not unkindly. "Mister Sanders is my father."

Flores surprised him with a smile, nodding her head. He could have sworn her face was flushed.

"I don't know what it was, Clay, that set things off," she continued, looking more relaxed. "Any of the above, all of the above, or something entirely different that I'm unaware of. I doubt we'll ever know. The cities were already a nightmare. Radio traffic from all around the region confirmed that, whether it was military bands, law enforcement and emergency services, or ham operators spreading the news. I don't know how they could have been any worse, or gotten any worse I should say, but apparently, they did. Now, it's like a huge riot that just rolls across the land. Almost scorched Earth from what little we've been able to hear."

"Is that what hit us today?" Clay wanted to know.

"I'd have to guess, but probably," Flores replied. "They don't bother with talking or bartering, from what we know. They favor scouting for a day or two and then attacking all at once. A few have shown some tactical moves, using enfilades and flanking maneuvers and what have you, but all we've heard of were small unit stuff. I don't think there's any one group, or that there's any real organization among them. But there are a lot of them. They're effectively completing what the plague didn't do. Wiping us out."

"We've experienced that today," Clay nodded. "I have to thank you for sweeping up the mess on the interstate for us, by the way," he added, and again she seemed to flush a bit in pleasure.

"You're welcome, Mis-, Clay," she caught herself. "For a moment as we pulled up I feared the worst, but then I saw all the casualties and decided you were giving them all they could handle. We just cleaned up for you, as you said."

"It took a lot of strain off of us, Lieutenant-," It was Flores' turn to hold up a hand and interrupt.

"If I'm calling you Clay, then you need to start calling me Triana," she told him. Clay considered that for a second before nodding.

"That's fair, and doable," he told her with a grin. "You guys took a lot of strain off us, Triana. While we would have stopped them, it would have hurt us more, and we've hurt enough, today." Bitterness crept into his voice as he thought of Stacey Pryor and Corey Reynard lying under a tarp behind T2.

"I'm sorry," Flores said gently. "It's like that everywhere. At least as far as we know. There's no more contact with either coast, or the north outside of intermittent contact with Fort Knox. I'm sure there are still people out there with functioning units, but I think they've shut them off and hunkered down, hoping to wait it out. Being on the air draws attention, and attention is usually a death sentence."

"Seems that way," Clay nodded, thinking of all the attention they had drawn to themselves since everything had begun. Gleason had used the Hummer to take Gillis to the clinic, so Clay leaned on the Cougar, then sat down on the bumper.

"You're welcome to share the bumper with me," he told Flores and then Greg. The former looked both relieved and pleased at the offer and hurried to accept it. Greg hesitated, looking around.

"I think I'm going to check on this line," he told Clay. "Also see if Gordy and Kev have made it back."

"Okay," Clay nodded. Greg walked away, the only sound being the crunch of snow and ice beneath his boots.

"Thank you," Flores said softly into the quiet.

"For what?" Clay asked, looking her way.

"For not throwing us out without giving me a chance to beg," she replied. "It wasn't for me. It was for the people following me. I would have left alone if you would have kept them and not me. They followed me because...because they looked to me for leadership and there was no one else. No one else and it was supposed to be my job, right? Only, I hadn't done my job very well, I don't think, no matter how pleased Major Whitten was with my improvement. There was no way to stay where we were, we just didn't have the bodies to make it secure. And there was too much ordnance still there to let a bunch like this," she waved toward the highway, "grab on to it."

"What kind of ordnance?" Clay asked, curious. In answer to his question, she reached into her tunic and withdrew a small notebook. Opening it, she began detailing what each truck was carrying. Clay listened with speaking, though his eyebrows did raise a few times at the mention of certain items. By the time she was half-way through her recitation, Gillis was returning, sliding to a stop a few vehicle lengths from the Cougar.

"They're all clean, sir," the young officer reported. "No anti-bodies, either. None of them appear to have even been exposed, the doctor reports."

"That is good news," Clay nodded. "Well, Lieutenant Flores, how about you go and get the rest of your folks. I'll have someone move that trailer, and you can all pull down to the front of the Troy Farm, the place where you met me before," he clarified at her frown. "I need to see about the rest of my folks and start…start seeing how badly we were hurt," he finished sadly.

"Yes, sir," Flores snapped to and then headed for her own vehicle.

"Faron, get Cliff or Roddy up here with something that will open the road," Clay ordered. "Then have it closed up when they're all through."

"Got it, Boss."

CHAPTER ELEVEN

Jose and the others were arriving when Clay pulled in at the Troy farm. Dismounting, he looked at his friend questioningly.

"I think we're good," Jose nodded. "We found their flank, including an attack angling for the Hill. Put paid to them all and walked our way down their line. No prisoners," he added.

"Good," Clay nodded. "Get a crew of civies together, with a strong escort. We need to glean the field and then start getting those bodies in the ground. They'll draw predators in this kind of weather where food is scarce."

"On it," Jose agreed. "I thought I'd take this same bunch back as security, though I hadn't started thinking on who would clean up."

"Use as many healthy civies as you can for the gathering, I guess," Clay mused, frowning. "If I can get caught up, I'll help, too. Try to leave the security troops in place for now. We may or may not have gotten them all. According to Flores, this is happening everywhere."

"Flores?" Jose frowned. "You've heard from the outside?"

"In a manner," Clay chuckled. He took the next few minutes to explain the events of the past hour. By the time Jose was caught up, a convoy of heavy vehicles was slowly moving up the road toward the farms.

"Well," Jose made a slightly sour face. "Wonders never cease, I guess. We'll get on with the business. I will pull Gordy for the backhoe, assuming you don't mind?"

"Do it," Clay agreed at once. "He needs a distraction after Corey died and Heath was wounded."

"What I was thinking," Jose sighed. "Damn shame about Straight Edge," he added, his voice going mournful for just a second.

"Yeah," Clay agreed. "Empty chairs, brother."

"Empty chairs," Jose agreed. "We're on the move."

-

The rest of the day was a beehive of activity that kept most of the farm from thinking over much about how many people were in the clinic in serious condition, not to mention how many tarp-covered mounds were behind Building Two. Some of those names caught a few people by surprise.

In a spare minute alone, Clay walked down the row, stopping briefly at each one to look at their faces. He knew them all, but two he knew much better than the rest.

"Good journey, brother," he murmured to Stacey Pryor's calm features. "Our travels together are at an end. You go on alone from here. The rest of us will see you soon enough." Returning the shroud to its place, he continued until he found the body of Corey Reynard.

"Corey, I am so sorry," Clay whispered. "If I could go back and not have that training mission, I would in a second, and yet without you four out there, we would have been hurting. Probably overrun. Thank you for defending us, kiddo. A trooper to the end," he patted the boy's still shoulder gently. "We'll miss you, Rey. We'll miss you and we won't forget." Replacing the shroud, he stood and examined the row. The names echoed in his head as he stood there, lost in thought.

Corey Reynard
Freda Fletcher
Eunice Maynard
Parnell Plank
Zayne Parris
Ellis Gates
Talia Gray
Stacey Pryor

He had sent for Greg once he realized Gray was among the dead. His friend had looked at the young woman's body, asked how she had died, and then returned to work.

Talia's leg wound had indeed cut her femoral artery. She had lost too much blood by the time medical aid made it to her and she had died on the table as Jaylyn attempted to treat her.

Freda Fletcher had suffered a head wound, and a wound to her neck as well. Field treatment in the ditch was not enough to save her.

Eunice Maynard had also suffered a head wound, an apparent ricochet that had gone through her left eye and probably killed her instantly.

Parnell Plank had bled to death of multiple wounds even as Raven Elliot had tried valiantly to save him under fire.

Ellis Gates had taken a steel core round between the panels of his vest, the bullet tearing him apart inside even as he looked unharmed other than blood seeping down his side.

Corey had died of multiple wounds, either from an automatic weapon or by being targeted by two or more decent shooters. He had died shooting, defending his home and the people he called family.

And Stacey Pryor. Hit just below the collar, his friend would have bled out in two minutes or so, according to Jaylyn Thatcher. She had almost whispered it in his ear, the sadness in her voice still easy to hear. She and her husband had gotten to know Stacey fairly well on their trek east.

Eight dead. Eight more wounded, some severely.

Savannah Hale had taken a round to the thigh. She would recover but would be out of action for at least two months as she healed and then returned to fitness for the field.

Jena Waller had a bullet wound to her left shoulder, just outside her vest. Lucky in that it had missed the shoulder joint, it was still messy, and would likewise require at least a month of recovery, and that was assuming all went well.

Keely Irwin's left arm was smashed, and she had an ugly gouge along the left side of her head. She was in what Jaylyn called a 'shallow coma' and might yet lose her arm. If she didn't wake up, then that would be the least of her injuries.

Heath Kelly had a broken arm, an in-and-out through wound on the meaty part of his left thigh, and a severe concussion. The last Clay had heard, he was still not tracking quite right, but had been medicated enough that he would rest easy even while he was forced to stay awake. His niece was going back and forth from Operations to the Clinic every few minutes, trying to check on him.

Matt Kenny was still unconscious and was suffering from massive internal bruising due to a high-powered round hitting him in the back. While his vest held, it couldn't stop all the kinetic force from the bullet. He would probably recover, but it might be weeks before he was back to battery.

Carol Kennard's left arm had been treated and she had been given light duty for the next week. Good fortune had favored her today.

Heather Patton. Clay shook his head as he recalled her being brought into the clinic, swearing that she was fine and should be back on the line. Jaylyn took one look at her arm and vehemently disagreed. Heather's left arm was not broken, exactly, but it was cracked and the wound that caused it full of dirt, rocks and even gunpowder residue. The memory of hearing about her efforts even after her arm had been broken managed to bring a smile to Clay's face, sad though it was. That girl was definitely a fighter. That was good. They would need fighters.

Mitchell Nolan had suffered a graze to his arm and a 'nick' to his left temple that was bandaged by Kait Caudell, who had added an admonishment for him to take it easy for the remainder of the day. He had laughed at her even as he retrieved his gear and left the clinic, a clearly amused Kait shaking her head slowly as she walked to the field phone and called the Troy House to inform Beverly Jackson of her orders.

Fourteen people gone or out of commission for weeks to come, two more walking wounded, and no telling how much psychological trauma to work through for some.

And fifteen people showing up at just the right moment to fill that gap. A coincidence that Clay could not help feeling uneasy about. Fate? Good luck? Harbinger of bad things to come?

He was too tired to think about it, and it didn't matter anyway. Flores' people had immediately joined in the work that needed done, the medical officers heading to the clinic, while the two medics ran back and forth to the trucks for equipment or supplies that the clinic didn't have. Others were either slipping into their own roles or else simply joining up with labor parties trying to fix the damage the farm had taken during the assault.

Crews walked the battlefield, collecting arms, ammunition and equipment from the dead. They could be traded away or used on the farm. Other items were evaluated during the search and either added to the pile or left with the bodies.

Behind them came the backhoe, collecting bodies to be dumped into a trench that was already dug. Leaving the bodies out, even overnight, was an invitation to any predators in the area, so that was also a priority.

"Everything is a priority," Clay muttered to himself, his gaze locked on the southern horizon.

"What's a priority, Cowboy?" a welcome and familiar voice asked from behind him. A genuine smile on his face, Clay turned and embraced a beautiful redhead with a rifle slung across her shoulder.

"Glad to see me?" Lainie Harper said softly, hugging him tightly.

"You have no idea," he sighed, his own hug just as tight.

"Oh, I might have an idea," she pulled back, looking at him. "You look exhausted, poor baby. Are you okay?"

"I'm as okay as I'm able to be," he took a deep breath. "Lost a lot of people today. Including Stacey and Corey."

"Corey?" Lainie was shocked. "And Stacey too?"

"And six more," he pointed to the row of shrouded dead he had just left. "Heath is inside with a head wound and a broken arm, among other problems. A lot of others are in there, too. Oh, and Flores showed up with a convoy and fifteen people, counting her. How about that?"

"Hey, you need to calm down, sweetie," Lainie frowned in concern and the normally taciturn Clay rattled on and on. "Take a deep breath and try to calm yourself. Flores was the mouthy lieutenant, right?"

"The first one," Clay nodded, after holding his breath and counting to ten before slowly releasing it. "She seems to have undergone a transformation since then. Being under fire will do that to you. She ended up as the senior officer left at their HQ, and we were their last hope. Brought us truckloads of presents in exchange." He pointed to the idled convoy out on the road.

"Well, that was thoughtful," Lainie tried to be encouraging. "Why don't we find a place to sit down, and you tell me about it. Okay?"

"Okay."

-

Flores watched as two of her better drivers maneuvered the vehicles her group had brought with them into a rough line behind the three identical buildings that most of the farm's operations seemed to be ran from. First had been the five-tons, now it was the semis. The Hummer and M-RAP had been designated to the far building known as T3. She was sure there was some significance to that name but had no idea yet what it might be.

Clay had wanted to know how many vehicles she had left behind her due to a lack of personnel. She had informed him there were two more Cougars, four more Hummers, and several civilian vehicles as well as some equipment, including an engineering vehicle that had survived the storm.

"Anything else?" he asked.

"Supplies and parts we didn't have room for," she had nodded. "No ordnance. I felt that was the most important thing. Not to arm these terrorists any better than they already were."

122

FIRE FROM THE SKY

"Good call," he had agreed.

She could tell he had something simmering behind that cool gaze but lacked the nerve to ask. The change in him from her first meeting was all but palpable and it took very little time for her to realize that what she was seeing now was the real Clayton Sanders. What she had seen before was a civil veneer that he tried to wear in order to be less frightening.

And it was frightening, not just intimidating. More to the point, several of the people working with him projected that same aura. A complete lack of concern about anything. It didn't surprise her that such a large group had been unsuccessful in attacking this farm.

It also made her exceedingly glad that Captain Adcock had not allowed her to antagonize Sanders any further than she had.

-

Zach finally found a minute to rest easy and reflect on the events of the day. He sat on a fence rail, looking southward once more. In the furthest southeast corner of the farm's territory was a new burial trench containing eighty-one bodies. Eighty-one. It made him wonder what the total number of people in the attack had been.

He considered the loss of Corey Reynard. A good friend and a brother for most of Zach's life. Like Kade. Both now gone, forever, and Zach hoped to a far better place than the one they had left behind.

Then he thought about Heath, lying in the clinic with a mangled arm, a bad leg and...issues, with his awareness. He closed his eyes and looked skyward, praying for his friend's well-being. That he would recover and still be the same old Heath he had known for so long.

"What'cha doing?" a female voice broke his reverie. He turned to see Kim Powers studying him from more than an arm length away. Smart girl.

"Just thinking about the day," he replied honestly. "I take it you're okay?"

"As much as I can be," she nodded, closing the distance between them now that Zach was aware of her presence. She ended up between his knees, her head resting on his chest.

"Talia was a friend," she said, her soft voice muffled as she talked into his coat.

"I know the feeling," he replied, wrapping his arms around her in a loose but firm embrace. "More than once, in fact."

123

"Sorry," she looked up at him. "I shouldn't act like I'm the only one."

"You aren't," he shrugged. "Everyone is dealing. Some more than others. Talia was okay."

"I feel bad for Greg Holloway," Kim continued. Zach nodded but added nothing. The two of them decided to be silent and still for the time being.

-

"You okay?"

Abigail Sanders' voice made Greg Holloway look up from where he was cleaning his gear. He smiled faintly at her and pointed to a spot next to him on the log he was using as a seat.

"I'm good," he nodded, returning to his work. "You?"

"We didn't have to do anything," she nodded, taking the offered seat. "Guarding the back door, so to speak."

"Has to be done," Greg assured her. "I'm glad you weren't up here," he added, not looking up.

"Don't have any faith in my shooting?" she chuckled, lightly bumping him with her shoulder.

"Don't want you having to do this," he shook his head.

"Oh," Abby didn't know what else to say to that. "I appreciate it," she finally did say.

"How's Leanne?" Greg wanted to know.

"Frantic with worry," Abby admitted. "Nothing she's been told has helped with that. She's too smart to lie to, so they have to tell her like it is."

"And how is it?" he asked, finally looking up. She blushed faintly at his direct attention but didn't look away.

"If he wakes up tomorrow tracking okay, then Jaylyn says he'll be out of danger," she reported. "His arm will need rehab, but she says it will definitely heal, and his leg is an afterthought compared to the rest, so long as it doesn't get infected. So, we wait for daylight, I guess."

"I hope the kid's okay," Greg turned his attention back to his gear. "Losing Corey is more than enough."

"I still can't believe it," Abby agreed. "Sam is talking to Terri Hartwell right now. She is…I guess distraught is not too strong a word," she decided. "Her and Corey were more or less a thing, and now…well, is now," she shrugged, a gesture of helplessness.

"I know the feeling," Greg nodded slowly.

"Sorry," Abby turned red as she realized what she'd said.

"For what?" Greg frowned, looking up at her. "What did you do now?" he actually grinned.

"Nothing!" she shot back, mock outrage playing across her features before softening. "I meant about Talia."

"Ah," Greg nodded. "Yeah, that was too bad. She was good people. Tough and determined. Dependable. We'll miss her." He sheathed his knife and began scrubbing at his web gear next.

"I meant...I mean you and her...I mean...." Abby ran out of words and just stopped, face redder than before.

"I know what you meant," Greg let her off the hook easy. "It's not like that. Never was. Friends, yes. She was good people, like I said. I enjoyed her company. I know everyone assumed we were more, but no. Just friends."

"I'm still sorry, then, since I was one of the assuming ones," she admitted. "I meant it in the nicest way," she added with a bashful smile.

"I know you did," he chuckled lightly. "She did a good job. Damn shame she got clipped on the way out. Still, you can never know. Another reason I'm glad you weren't part of all this," he added, his voice serious. Once more Abby felt a blush spread across her face.

"I'm fine," she promised him, leaning over until her shoulder touched his, where she let it stay. "I'm just fine."

-

Gordon Sanders felt a sadness settle over him as he rode into the area around the giant buildings his son had built on the Troy farm. Even though the battle hadn't reached here, it still made an impact. Several people sported bandages or worked to repair gear broken during the battle. Gail Knight had left to report to Jose Juarez now that she was on the premises. Charley Wilmeth had stayed near Gordon, not being a part of the defense forces.

"I'm going to see if Clayton is inside," Gordon told her, swinging down to the ground. "Mind holding on to my horse for me?"

"Not at all," Charley smiled, taking the reins. "We'll just be here, waiting for you."

"Thank you," Gordon smiled back, then stepped inside Building Two.

Into a maze of organized confusion. He saw Leon walking out of the radio room and waved.

"Hey, Grandpa," Leon smiled ever so slightly. "What are you doing here?"

"Just checking in to see how things are," Gordon replied, hugging Leon tightly. "Everyone okay?"

"No, not everyone," Leon's smile faded. "We lost Corey Reynard, among others. And Heath is unconscious over in the clinic. Leanne is with him now."

Gordon felt the weight of what Leon had said settle on him, feeling weak for a moment.

"Corey," he murmured. "He was a good boy. And Heath is in the clinic, you say?"

"Yes, sir," Leon nodded. "He's in bad shape, too," the teen added softly. "I don't know what Leanne will do if…I mean, she and Heath…." He didn't finish, just trailed off lamely, not knowing what to say.

"I know, son," Gordon patted Leon's shoulder. "I know. I'll step inside and talk to Patricia when I can. Where is Clayton?"

"Probably out back, somewhere," Leon shrugged. "He was watching them bring in those new vehicles, and also that's…that's where Stacey Pryor and Corey are…laid out."

"Pryor, too?" Gordon asked. "How many others?"

"At least five more dead that I know of, but there may be more. I don't know exactly how many wounded, but several are hurt pretty badly," Leon reported. "It was a hard fight."

"Most of them are for someone," Gordon assured him. "I'll see you later, son."

"Yes, sir."

-

Patricia Sanders saw her father-in-law enter the clinic and moved to his side.

"Hello, Dad," she smiled tiredly.

"You look tired, Pat," he smiled. "You okay?"

"I'm a little old for this kind of action," she laughed softly. "Everything alright?"

"I guess as much as it can be," he replied, catching sight of his granddaughter sitting next to a still figure. "How is she," he nodded in Leanne's direction.

"She alters between fussy and flighty," Patricia replied. "One minute she's literally throwing a fit for information and demanding to know everything we've done, the next she's disappeared, probably to Operations, or maybe to Clayton's office to hide. Then, she's back and no one saw her come in."

"Is she in the way?" Gordon asked. "Hindering you at all?"

"No," Patricia's voice was kind. "She's worried sick and dealing with it as best she can. She's very young to be going through something like this, Dad."

"She is that," he nodded. "Well, if she becomes a problem, let me know and I'll take her home. Maybe to her grandmother. Either way, I'll move her out of the way for a while. She looks like she needs some sleep, anyway."

"Almost certainly, but so do most of us after today," Patricia agreed. "I'll call if we need you."

"Take care of yourself, Pat," Gordon encouraged before leaving.

"Right," her answer came after he had gone.

-

"Watches will be in two hour increments tonight," Jose ordered. "Everyone is tired. We'll double up on the patrol numbers as well. Stronger patrols and maybe add one as well. Reaction force can sleep, but only if they're geared up. We'll see what tomorrow brings before we change things back to normal. I want a Hummer and a Cougar four-wheel on the pad, ready to move, at all times. Questions?" There were none.

"Let's get separated into new watches, then, and get our game faces back on," he ordered. "We've got people holding the line that haven't had a break yet. Let's get them relieved so they can get warm, rest and eat. Move out."

The meeting broke apart, leaving Jose alone for the moment. He was surprised to see Martina Sanchez, his significant other, coming his way with a food container.

"Since Mohammed won't come to the mountain," she teased, handing him the dish. He removed the top and immediately began to eat.

"It's not going anywhere, *Amanté*," she teased, smiling. "How are you faring, *mi Vida*?" her voice softened, and her facial expression grew more concerned.

"About as well as I can," he shrugged, slowing his ravenous eating. "I'll miss him. It was good to have him back even for a little while."

"I am sorry, Jose," she held his arm gently, resting her head on his shoulder. "He was a good man."

"He was at that," Jose agreed. "One of the best."

Similar discussions were taking place all over the farm. They had lost more people today than had been lost in total since the beginning of the disaster that had been the Storm. This time, there would be many empty chairs. While life would continue for the rest, they would be poorer for the absences.

Some emptiness could not be filled.

CHAPTER TWELVE

The farm remained busy through the night. Those not on watch tried to sleep a few hours or else worked to ready gear and equipment for another day of fighting should it happen. The clinic was a beehive of activity even after everyone had received initial treatments. Visitors came and went, people slipping in to see comrades or ask about their prognosis, but only as they had time from other duties. The medical staff slept in two-hour shifts, buoyed by the arrival of the medical personnel that had accompanied Flores. Their presence meant that the farm's medical corps could actually sleep rather than just catnap.

By sunup, everyone had been able to eat at least one hot meal, sleep at least two hours if not more, refill canteens and ammo pouches and warm up. Most took the time to change socks to protect their feet from the cold and wet conditions, but no one hit the showers. Returning to the cold with wet hair and damp skin and clothing was just asking for sickness and recovering from such things was no longer a matter of a shot or a round of antibiotics.

Leon used one of his drones to recon the farm's perimeter once the sun was above the horizon, giving him light to see. Clay watched silently over his nephew's shoulder as the drone's camera dutifully revealed what there was to see.

Which was nothing. There was nothing to see. Whoever had been responsible for the attack had departed completely. The collection of vehicles and horses that Jose had reported were gone this morning, the road empty of any traffic or signs of life at all.

"All clear, Uncle Clay," Leon said finally, once he had made a circuit of the farm. "Might be a body or two in the shadows, of course, and maybe even someone alive for that matter, but the camera is pretty good, and I took the pass as low as I could. Whatever was left of them is gone."

"Good," Clay said firmly. "Thanks, Leon."

"Hey, it's what I do."

-

"We appear to be in the clear for now," Clay told the assembled officers and NCOs. "That may last for hours, days or forever for all I know, but right now we're okay. Flores, I want you to get with Jose and

129

plan a mission to return to your old HQ and pick up anything of value you had to leave. That includes vehicles. If you didn't have fuel for them, take enough to get them back here. I want this mission done in one day, mind you. Leave early and back as soon as humanly possible."

"We'll return to regular watches tomorrow," he continued. "No sense in driving our people into the snow if we don't have to. We're going to have to do some building, but that's going to have to wait for better weather. First thing going up will be the new towers. They would have been nice to have yesterday." A chorus of 'Amens' agreed with him.

"We'll likely have to undergo a reorganization soon. We've got so many people gone or down, our old chart won't work anymore. But we can make it with patchwork for a week or so, I think. I'd rather it not go much longer, though, since we'll need to have new units training together. It was superior training and organization that got us through this with so few losses. I know it doesn't seem like few to those of us who lost friends, but the people who have seen combat before know better. If we hadn't had our people so well trained, we'd be dead or wishing we were by now. We will continue our training regimen without letup, other than the next five days or so while we work to get back on track. Everyone can use a little rest, I think, and time to get over the shock of battle. For some of us, yesterday was the first taste of combat. They're likely to need help getting over that. Be sure they get it."

"That's all I have. Jose will take over the meeting as head of security. Lieutenant Flores and I have to check on some other things. Good work, yesterday, everyone. Make sure you tell those assigned to you that, too."

-

In the aftermath of the battle, Clay had not had the opportunity to meet the people who had arrived with Flores. He was taking the time to do that now, with each member of her group introducing themselves and explaining their specialty.

"Staff Sergeant Chandler Smith, sir," a beefy looking NCO said first. "31 Bravo." The designation for Military Police officer. "Thirteen years, sir. All of it as an MP, and as a civilian LEO." Smith stepped back and a tall black man stepped forward.

"Corporal Emmett Beaumont, sir, also 31 Bravo. Originally from Louisiana, sir. My family moved to Nashville when I was ten. Three years and change in uniform, sir. Attending Tennessee Tech when the world went dark." Beaumont stepped back into the line, replaced by another who was not quite as tall.

"Corporal Dax Cooper, sir, and I'm also 31 Bravo. Five years in. From Springhill, Tennessee. Rutherford County S.O. in civilian life, and CJ major at MTSU."

"Corporal Ian Towner, sir," the next man stated. "Medic. An EMT for Metro Nashville Fire Department, sir, in civilian life."

"Corporal Regina Braddock, sir," a willowy brunette stepped forward. "Medic. RN student at Vanderbilt, sir."

"Lieutenant Candida Guerrero, sir," a short Hispanic woman was next. "Physician Assistant. I was also a PA in the civilian world and worked in the campus medical office of MTSU."

"Lieutenant Krysten Sands, RN," a statuesque blonde with a no-nonsense look about her stated next. "I am also an RN in civilian life, working as a Cardiac RN for a heart surgeon. I'm originally from Centerville, Tennessee, but was living in Nashville when the lights went out."

"Sergeant Nessa Winfield, Unit Supply Specialist," an athletic looking black woman stepped forward next. Clay estimated her to be late twenties to early thirties. She looked as if she had probably majored in every sport available in whatever college she had attended.

"I'm from Smyrna, sir, and was working as a warehouse supervisor before the calamity unfolded."

"Jorie Sunday, sir, PFC. 12 M Firefighter, sir," a very young man with near copper colored hair didn't quite stammer. "I was from Nashville, sir, but grew up in foster care. I'm hoping...sorry, sir. I *was* hoping to make the Metro Fire Department with my training in the Guard."

"Sergeant Sara Yamaguchi," a woman of Japanese descent went next. Probably in her early thirties, Clay guessed. "91 F. I'm a fully certified gunsmith, including the manufacture of firearms of any type and caliber. I'm also fully trained and experienced in artillery repair and all crew served heavy weapons."

"Sergeant Pacifico Aroha," a tan skinned woman who was what Clay's father would call sturdily built stepped forward. Her face, neck and arms were decorated with several tattoos that looked somewhat familiar. Clay had a feeling he knew where she was from.

EMBERS

"I am a wheeled vehicle mechanic, 91 Bravo," Aroha continued, her accent becoming clearer now. "As you may have guessed, I am not from these parts." It came out as 'paahts'. "My family moved to America after the Christchurch earthquake of 2011. My father was an engineer and we settled in Springhill when he went to work for GM. He and me mum died in a auto vehicle crash five years ago. I've no other family save in New Zealand. As for me, if it can be made to run, I can make it run."

Clay caught himself before he smiled as the confident young woman stepped back into line. He wondered what Jake was going to think about Pacifico Aroha.

"Warrant Three Carl Ely," a man who was obviously older than the rest stepped forward almost lazily. "Combat Engineer. Twenty-two years, twelve of that on active duty somewhere or another." And that was all as Warrant Officer Ely returned to the line, clearly less than impressed with being there.

"Sergeant First Class Charles Swift, sir," the next man in line stepped forward. "Carpentry and Masonry Specialist, sir. Fourteen years' experience in military and civilian life." Swift was heavily muscled and had an air of competence about him that could only come from successful application of a chosen field. He would be a major asset to the farm. The last soldier, a Hispanic female, stepped forward.

"Specialist Valentina Santiago, Interior Electrician, sir," the young woman informed him. She was dressed in BDU pants and a t-shirt that said 'Let Me Twist Your Wires'. There was look about her that spoke of a misspent youth and an attempt at a misspent adulthood. Clay liked her at once.

"Let me welcome all of you to the Farm," Clay told the assembled group. "I'm not going to lie; I've heard some specialties in here today that make me extremely happy. All of you have talents that we can sorely use and will greatly appreciate. We're a bit rushed with everything right now, as you can see for yourself, so your welcome may leave a bit to be desired, but the houses are warm, the food is hot and filling, and we have hot water showers." A ragged cheer went up from the group at that, making Flores smile.

"I hope you all will enjoy being here as much as we will likely enjoy having you. If you have a question, just ask anyone in uniform. Our uniforms are black for the most part, though your fellows that were already here under Lieutenant Gillis are usually wearing digicams. But

132

any of our uniformed personnel will be able to help you. I can't promise you easy living, but compared to the rest of the world, we're in an oasis. Protecting it is the rub, as you saw today. But we're hopeful, and your arrival has added to that hope. I'll get out of your way now, and let you get unpacked. Someone will be around tomorrow, probably, to introduce you to your opposite numbers here on the farm, assuming you have one. That is all," he added to Flores.

"Yes, sir," she snapped to. "You heard the man, folks. We're home! Go unpack and settle in. Tomorrow we go back to work."

-

"Okay, kid?"

Gordy Sanders was sitting atop a Hummer, having crawled out of the turret to get there. The vehicle was parked behind the buildings, facing north, away from everything. He was staring into the sky toward the horizon, occasionally taking a sip of clear liquid from a fruit jar.

He turned to see Mitchell Nolan standing on the ground, looking up at him.

"Fine," Gordy nodded, turning back to his examination of the winter sky.

"It's perfectly okay not to be fine after something like this," Mitchell told him. When Gordy didn't answer, Mitchell climbed into the Hummer himself and was soon crawling out onto the roof to join the teen. He reached over and took the jar from Gordy's unresisting hands and took a sip. He instantly regretted it.

"Holy shit," he gasped, shaking his head as his eyes watered and then closed. "Where in the hell did you get this shit? From a gas tank?"

"Made it myself, thanks," Gordy replied, taking the jar back. "Charcoal filtered and laced with peaches. That's how I got that smooth, refined taste."

"That's smooth? And refined?" Mitchell demanded. "You know, *refined* makes it sound like gasoline. Is that stuff *supposed* to be rocket fuel?"

"It's supposed to be sour mash," Gordy took another sip, apparently unaffected by the high alcohol content. "Excellent sour mash, in fact, if I do say so myself." He took yet another sip before sighing.

"Me and Corey made it last year, after harvest," he said finally. "Real bitch to find the sugar, too. Had to make it with sugar beets, which is not nearly as easy as using granulated sugar, by the way. Had to cook

133

that down first, then the corn, then…well, you get the picture. Anyway, this was the last jug. We only made three gallons in the end. We were going to share this one on the Fourth of July this year. I decided that wasn't going to work out and figured I'd just drink it myself."

"You know, kid, this ain't-," Mitchell began, only to be cut off.

"Really don't want to hear it," Gordy said softly. "Really don't. Heard it already and heard it all before."

"Understandable," Mitchell nodded. He had been about to tell Gordy it wasn't his fault that Corey was dead, and Heath was injured. Apparently, someone else had already done that.

"Look, far be it from me to interrupt a man who's celebrating a friend's death," Mitchell slipped back into the turret and stood there. "Just…know if you need to talk to someone who can understand, we're all here for you. Okay?"

"Thanks," Gordy nodded, but didn't look at him. "Keep it in mind."

"See you around, kid," Mitchell patted Gordy's leg and disappeared down the hatch.

Gordy didn't even notice the older man get down and walk away.

-

Heath Kelly felt as if he were floating in a sea of dark. Which was odd, since he'd never actually been near the sea. How would he know what it was like? Closest he had been was swimming in Wheeler Lake, or Lake Chickamauga. And they were nothing like big as the sea. Any sea.

Yet, here he was, adrift in…nothing. And despite being adrift in that nothingness, he could almost swear he could hear Leanne Tillman's voice. Calling him. Talking to him. He couldn't quite make out the words, but he recognized her voice.

He spent a minute trying to figure out how he had come to be in his present predicament, deciding that following his way back to the last thing he could remember might tell him something. He had to pause for a minute and think about that since he couldn't seem to remember where he'd been. It had been cold, though. He remembered that very vividly. Cold and damp.

Suddenly he remembered. He'd been on a baby-sitting job with Gordy, Corey and Kurtis. Watching over a training mission for the older teens that were learning new skills. He had thought it was a rough lesson at first, but Gordy had pointed out that if they had to do things in this weather during an emergency, then training in this weather would come in handy. Heath had to admit that was true. It was still a hard lesson.

But something had happened during that lesson, hadn't it? He strained to remember and suddenly heard Leanne's voice get a bit louder. Not clearer, just louder. He wondered sometimes how she could be so loud when she was so small.

He had never asked her about it, however. That would be tantamount to suicide.

Suddenly, in a rush of seconds, everything came back to him. Intercepting an attack on the farm, sending the 'kids' to the Plum Farm with Gordy, Corey getting-

Heath's eyes shot open.

-

"I know you can hear me, Heath," Leanne wiped her boyfriend's forehead with a cool cloth, wiping the sweat away. The clinic wasn't overly warm, but he was under a heavy blanket so maybe that was it.

"I know you can hear me, and I know you're okay," Leanne continued, wringing the cloth out and starting again. "I just won't accept anything else. Do you hear? Jaylyn says if you wake up okay, then you're out of the woods, so that means you have to wake up okay. Okay? For me, you have to-,"

Leanne stopped short as she realized she was looking right into Heath Kelly's eyes.

"H-Heath!" she exclaimed suddenly. "You're awake!"

He opened his mouth as it to speak, but nothing came.

"Oh! Oh, here!" Leanne fumbled with a cup and straw, almost forcing the straw into his mouth.

"Leanne, don't shove it up his nose, alright?" Kaitlin Caudell warned as she arrived to check on Leanne's near yelling. "Well, look who's awake, hey?" she smiled at Heath. The teen used the straw to pull deep on the water, drinking as if he'd never had water before. He choked slightly and began to cough, prompting Leanne to remove the straw from his mouth and then grab the washcloth to wipe his mouth and chin.

"I'm sorry!" she exclaimed, wiping hurriedly at his face. "That was me! I'm sorry!"

Heath tried to lift his left arm to stop her and found he couldn't. Using his right to stop her motion and gently push her away, he looked down at his left arm to see it wrapped at an angle and strapped to his body.

"Leanne, I need to get in there, sweetie," Kaitlin said gently. "Give me a little room, okay? You don't have to go anywhere, just…let me work. 'Kay?"

"Okay," the small teen nodded, stepping back and then moving to the head of the bed, behind Heath's prone figure.

"Heath, can you hear me okay?" Kaitlin asked. Heath nodded, still looking at his arm.

"Look at me, sweetie," Kaitlin gently took his cheek and turned him her way. "There you go. I need to look at your eyes. No, no, look at me," she chided when he went to look at his arm again. Reluctantly he turned his gaze back to her.

"There you go," she soothed. "I'm going to check your pupils, okay? Bright light coming." She flashed her light in each eye, noting the pupil reaction.

"It's good, right?" Leanne all but demanded even before Kaitlin was finished.

"Leanne, let me work, sweetheart," Kaitlin said again, gently. "Be patient. You've been patient all this time, so just keep doing that. Heath, is your head hurting?" He took a deep breath and nodded slowly, eyes closing.

"No, Heath. No, keep your eyes open for me. You've slept long enough for a few minutes, and we need to talk to you, okay? I want you to focus on my-, Heath! Look at me!" she snapped. He opened his eyes again, his look telling both Leanne and Kaitlin what he thought about that situation.

"Now, I want you to focus on this light, Heath," she held up her small penlight, the light from it making the top glow. "I want you to follow it as I move it around, okay? Heath, I know you hear me," she chided a Heath appeared to be on the verge of becoming mulish.

"Dammit, Heath, help her help you!" Leanne suddenly exploded. "Stop being so childish and do what she says!"

Giving Leanne a near malignant glare, he then turned his sullen gaze to the nurse, who was waiting patiently with her light still in the air.

"Good deal," she smiled at him brightly. "Just follow the light for me, Heath." She slowly moved the light side-to-side before moving it slowly up and then down. Heath dutifully followed the light's movement without pause or problem.

"Excellent," Kaitlin beamed. "Now we just have to wait for Doctor Thatcher-,"

"-who is here," Jaylyn's voice cut in as she arrived at bedside, looking as if she had just been awakened, which she had. She stepped in and proceeded to check Heath's pupil reactions herself, then looked at him for a moment in silence.

"Open your eyes, soldier!" she snapped as Heath's eyes once more drifted shut. His eyes opened at once, focused on her.

"Better," she nodded, her voice easing. "Can you talk to me, Heath?" she asked him. "You can talk about anything you want, so long as I can hear you talking." He frowned at that, as if questioning why it was a big deal.

"Talk to me, Heath," she ordered, returning his frown. "Say whatever you want to, but speak to me. Now," her voice was suddenly firm and sharp.

"Doctor, don't-," Leanne started but fell silent as Jaylyn's dark gaze flitted to her for a brief second. It took a great deal to cow Leanne Tillman into silence. A small grin appeared on Heath's face at that. Jaylyn caught it and smiled at him.

"Found that amusing, did you?" she asked, and he nodded slowly. His eyes started to close again even as he nodded.

"Heath Kelly!" Jaylyn snapped, her voice ringing not only with medical authority but military authority as well. Once more Heath's eyes popped wide open, locked on her.

"You can sleep after I hear you speak, soldier!" Jaylyn's voice rang across the clinic. "Now talk to me!"

"Your hair looks a little rough, Doc," Heath managed to croak out, after looking her over. Leanne had to cover her mouth to try and hide a giggle and Kailin laughed outright. Jaylyn frowned mightily at Heath for a few seconds before her face split into a broad smile.

"And whose fault is that, Heath Kelly?" she laughed. "You've had us worried sick, young man. Some more than others," she nodded to where Leanne was looking at him.

"Corey?" Heath rasped out. "What happ-,"

"That's a story for another time, Mister Kelly," Jaylyn told him firmly. "You worry about your own condition before we talk about anyone else."

"'m okay," his rough whisper was sounding more like him every minute.

"You are most certainly not okay!" Leanne huffed, tears streaming down her face.

"She's quite right, Mister Kelly," Jaylyn nodded. "You are in no sense of the word okay. You will be, however," she promised him with a gentle smile. "You will be."

News about Heath awakening had spread quickly. Good news was hard to come by at the moment, so the word that one of their more seriously wounded comrades would eventually be okay was excellent news and a great boost to morale.

Amanda Lowery, still recovering from a gunshot wound she had received before Thanksgiving, was being ferried to the clinic later that morning by none other than Xavier Adair himself. With so many being treated after the battle, Amanda had been removed from the clinic and carried home, her condition being cautiously evaluated as well enough to lie in bed at home. This morning she had to return, however, as she was still not healed. She had started a series of supervised exercises designed to help her get back her lost musculature and needed to continue those so that she didn't lose any progress.

"Probably should have just stayed home, today," Amanda noted sourly. "Lot of people worse off than I am right now."

"While true, if you were to neglect your own recovery, you would soon join those who are worse off," Xavier reminded her. "It would be in everyone's best interest if your recovery is not inhibited. We lost a great many people yesterday, Miss Lowery. Getting some back will be a great help as well as a boost to everyone's morale."

"Even an idiot like me?" she demanded.

"Even someone as mentally deficient as you," he assured her, then slowly counted to three.

"What?!" the explosion came right on time. "Are you calling me an idiot?!"

"Not at all, my dear Amanda," Xavier replied with a straight face. "You called yourself an idiot. While I may or may not agree, it's always best in my experience to humor the sick and the injured so as to encourage their recovery as much as is possible. I was, therefore, merely assisting you in your ongoing recovery. Nothing more."

"Jackass," Amanda growled softly.

"That is the rumor."

-

Nate Caudell eased through the woods south of the farm, following the trail left by the assaulting force the day before. He already knew where they had started so what he was really doing was looking for anything that would help identify the group, as well as looking for anyone who had escaped the battle but remained behind.

He raised his fist into the air suddenly, stopping short. Behind him, Zach Willis and Kevin Bodee froze, each to one side of the trail.

Nate studied the ground before him carefully before reaching out and stirring the leaves around.

"Blood," he said to the other two. "So at least some of their wounded made it out of the fields." With that he was on his feet, and the search continued.

While they might or might not find anything of value, knowing that the woods were as empty as the drone pass made it look would be a great help. There were other projects in the planning stage that would proceed much easier if the coast was clear.

-

"We'll take your three MPs for sure," Jose said, looking at a list in his hands. "Maybe the supply bunny since they can obviously drive. I don't want to risk the medicos, or the armorer either. The mechanic might be a good inclusion, however, in case something breaks down."

"Okay," Flores made a note of her own. "I suggest we take as few vehicles with us as possible to get there, though I imagine that goes without saying. It would be ideal to take one of those gun trucks you have out back, but we'd probably have hypothermia by the time we got there."

"We can take...hm," Jose paused, comparing equipment lists. "We can move the canvas top from one of the other trucks to a gun truck," he said finally. "Add to that a six-wheel Cougar and a Hummer, and that's a pretty strong force with room for everyone. Hm," he studied on that for a few more minutes, then leaned out of the office door. He spotted Mitchell Nolan right away.

"Mitch!"

"Yo!" the taller man turned to look at him.

"Get a crew together and get one of the five-ton canvas tops put on a gun truck, please," Jose instructed. "We'll be taking it with us to their HQ, so have Jake look it over and find out which one he recommends."

"Will do," Mitch waved and started for the door. Jose pulled his chair back inside the office where he began studying the map.

"You came this way, yes?" he traced a route along the map.

"We did," Flores nodded.

"No obstacles in the way, or any troubles?" Jose asked, looking at her.

"No, actually," Flores admitted. "And I honestly expected it. It's possible that the Hummer and Cougar were enough to prevent it, but I really doubt it. Not this late into the game."

"Agreed," Jose nodded absently. "So, either you happened to choose a great route, or else everyone was bundled up somewhere trying to stay warm."

"That does sound more likely," she agreed.

"Okay, we need a minimum of six drivers for the military vehicles. We'll be taking Beast along with a flatbed for that engineering vehicle."

"About that," Flores said before Jose could continue. "We have an M-9 armored bulldozer, with attachments. That's a heavy load. There's also an M88 heavy vehicle recovery unit. Honestly, I don't see what help it would be to you, but if you think you need a heavy wrecker so to speak, it's just sitting there. My point, though, was I don't know if one truck can carry the dozer and all of the attachments."

"We'll ask our resident expert," Jose nodded his understanding.

-

"Show me the route," Ellen Kargay said quietly. Jose held up the map without a word, showing her the pencil marked route they planned to take.

"We came in this way," she pointed to one spot. "That's a fairly high incline, maybe four degrees. It's short, though, and pretty much straight on the four-lane area. So long as I can start up at a go, I can make it. If I have to stop at the bottom, or worse on the way up, then maybe not. That's a lot of weight."

"So other than the risk of stopping, Beast can handle the weight?" Jose asked her.

"Sure," she nodded. "It will be the bulk that would interfere. You say there are three attachments?" she asked Flores.

"Yes," the young soldier was a bit intimidated by the hulking blonde and didn't want to risk saying more than she needed to.

"May have to load one of the attachments somewhere else if we can't find room on the trailer, but if we're careful, and the dozer is almost empty of fuel, we should be okay, I think. Be thinking about which attachment you want to leave behind, just in case. I assume the blade is an attachment and is already connected?" she asked.

"It is, yes," Flores nodded again.

"Yeah, we can do this," Ellen told Jose. "I won't say it's no problems since it will be nothing but problems in all likelihood, but we can make it."

"Great," Jose nodded his thanks. "That's all we needed. We'll be heading out before light in the morning."

"We'll be ready," the trucker promised.

CHAPTER THIRTEEN

For once, things worked exactly as planned. The group headed to the former headquarters left before dawn, using NVGs to see the road and any obstructions. Roddy Thatcher had been pressed into service to drive a second semi behind Ellen and the Beast, just in case there was something there that the farm could benefit from.

While there were no munitions remaining at the former HQ facility, there were plenty of other needful things scattered about the facilities. Some of the group took the time to strip the area as clean as possible while the rest worked to ready the huge, armored bulldozer for transport. With the dozer loaded and ready, attention was turned to other equipment.

Jose had argued against worrying with the tank recovery vehicle, but for some reason Clay had wanted the damn thing. Jose couldn't see the need, seeing as how the farm didn't have even one tank, but Clay was adamant that they try. So, Jose and company worked to get the massive vehicle loaded onto a flatbed trailer that was far too narrow to carry it in Jose's opinion. When they were finished, he went from one side of the trailer to the other, noting how precious little of the vehicle's tracks were actually on the flatbed. When he had pointed that out to the two truckers, both had just shrugged.

"I've hauled worse," the two had said almost in unison, then laughed as they returned to work. Jose didn't think that was very funny but decided if the two drivers were okay with it, he would let it be. He was glad he wasn't driving either truck, however.

The operation went off without a hitch, including the return trip. Despite Jose's worries, the two trucks made it fine with their heavy loads, the other vehicles spread out around them. So well did things go that they were back on the farm well before dark, which no one had expected.

"That went well," Clay noted as others worked to secure the loads and vehicles in their proper places.

"Too well," Jose nodded, still eyeing the heavily loaded flatbed trailers with no small trepidation.

"Don't jinx it, man," Clay warned, concerned.

"I don't have to," Jose shook his head. "Something this complicated goes this easy, you can bet your ass that something is going make us pay for it."

"Maybe we paid in advance," Clay shrugged. "We had a hot one day before yesterday."

"True," Jose mused, lips pursed in thought. "Maybe that's it."

-

Everyone had their own way of dealing with the death of those close to them. There were losses to every group on the farm, and each would deal with their comrade's final arrangements with support from the rest of the farm.

Except for one group.

One group would mourn in private.

-

"Where you guys going?" Kim asked as she saw Clayton and Xavier, dressed identically, walking toward the vehicle park.

"We have something we need to take care of, my dear," Xavier replied, Zach nodding in agreement. Neither stopped nor even slowed.

"Need any help?" she asked.

"No," came the reply, in unison.

"Oh," she was taken aback by the abrupt reply. "Uh, okay then," she half-waved at their backs. "See you later!"

"Of course, dear girl," Xavier said, not bothering to turn around. "Do be careful."

Kim waited for perhaps fifteen seconds before deciding to follow the two. She had made only three steps when a voice stopped her.

"Where ya going?" Petra Shannon's voice made Kim jump slightly.

"Uh, well, I was, ah, gonna follow those two and see what they were doing," she admitted.

"You're kidding, right?" Petra frowned. "It's the funeral for Stacey Pryor and Corey Reynard, Kim."

"Oh, jeez," Kim felt like slapping herself. "But wait. Why aren't the rest of us part of it?"

"Because we aren't part of that little group, sister," Petra replied. "They have their own ways of doing things."

"How do you know?" Kim demanded.

"Beverly Jackson mentioned it earlier," Petra informed her.

"What are they doing that we shouldn't be there?" Kim asked.

"I think it's just something private, and we aren't meant to participate," Petra shrugged. "Beverly didn't elaborate."

Kim thought about that for less than a minute before making her decision.

"I'm going to see what they're doing."

"Really shouldn't," Petra warned, though she walked along with Kim.

"I want to know," Kim shrugged. "You can go or stay. Up to you."

-

"It won't seem right without ole Corey," Titus Terry observed mournfully. "Won't seem right at all. Now him and Kade both gone, man," he shook his head slowly.

"Heath laying in the clinic, too," Zach nodded. "Six has become three all of a sudden."

"Dude, this wasn't your fault," Kurtis said gently as Gordy stared rigidly at the figure of Corey Reynard.

"I'm the one that left you there," Gordy replied, his eyes never leaving Corey's body.

"And we were the ones who figured you were the guy for the job, man," Kurtis reminded him. "All of us, including Corey. Hell, it was Corey's idea."

"I told him it was a stupid ass idea," Gordy nodded slowly.

"It was a fine idea for the spot we were in, Gordy," Kurtis objected. "And we gave the bastards hell for a long while, don't forget. We did our job. You start saying all of this was because of you then you start detracting from what Corey and Heath sacrificed for the farm, man. That ain't right. It ain't right and what's more, you know it ain't right."

"He's telling you straight, bro," Titus agreed. "Hell, it wasn't none of our fault what happened to Kade, was it?"

"No," Zach answered that one. "No, it wasn't. And this wasn't anyone's fault outside the people who decided to attack this farm and the people on it. Kurtis is right on the money, Gordy. We did our jobs. Stacey did his job. So did the others."

"True," Gordy nodded. Reluctantly.

"So, ease up on that fault laying, man," Titus ordered. "Ole Corey would be mad, hearing you say that crap, dude."

"Especially if you were trying to blame him," Zach laughed softly. "Remember when he broke Old Man Tilson's window with a baseball?

144

He got so mad when we ratted him out, even though he was guilty? I can still see his face all red and cheeks puffed out," he laughed again.

"I told him later, what else was we supposed to do? Take the blame for you?" Titus was laughing now, his head bobbing. "And he said 'that's what real friends would do, yeah!' I laughed right in his face for saying that!"

Across the way, a similar discussion was taking place among the others.

"Man, ain't this some shit?" Shane shook his head. "Survive being in the shit all over the world and be done in by a redneck with a deer rifle right here at home?"

"Yep," Mitchell Nolan nodded.

"Life is rather like that, is it not?" Xavier mused. "I shall miss Edge very much. A good man to be sure."

"Remember in…what was the name of that town? Hisvasta…no, Hivasta, or something. Anyway, remember he stole that chicken and the old woman who owned it saw him and chased him down the road with a broom?" Tandi was laughing by the time he got to the end of his tale.

"Boss made him go back and pay for it," Nate chuckled. "Had to work for the old woman for three days."

"Chicken wasn't bad, though," Kevin reminded them.

"No. No it wasn't," Jose smiled at nothing, somewhere out in the dark.

And so it went for a while. Stories, memories, good times and bad. Finally, far sooner than it seemed like it should have been, Clay stood before them all. Silence fell across the group as they settled in. It was time to say goodbye.

"Here we are again," Clay said gently. "Seems just when we think things are settled and calm, we end up here again. A warning, perhaps, not to become too comfortable, lest we become weak. Complacent."

"Two brothers lay before us tonight, lost to us in combat, in defense of home and family. Two good men who gave selflessly of themselves when others hid. Time and again these two have been there for us when we were in need. Going forward, we will have to be there for them, because tonight, they leave us behind."

"Tonight, we say goodbye as our brothers shake off the mortal coil and step beyond, step forward into whatever awaits us all. These shells, these husks are all that remain, entrusted to us in order that we might bid our brothers farewell." He took a knife from his side and cut his palm without so much as a grimace before handing it to Jose Juarez.

Jose repeated the gesture and then passed the blade to Mitchell Nolan, who in turn passed it to Shane Golden. The blade slowly made the rounds until all stood in the dark with blood pooling in their palms.

One behind another they trooped by their fallen brothers and left a handprint of blood somewhere on the body. No one spoke, the silence like a blanket in the wintry night. Clay was last on both sides of the pyre. Finished, he stepped back, blood dripping from his hand.

"Your battles here are done," he said gently. "May the peace denied you in this life, be waiting for you in the next. We will see you again."

Finished, he nodded to Jose and Gordy before taking his place among the rest. There were no more words to say.

Jose and Gordy each took a torch, a wood and tarlike construct that would not have looked out of place a thousand years before and walked to the pyres. Without a word between them, the two chose a side and walked down the pyre, dragging the torch behind them to light the wood beneath. That done, the torches joined the pyre as the two returned to their comrades.

The entire group would wait in silence until the pyres and their contents were nothing more than embers and memories.

-

"What the hell is on fire back there?" Flores asked, alarm clear in her voice.

"Nothing you need worry over, *Chica*," Martina Sanchez said quietly. "Just brothers saying farewell."

Flores looked like she wanted to pursue the matter, but suddenly changed her mind.

"So long as you're sure it's not something for us to be concerned over," she nodded, sitting down again.

"It's not."

-

Kim Powers had long since abandoned any form of stealth as she watched the funeral pyres light the night sky. She had watched the entire 'service', feeling as if Petra was right and that they were intruders. Interlopers who had no business being there. No business seeing what they did.

146

"What are you two up to?" a quiet voice asked from behind them. Both young women whirled to find Lainie Harper watching them curiously.

"Uh, we uh…we were just, ah…." Kim stammered while Petra remained quiet.

"You really shouldn't be here, girls," Lainie said simply. There was no judgement in her voice, no sense of scolding, just a cautioning tone.

"We figured that out," Kim admitted. "Petra had said it all along," she added, covering for the friend she had drug along. "She mostly came along so I'd not be alone."

"You're a good friend," Lainie told Petra, smiling tiredly. "C'mon you two," she motioned. "There's some hot tea around front. And you really shouldn't be here."

The two followed her, looking back only once.

"So why do that?" Petra asked as they neared the front of T1.

"It's just their way," Lainie shrugged. "The men with Clay are all commandoes, but you know that, I'm sure. The boys, they were trained to be like them, and they are. This is the second time for each group that they've lost someone."

"And they just…burn them?" Petra pressed, trying to understand.

"It's their way," Lainie shrugged again. "To them, it's an honor that was earned on the battlefield. Not something to be shared. They mourn by celebrating the lives of their friends. It's a ritual as old as war, I suppose. Something we aren't really meant to see or to understand."

"You've seen it before," Kim suddenly realized. "You've seen this before tonight."

"Two times too many," Lainie nodded. "We'll all likely see it again. I'd love to hope, to think, that all the rest will die of old age after tonight, but I realize that they are the ones who leave the farm to go and do what needs to be done for us. That means the odds are long against it." She paused, looking at Kim meaningfully.

"If you're serious about Zach, then you need to know what you're getting into, sugar. You have to be prepared to see him lying on one of those pyres one day. Okay?"

"I…I-I don't…" Kim was suddenly unable to get her words to work for her as the weight of what Lainie had said settled upon her.

"Just a friendly warning, sweetie," Lainie smiled softly.

"I, thank you," Kim finally managed, deep in thought.

147

"You're welcome."

-

There were six other funerals on the farm for the fallen. Soldiers mourning their dead with honors, friends mourning friends with eulogies and not a few tears. All six laid to rest in the small but growing family cemetery on the Sanders' farm.

The next week was a quiet and solemn time as the living worked to recover from their losses as well as repair the damage to the farm and their own psyches. For many, it had been their first taste of combat. Losses to random violence, illness and other predations that had haunted the land since the Storm did not quite measure up to the violence of engaging in actual combat and seeing someone next to you killed or maimed, while you remained uninjured.

The worst damage done was not in seeing the violence, but in realizing that it could just as easily have been their own light snuffed out. No rhyme, no reason, just the luck of the battle and a bullet with your name on it.

Not every psyche was strong enough to accept that risk.

-

"You've never been deployed, have you Private Abramson?"

"No, ma'am," Abramson replied softly, shaking his head. "We...we joined up after the deployment to Iraq. Would have gone for the next deployment if there had been one."

"So, this was your first time under fire, then?" Beverly asked gently.

"Yes, ma'am," he gave a nod this time.

"When you say 'we', you mean Corporal Parris and yourself, right?" she clarified.

"Yes, ma'am," Abramson nodded again. "We been together since boot. He was my friend."

"This has hit you particularly hard, then, hasn't it?" Beverly asked sympathetically. "He wasn't just a fellow soldier, but a friend as well."

"Yeah," he replied, then straightened. "I mean, yes, ma'am," he sharpened his reply into military correct politeness.

"That isn't necessary, Private," Beverly told him. "I'm not in your chain of command, nor am I in the service at all. I'm just a civilian trying to help."

"Thank you, ma'am."

Beverly fought off a sigh at the response. It wouldn't help, and it might be harmful. There was no doubt that this was going to be a long road. Still, it was her profession, and she was grateful that she could make a meaningful contribution to the farm and the people who defended it.

It wouldn't make this go any easier, however.

"So, tell me about you and Corporal Parris, then," she turned her attention back to the soldier before her. The sooner she made inroads into the problems, the sooner she could begin finding possible solutions.

"Tell me about your first meeting."

-

"Hey, kiddo," Clay said gently, walking up to Gordy. The younger man was staring south, across the empty fields and pastures. It was an empty, unfocused stare, the kind someone lost in thought might have.

"Unc," Gordy turned his way, nodding. "Finally get a break?"

"Yeah," Clay sighed. "Won't last long, but maybe I'm caught up enough to get a nap or something. Eat a real meal."

"Good luck with that," Gordy snorted, turning back to his examination of the southern horizon.

"You can't keep this up, Gordy," Clay said flatly, opting for directness over the beat-around-the-bush approach.

"What do you need me to do?" Gordy asked at once, giving Clay his full attention.

"Nothing at the moment, and that's not what I'm talking about," Clay raised an eyebrow.

"I know what you're talking about," Gordy nodded, once more turning his gaze away.

"Then you know it has to stop," Clay replied plainly. "You can't keep this up. Nothing that happened was your fault. Not Corey, not Heath. The fault lies completely with the people who attacked us. And Corey and Heath defended this farm in the face of overwhelming odds, along with Kurtis."

"You four were out there specifically to watch over those kids and make sure nothing happened to them. That was your job, Gordy. One you did very well in addition to defending this place. Leaving aside that it gave us time to prepare to defend the farm that we'd have not had if you hadn't been there."

"I know," Gordy sighed, looking down at the ground. "But I...I was in charge. I left them there, and now Corey is dead and Heath...I hope Heath recovers. For Leanne as much as his sake. They deserve better."

"We all deserve better, Gordy," Clay rested a hand on the taller teen's shoulder. "We all do. If we're lucky, we get it. We're not always lucky. But we're a hell of a lot more fortunate than probably ninety-five percent of the entire world right now. That may be all the luck we get."

"Thought of that, too," Gordy agreed. "But I can't help but feel responsible, because I was supposed to be in charge." Clay studied his nephew for maybe half-a-minute before coming to a decision.

"Listen, kid," he said flatly. "Being in charge, being responsible, feeling responsible all go together. They're a matched set. You're going to have to get used to that, because one day you'll probably be running this place. Hopefully not for a while, since that would mean I was gone, but still. And when you are, you're going to have to make tough calls. Calls like leaving your friends to engage a superior force because they're the best for the job. Better than you, because you need to do something else. Because you're in charge."

"That is never going to change, Gordy. That feeling of responsibility, that feeling of guilt, even. It will stay with you always, and it will make you second-guess everything you do, for fear you will make a mistake and cost someone their life. That will never change."

"How do you deal with it, then?" Gordy didn't quite demand.

"I stay busy," Clay shrugged. "I accept that since I'm in command, I will always be called upon to make hard decisions that no one else will make. That I can't pass the buck any higher because it literally stops with me. Why do you think I was so glad to see Adcock roll in here?" he chuckled. "For a little while I was able to pass along those hard calls to someone else, at least when it wasn't something directly farm related. Now, it's back down to me. It is what it is, Gordy. For me now, and one day for you. You can't let it eat at you, either. And Corey nor Heath either one would want it."

"I know," Gordy agreed. "It's just a lot, that's all," he finally added.

"It is, and no one your age should have to deal with it," Clay said at once. "In the army, you'd be at least nineteen and probably closer to twenty-one. Even with OCS after Boot or AIT, you'd still be much older, and you would have had at least some training with people like Beverly, and with NCOs who knew what combat was like, in dealing with things like this. You've got none of that. And that's my fault," Clay added finally, as if the winds had left his sails.

"Now who's feeling guilty and responsible?" Gordy asked, a wry smile on his face.

"I told you it never goes away, kid," Clay shrugged. "I'm sorry you have to learn all this at your age, Gordy. Hell, I'm sorry you need to learn it at all. You should be playing football and chasing girls and sneaking out of the dorm to party. But I can't change what is. If I could, I would."

"I know," Gordy snorted slightly. "I promise I do. And I don't blame you for any of this. I don't really blame myself, I guess. If it were anyone else in my place, I'd likely be one of the first to tell them just what you've told me. I think…I think it's because it was Corey, and Heath. That's all. Because it was my friends. And I know that's something you understand better than anyone here."

"Too true," Clay gave him a tired smile. "Are you going to be okay?"

"I will," Gordy promised, looking brighter now. "I promise, I will. Thanks, Clay."

"I'm always here if you need me, kid," Clay slapped his back gently. "Now, I'd suggest you go and visit your girl up in Tower One. She's filling in for Heath until he's back to battery. Go see her. Relax. Take a picnic with you. Enjoy life, man. While it's there."

"Sounds like good advice," Gordy smiled.

"Only kind I give!"

-

Clay decided to be slightly selfish and use his ATV to go home to eat. There were others on the farm, not to mention several ATCs and numerous golf carts. The carts didn't do well in mud but the snow didn't seem to trouble them too much.

He walked into his house to be met with warmth of the hearth and the smell of baking bread. As he shucked his wet boots and coveralls off at the door, Lainie came to meet him.

"Hello, my Cowboy," she kissed his cheek as she helped him get his overshirt off. "How are you, my baby?"

"I'm tired, if I'm being honest," he admitted. "How are you, sexy?" he wrapped his arms around her and kissed her 'like he meant it', as she often called it.

"Oh, my," she almost purred. "I'm fine, now," she giggled outright. "I hope you're here for a little while?" she asked, studying him closely.

"I don't honestly know," he shrugged. "Still a lot to do, and that's without trying to assimilate Flores' bunch into the farm. We got a lotta hands missing from the work force, too."

"I know, but you've been going almost non-stop for five days, now," she countered. "You have to take some time off to rest or you'll be right back in the same shape as before. Please don't do that, Clay. Please. Last time was scary enough."

She was referring to an incident where he had worked himself into exhaustion. All that had saved him from even worse problems was that he happened to be with Jaylyn Thatcher in the clinic and she noticed the danger he was in. Two days enforced rest had helped him a great deal, and Lainie had been careful to watch him since.

"I promise I won't let it get like that again," Clay assured her. "In fact, hold on just a minute," he smiled at her before picking up the field phone and winding it.

"Operations, this is Deuce," his nephew answered at once.

"Deuce, this is Bossman," Clay said. "I'm taking the rest of the day off. Send someone to my house to get my ATV and bring it back down for you guys to use. Even if you don't need it, I don't want it sitting out in the weather. I'll be available if I'm needed, but I hope you don't need me. Okay?"

"Got it, Unc," Leon replied at once. "I'll send someone up there ASAP. Try to get some rest. I'll leave a note not to bother you unless it's absolutely necessary."

"Thanks, kiddo." With that he replaced the phone in its bag and faced Lainie with a grin.

"How's that?"

"That's excellent," she beamed at him.

CHAPTER FOURTEEN

Winter gradually gave way to spring. With no follow-up attack from the group that had attacked the farm during the snowstorm, the farm residents began losing the tension that had dogged them for weeks. Work progressed slowly during the remainder of the winter season due to both inclement weather and a lack of personnel who were able to perform some chores. Clay and the others were forced to prioritize some projects over others, not always to a good reception by the residents. Still, no one wanted to go through another attack like the one that had claimed so many of their friends and family.

By the time spring was upon them, five new towers formed a strong semi-circle around the farm, running from the western edge behind the Hill to the eastern edge along the highway to the north area beyond the road. Each was covered and lined with four to six inches of dirt between two strong log walls. The towers were not impervious to damage, but it would take a strong weapon to reach the personnel inside. The engineering vehicle and recovery vehicle brought from the abandoned headquarters had been a huge help in getting the towers up and finished, cutting days off the job.

The training schedule had been upped as well, security personnel working harder than ever to be in the proper shape both mentally and physically should another massed attack ever reach them. Jose Juarez, Greg Holloway and Sean Gleason were harsh task masters, running the participants through seemingly endless drills and trials to strength body and mind as well as skills and ability.

The wounded slowly returned to duty, forced to essentially start over in some cases after languishing in bed or rehab, out of action for far too long.

-

"C'mon, Mavis, you can make it!"

"Stop…calling…me…Mavis…dammit!" Amanda Lowery grunted out as she struggled through her pushups. "I…hate you…so…much!"

"Aww, sweetie, you don't hate me!" Kim Powers chuckled as she did her own workout right beside her friend. "I'm basically your physical therapist, you know!"

153

"Ano...ther...good reason...to really...hate you," Amanda gasped out as she neared the end. "Oh, thank God," she groaned as she finished, collapsing on the ground.

"Now, see there?" Kim laughed. "That wasn't so bad, was it? You just got to apply yourself, that's all!"

"You are so lucky that I'm almost dead here," Amanda gasped, chest heaving as she forced air into her lungs. "If I wasn't, I would definitely kill you."

Amanda had slowly been getting her conditioning back for the last three weeks. She was still a bit sore, but Jaylyn had assured her that she was cleared for a full workout, so Amanda had been giving it all she had. She was very close to being able to requalify thanks to Kim's incessant 'help'. Amanda would die screaming before she admitted it, but if not for Kim pushing her, she would have already quit.

"You're very close to getting back, though," Kim lay on her back, also gasping. She had done almost twice as many pushups as Amanda so that she didn't look as if she had quit on her friend.

"I know," Amanda nodded as she struggled to sit up. "And despite hating you, I appreciate the help. I promise," she held a hand up as if swearing an oath.

"That's so sweet!" Kim smiled, still on the ground.

"I got to get some water," Amanda groaned as she got to her feet. "Thatcher was very insistent that I stay hydrated."

"Are you done for today, then?" Kim asked, rising to her feet as well and brushing off her clothing.

"I think so," Amanda nodded. "I've pushed myself about as hard as I dare to, I think. I do not want to go backward, even if it takes me a little longer to get back."

"I understand," Kim nodded. "Are you working out with Xavier at all?"

"No," Amanda scowled a bit at that. "He's helping someone else right now."

-

"Well done, Miss Tillman!" Xavier applauded as he came to his feet. Leanne had just succeeded in throwing him for the first time. First time without him allowing it, that is.

"Thanks!" the teen beamed at him. "Promise you didn't let me, right?" she looked at him carefully.

154

"I promise you faithfully that you did that all on your own, my dear little honey badger," Xavier smiled at her. "Well done, indeed. And with that success, I think it's time we called it a day, don't you? I suspect you have other matters you wish to devote your time to, do you not?"

"Yes, I do," Leanne nodded, biting her lower lip slightly. Heath was getting his 'final' checkup today. Final meaning the one that would clear him to start working out so he could get back into shape. He would have to submit to daily checkups for the first week, and at least weekly checks until he was completely cleared. Assuming he made it through the examination today.

"Do tell young Mister Kelly that I wish him well," Xavier smiled. Leanne's face reddened slightly at that, but not nearly like it once had.

"I will," she smiled at him as she gathered her things. "Thanks."

-

"How is that?" Kaitlin asked as she gently pulled Heath's left arm straight out from his shoulder. "Any pain?"

"You know there is," Heath told her quietly. "I imagine it will hurt from now on, in fact."

"Be that as it may," Kaitlin said patiently, "I have to ask as I go. Help me to help you, Heath, okay?"

"It hurts along my upper arm, in the triceps area, and down through my elbow and maybe a little lower ever so often."

"Better," Kait smiled lowering his arm. "Now, you do it yourself. Let me see how well you do."

Heath slowly but steadily raised his left arm until it was straight once more, exactly like she had done. He grunted once but didn't grimace in pain as she had expected.

"Don't hide the pain, Heath," she warned.

"How can I hide the pain when you know almost every move that I make hurts?" Heath demanded, though respectfully.

"Point," she decided not to argue with him. "Run through the strengthening exercises for me and let me see how you do."

Heath was holding both arms out straight, making small circles in the air when Leanne arrived. It reminded her of P.E. class back in high school. She thought about school for only a second before putting it from her mind. She had looked forward to being challenged at university, but that was not going to happen anymore. Thinking on it was not helpful.

"Hey, you've got an audience," Kaitlin teased him slightly. "Okay, that's good, Heath. Go ahead and lower your arms. I think you're good to go, bud. We'll have to see what Doctor Thatcher says, of course."

"Of course," Heath snorted. He started to put his shirt on but then realized it was useless since Thatcher would just tell him to take it off so she could see his scars. As if his thinking of her had summoned her, Thatcher chose that moment to walk in.

"Morning all!" she smiled as she took the chart Kaitlin offered her. In this case, chart meant tablet since that saved on paper. The twins had secured hundreds of tablets and smart phones in order to be able to use them as map holders, dictionaries, even schoolbooks.

And medical charts.

"Looks good," Jaylyn nodded as she perused Kaitlin's information. "What do you have to say, Heath?" she asked. "How confident are you that your arm is back to one hundred percent?"

"I don't expect it to ever be one hundred percent again, ma'am," Heath replied at once. "I expect to have trouble with it for the rest of my life. And to hurt like the devil when it comes on to rain."

"Very likely, I'm afraid," Jaylyn nodded, impressed that Heath had not tried to 'snow' her by assuring her he was completely fine and ready to go. "Especially the weather sensitivity. Lift your arm for me," she ordered suddenly. Heath raised his arm for her, grimacing slightly as he did.

"Don't hide the pain, Heath," she warned. Heath snorted at that, shaking his head.

"Do they teach you to say that in medical school?" he asked the two women. Kaitlin laughed softly as Jaylyn gave him a mock glare while moving to his hand.

"We need to know if you're hurting, Heath," she admonished gently. "I'm going to push down on your arm. You need to work against me. If the pain increases, or if it hurts in a way that it doesn't right now, I want to know about it right away. Ready? Here we go," she added when he nodded. She slowly began to push down on his hand, trying to force his arm down. Heath managed to hold against her, though he did show the strain on his face as well as in his trembling arm.

"That's enough," Jaylyn said finally, satisfied. "Any pain that would be different or worse than you've been feeling? Any new pains at all?"

"No, ma'am," Heath replied after considering the question for a moment. "It's just pain that I already had, that's all."

"Good," she nodded slowly, looking again at the tablet. "I think we can release you to begin working out, Heath, with a couple of admonishments. First, I want to know at once if there is any new pain at all. I don't care how simple or slight, if it's a pain you're not used to, I want to know it. I mean right away, too. Get me?"

"Yes, ma'am," Heath nodded, slipping his shirt on. "What else?"

"I want you to go slow for the first week to ten days, and I want to see you here for a checkup at the end of the workday. Every day, Heath, at least for those ten days. That is not negotiable, either. I need to be able to monitor your progress. We need to ensure that you aren't overdoing it. I know you want it all back, and you'll get it. It just takes time, that's all."

"I can do that," Heath promised with a nod. "I'm patient enough to know I can't just start out where I was. I'll get there when I get there."

"Good attitude," Jaylyn smiled. "With that, I think it's safe to release you into the custody of this pretty young woman, here," Jaylyn smiled at Leanne, who blushed.

"That sounds good," Heath smiled slightly, winking at Leanne, which made her smile brightly.

"Okay, you two," Kaitlin laughed. "Play footsie somewhere besides here. Shoo. Go."

"Thank you both for everything," Heath told the two women. "I appreciate it very much. I thought…I thought at first, I was going to lose my arm, or at least lose the use of it. Thank you for saving it. I wouldn't be much use without it."

"Fan of history, Mister Kelly?" Jaylyn asked suddenly, studying him.

"Depends on the history, I guess," Heath shrugged. "Why?"

"Horatio Lord Nelson was an Englishman," Jaylyn commented. "Had a somewhat storied career, including a failed landing action that cost him his right arm. He was right-handed. He spent the next several years at sea, rising to the rank of Admiral and doing great damage to the French and the Spanish fleets before being killed in action whilst leading the English fleet to victory at the Battle of Trafalgar. All that with one arm, mind you," she raised her eyebrows slightly.

157

"Moral of the story, Mister Kelly," Jaylyn finished, "is not to count yourself out so quickly. Nelson actually had his damaged arm amputated as quickly as possible and then returned to the bridge and continued leading his ships. Just something to think about. Have a good day, you two," she smiled suddenly and then was gone, Kaitlin following.

"How 'bout that," Heath looked at Leanne.

"How 'bout that, for real," Leanne smiled, then immediately embraced him. "I'm so glad for you," she beamed up at him.

"Thanks, sweetie," Heath grinned at her. "I'm hungry. Wanna take me to lunch, Miss Tillman?"

"I would be delighted, Mister Kelly."

-

Not everyone had recovered so well.

Keely Irvine had held on for two weeks in her shallow coma before succumbing to her injuries, bringing the death toll to nine. Her death had, in some ways, been harder, coming as it did so many days after the battle. Perhaps, some thought, because she alone had died on that day.

Matt Kenny had been slow to recover, Jaylyn deducing that his heart and lungs had been bruised by the round his vest had stopped. Kenny had suffered in silence, however, grateful that the damage wasn't worse. He would heal and that was a gift.

Not all damage was physical, either. Beau Abramson had never recovered from Zayne Parris' death, and from the horror of removing his friend's helmet. He had met with Beverly several times, but the only thing she could get out of him other than his nightmares about his friend dying over and over was anger at Carrie Jarret for not 'helping' Parris. Tandi Maseo had assured Abramson that there was no help for his friend. Dead could not be treated and that was a fact.

Jarret had expected that attitude and had simply ignored it. She had done her job and done it well, she had been assured. That was good enough for her. She felt bad for Abramson losing his friend, but not guilty. She had warned him to keep down.

Several others had gradually come forth over the weeks after the battle, coming either to Beverly Jackson or else searching out a veteran of other battles to talk. Some sought absolution for killing other humans, a few looked for answers as to why someone right beside them had been killed or wounded while they, themselves, were unharmed. A couple

158

just wanted to talk about their experience on the battlefield. Talking it out sometimes seemed to help.

Abramson was eventually relieved of any security responsibilities and given other work. Clay and the other leaders encouraged their people to go out of their way to continue engaging the young man, and not treating him as weak or lacking in some way. Combat was not for everyone, and losing a friend was a shock to the system no matter when or how it happened.

Some, however, came into their own once the battle had joined.

Heather Patton had practically roared like the proverbial lion as she fought along the eastern line. The story of her having to be pulled into the mule even as she kept shooting had swept through the more experienced commandos and earned their respect. The addition of her rummaging through her dead team leader's pockets for the detonator to the Claymore mine left behind them, then setting it off to curtail any pursuit, had also caught the attention of several people, Clay and Jose both among them.

Her arm, while not broken nearly as bad as Heath's had been, had still required six weeks to get a clean bill of health from Jaylyn Thatcher. Members of what was now being referred to as the 'first team', including both Clay and Jose as well as Greg Holloway, began to visit her almost daily for training sessions in tactics and information, preparing her for bigger things once she was cleared to return to action.

Once she was returned to duty, both she and Carrie Jarret found themselves with an invite to try the wrought iron tough training of the Skull and Bones. Both young women were eager to prove themselves and were working hard to prepare for the difficult course, which would begin when Heath Kelly was able to participate. Amanda had looked upon them with a quiet jealousy, wishing she could join them. Xavier had observed her watching them one day as he 'helped' her in place of Kim Powers.

-

"My dear Amanda," his voice was gentle and serious. "I see you following Miss Patton and Miss Jarret with rapt attention as they train. Could it be that you also wish to be added to our ranks?"

"Maybe," Amanda replied sullenly, wiping the sweat from her brow. "Why? Is that so bad? Or wrong?" she almost challenged.

"In absolutely no way," Xavier replied seriously. "Indeed, you have the same fire they do, and the same mental toughness. You will have to convince Bossman that your equipment lapse was a one-time only event, however, before he would allow you to follow them. He will not tolerate that kind of foolishness among us." He paused, looking at her carefully.

"You also need to understand the risks of wearing the Skull and Bones, Amanda," his voice was suddenly very serious. "We take missions away from this fair haven of ours, you know. Missions that invariably require nasty actions fought in dark and in silence. The risks are high enough for men, but for women it will be somewhat increased, given the nature of the people we often encounter. If you would join us, you must be prepared for that."

For once Amanda didn't reply with a snarky comment, sensing that Xavier was imparting serious and good advice to her. She considered his words for some time before nodding slowly.

"I get it," she replied. "I do. But the same thing could have happened here, too," she pointed out. "What if that group had overrun a position I was in? Would they have killed me? Or tried to take me with them? And into what from there? Life itself is a risk these days, X. Seems to me that the better trained I am, the tougher I am, the better off I'll be. Right?"

She was shocked to see a broad smile bloom across Xavier's face. Perhaps the first true smile she had ever seen from him.

"Well put, Amanda," he nodded. "Very well put, indeed. If you wish to make the attempt, then Zachary and I will assist you in preparing. But remember what I said about Bossman; you will have to convince him."

"I'll work hard to do just that," she promised. "And thanks, Xavier."

He froze for a second at her use of his actual name, something almost no one did. At first, she feared that she had done something wrong, but then he had smiled again, somewhat softer this time, and nodded once more.

"You are most welcome, Amanda."

-

"We have to start making some changes," Clay mused as he lay on a blanket, hands behind his head while he stared at the ceiling above him.

"What kind of changes?" Lainie asked him, rising on one elbow and resting her head in her hand. It was a rare quiet moment for the two of them.

"Start easing toward some sense of normalcy," he replied. "We'll plant soon, and that will include a lot more acreage for gardens this year. Not to mention other crops that people may find useful. We can start trading some. We've got a surplus of captured guns and ammo. Stuff we'd never use I mean. We can open a store with all that stuff. We'd need to figure out what we'd want to trade for everything. Stuff we need, you know. Maybe make a list of what we want and what we'll pay or trade for it."

"Pay?" Lainie asked. "With what?"

"Gold, silver, maybe even brass or copper, that kind of stuff," Clay shrugged. "Leon had a lot of silver dollars, and I've still got some gold coins. We could start a bank," he rose from where he was laying to mirror her stance.

"A bank, huh?" Lainie raised an eyebrow at him. "And do what with it?"

"I have no idea."

-

"Well, start by paying people for the work they do on the farm, I guess," Leon scratched his jaw absently. He was starting to shave, and it left his skin itching. He figured it would only get worse. "Not for the gardens and stuff. That's work they're doing for themselves. If we plant a truck patch garden, we can pay people for that, I guess, but then we own the produce and are free to trade it away. That kind of stuff."

"It's going to be hard to make change for a silver dollar, you know," Leanne mentioned, frowning. "You're looking at basing everything on dollars and that's going to get expensive in a hurry. Inflation is already going to be difficult."

"Inflation?" Clay grunted. "All I'm trying to do here is start-,"

"-start over," Leanne cut him off, something she rarely did. "You're going to reintroduce a specie-based economy into one that has, for going on two years now, been barter based. First of all, it will be difficult to get precious metal coins into the hands of those not part of the farm. Secondly, those without will just have another reason to hate 'those Sanders', and you'll have trouble with people committing violent crime to steal from others. You'll have goods no one can 'afford'," she used

161

air quotes for the word, "and precious little money in circulation. It's asking for every economic ill we had before the Storm to come roaring back."

"So, we can't do it," Clay sighed.

"I never said that," Leanne and Leon spoke in unison.

"Let us work on it," Leon told his uncle. "We'll try and come up with something. Besides, who are we going to trade with?"

"Yeah," Clay nodded slowly.

CHAPTER FIFTEEN

"What's the occasion?" Gordy asked as he noticed Leon working to ready Deuce's Place for 'business'.

"If I got my calendar right, then it's Saint Patrick's Day," Leon informed his cousin. "More or less," he shrugged after a pause. "Anyway, we got plenty of reasons to celebrate."

"Makes sense," Gordy nodded. "Need any help?"

"Sure! You want to set those chairs up for me?" he pointed to some folding chairs. "Also, make sure the monitors and the games are up and working, please? That's about it, really. The rest is just getting all this ready back here," he motioned to where he served drinks and cooked hamburgers and beef hotdogs.

"I can do that," Gordy promised and got to work.

"So, what have you been doing?" Gordy asked after a minute. "I haven't actually got to talk to you guys much, lately."

"Well, you're an uncommonly busy and important individual, Little Boss," Leon grinned at his cousin. Gordy shook his head with a wry grin on his face.

"Seriously, though, the big thing Leanne and I have been working on of late is trying to establish a real economy, one based on specie I mean. Uncle Clay wants to open a bank, even. We're trying to figure a way to make that work when the smallest denomination we have at the moment is a silver dollar. We're thinking about sandcasting coins of our own, but we're not sure just yet if they would work out."

"Wait," Gordy stopped, looking around at his cousin. "We'd have a real bank? How would that work?"

"Good question," Leon admitted. "So far that's about all we've got is a bunch of good questions. But unless we figure out a way to get around the whole lack of coinage thing, I don't know that we'll get much further. And to be honest, the barter system seems to be working okay for now. I think we're a little way off from needing a bank and money, but Clay really wants it done, so Leanne and I are working on it."

"Hm," Gordy nodded and returned to work. He needed to talk to Sam.

-

"A bank, huh?" Sam shifted in her seat as she surveyed the land beneath Tower One. She lowered her glasses and looked at Gordy. "I will really be glad when Heath gets released to work," she made a fake grimace. "That ladder is getting old."

"Doing great things for your legs, though," Gordy winked playfully as he pointed to her short's clad legs. Sam blushed a full red immediately, but grinned, pleased by the compliment.

"Well, aren't you just a charmer this afternoon," she laughed. "Though I accept your comment in the spirit with which it was given, and thank you kind sir," she bowed slightly. "Ya jerk," she added with a giggle.

"You do look good, Sam," Gordy promised.

"Thanks," she bit her lower lip slightly for a second. "Anyway, about this bank."

"Well, I remembered you have a lot of what you called junk silver," Gordy shrugged. "Mostly quarters and dimes, I think?" She nodded.

"Then you might want to talk to Clay or at least to the twins," Gordy went on. "You might get in on the bottom floor of the next big thing around here."

"It does sound like a good opportunity, assuming it works," Sam nodded thoughtfully. "And I don't have to invest all of it, anyway," she added, mind still exploring the possibilities. "It sounds like I'm the only one with the smaller denominations in silver, so that would make my help more valuable, right?"

"Oh, I think you and the twins are going to be haggling for a while," Gordy chuckled. "I can't wait to see this."

-

"*Sixty percent*!" Leon goggled at Sam. "Have you been in Doctor Thatcher's drug plants?!"

"It's a good return on my investment, that's all," Sam worked to stifle a grin. She had no intention of demanding such a ridiculous sum but twisting the twins was a favorite pastime of many.

"Good return," Leanne snorted. "More like highway robbery. And while I admit that having a supply of smaller silver coins would make the bank idea more viable, we can manage without them."

"Oh?" Sam asked, eyebrow raised. "By melting down your larger silver coins, I guess? Making a mold to cast smaller coins?"

164

"That's right," Leon nodded once, firmly. "We already tried it, and it worked just fine."

Sam knew that wasn't the entire truth, as each time they cast a new coin it destroyed their mold. At that rate, they would need to cast two at the time just to pay for the molds.

"I wouldn't say needing to rebuild a mold after each cast is 'just fine', Leon," Sam countered. "Fine. Fifty percent, then."

"Not a chance," Leanne refused immediately. "Not short of Uncle Clay demanding that we accept," she looked to where Clay sat in the corner, grinning at the exchange. He immediately held up his hands.

"Don't drag me into this," he ordered. "I'm just watching the show."

"Same here," Gordy chuckled, drawing a mock glare from Sam and a nasty little snicker from a highly amused Lainie.

"Then no," Leanne said flatly.

"Wow," Sam shook her head slowly. "I can't believe the two of you would begrudge someone the chance to make just a little, *itty*-bitty return on her money." It was all she could do at this point to keep a straight face.

"Itty-bitty?" Leanne all but screeched. "Five percent *might* qualify as itty-bitty! Ten would be more than reasonable! At best, at *best* it should be matching funds for percentages. Leon and I may not have any silver or gold of our own, but it's our labor that will make this work or not!"

"All right, fine," Sam decided to draw things to a close. "Because it's you two, and because we're practically family, I'll settle, and this is robbery mind you, I'll settle for three percent and a working share based on what I put into the depository."

"That's still too...wait. What?" Leon frowned as his brain caught up with his mouth.

"God, you two are so easy to wind up," Sam laughed so hard she was holding her stomach. "You're so smart that you're ridiculously easy to fool!"

Clay remembered Leon the Elder saying the same thing once, when they had 'tricked' the twins into helping them. It made him smile to see someone else doing the same thing, since it wasn't hurting them at all.

"Well, that...that's fine, then," Leanne tried not to stammer. "Whatever," she added, feigning disdain of the entire idea.

165

"Aw, don't be like that," Lainie snickered again. "She got you two good, and all in good fun. Go ahead and admit it. You do need her help, after all, and she did agree to your terms. More or less," she added with a grin.

"That is true," Leon sighed. "Still not cool, though," he muttered with a fake glare in Sam's direction.

"It's hilarious," Gordy laughed at his cousins. "Man, you two suckers got *played*!"

-

"Paid?" Titus Terry looked at Gordy. "Like, money paid. Real money, you mean."

"I mean," Gordy nodded. "Don't count on it just yet, mind you, but it's being worked on. We may have a store and a bank before long. Give people a chance to make money on their side gigs and stuff. Don't know exactly how that's going to work, but then I'm not in on the planning, so that won't matter."

"Paid," Titus mused. "And a store? Really? What could a store possibly have?"

"People are making stuff, man," Gordy shrugged. "Gram and some of the others are making cloth and thread, though I admit it's a slow go. Some are making leather gloves and coats and what have you. Knitting socks and underwear, too. Guns, knives and what have you that we've taken from people who attacked us. I mean, if it works, it could be awesome."

"Sounds like it," Titus nodded slowly. "Imagine being able to go on a real date, even. Get a chance to be a big spender," he laughed.

"Ain't it the truth?"

-

"I'm not trying to rain on your parade, Cowboy," Lainie laughed softly. "I'm just saying that this bank thing may not be the smooth operation you think it will. Nor the store, either. I hope it will, mind you, because that would mean things getting back to normal even if only here. But you're talking about rebuilding an economy on your own. A micro economy at that, with no support from outside other than goods you might take in trade. It's a big change from how it's been since the Storm."

"That is true, but the longer we wait to try and get back to normal, the harder it will be to get it done," Clay replied. "We need to shake people lose from being entirely dependent on the farm. Everyone needs a job or a business of their own in order to create at some semblance of a normal economy. Once upon a time, small towns were almost isolated, just like we are now. While it wasn't easy, they usually made things work. If we're careful, we can make it work, too."

"You're going to have some people complain about 'fair shares'," she warned. "You know that. Right?"

"I expect it, yes," Clay nodded. "But we have taken care of people all this time with a bare minimum in return. The farm will pay for labor, starting with planting season this year. We'll also pay those who are working daily with the cattle, hogs and horses. People like Terri and Dee, for instance, and Charley Wilmeth and Gail Knight. They're working with Dad almost every day."

"Plus, we'll be paying everyone on the security detail. A lot of them do that almost full time as it is, plus work on at least one other job. Most of them do more than the rest, and I'll reward them for it."

"Just asking for problems, right there," Lainie sighed. "People will be demanding to get the same pay as someone who works all the time and screeching about how unfair it is when they don't get it."

"They'll just have to screech," Clay shrugged. "This is how it's going to be."

"Remember that I told you," Lainie snorted. "And good luck with that. Really."

-

It was two weeks before Lainie and the twins along with input from a few others had managed to get just the idea of a bank and store straight enough to finally begin planning the operations of said institutions. Planning that was constantly and consistently met with problems and roadblocks, all of which needed to be planned around. Worse, word had traveled like a wildfire through the farm population about the project and the plans, leaving people not already assigned to one of the 'good' jobs scrambling to get their name in the hat.

Two of those people caught Clay completely flatfooted as he had forgotten them altogether, including the operation they oversaw.

"What about us?" Tammy Denmark asked as Callie Weston nodded from behind her.

"Uh, what about you?" Clay asked, confused. "I'm going to need more to go on than that," he clarified. "What are you asking about again?"

"About jobs," Tammy stated. "We're kind of tied in where we are at the moment because of how we came to be here, remember? Are we going to be able to apply for and compete for these 'jobs' everyone is talking about?"

"Uh, don't you already have jobs?" Clay asked, still not seeing the problem.

"Are we going to get paid for the orphanage, then?" Callie asked. "We were basically doing it in return for not being sent away, remember?"

"Oh," Clay finally realized the problem. "Well, no, you're not going to be sent away, for one thing. Both of you have worked hard and haven't caused a problem of any kind. Far as I'm concerned, you're as much a part of the community here as anyone else. As to jobs, we'll most likely keep the same crew operating the orphanage that we have now. You two, Lila Webb and Trudy Leighton. And yes, of course you'll be paid. I'm sorry I didn't realize what you were asking about. I mean, you two do want to stay there, right?" he asked almost as an afterthought, realizing this was something else he'd just taken for granted.

"I mean, well, yeah, of course," the two women talked over one another in their rush to agree. "We just wanted to see if we could work for pay, like some of the others. We'd like to be able to earn a living, such as it is."

"Well, you'll be on the payroll at the orphanage," Clay assured them. "We haven't set down any kind of pay scale yet, but when we do someone will let you know. Are you two sure you want to continue there? Once this gets started you may be locked into that position for a while. For you to be able to leave, we'd have to find someone willing to replace you. That may not be a given, you know?"

"I'm sure," Callie replied at once. "Honestly, I don't think it'd be good for the children for all of us to up and leave, either. They've become accustomed to us as their caregivers, and I honestly don't know how they'd respond to all new people."

"True," Tammy was nodding, frowning in thought. "I hadn't really considered that, either."

"Well, neither had I, to be honest," Clay agreed. "So, that's just another reason for you two to stay, and be paid. Now, like I said, I don't know what any of the pay scales are going to be yet, so if it's not what you expect, please don't be disappointed. We're having to do this from the ground up and we're bound to hit some rough spots. Please be patient."

"Will our job still include room and board?" Callie asked, clearly trying to calculate her needs and that of her own child.

"Of course," Clay nodded. "And we'll still try and rotate you out of there at least one day a week to work outside, like in the gardens. And give you a day off, too. Might not be every week," he warned. "I can't remember the last day off I had where I wasn't sick," he chuckled.

"People in the old days didn't get a day off at all," Tammy shrugged. "We'll make do, I promise."

"I never doubted it," Clay smiled. "And thanks."

-

"I did warn you," Lainie told him over lunch.

"To be fair, they weren't complaining, or demanding," Clay pointed out to her. "They were concerned and not a little nervous. Scared may not even be too strong a word. Now they're reassured and have gone right back to work."

"Not everyone will be that easy, Cowboy," Lainie shook her head. "As a former manager and business owner, I'm telling you what I know."

"You were a business manager, weren't you," Clay murmured, a statement rather than a question. "Even had an Associate's in Business Management, right?"

"Yes," Lainie drew the word out, wary. She didn't like his tone. "Why?"

"Just happened to think of it," he shrugged. "That's all."

-

Darrell Goodrum wasn't the same disagreeable man he'd been before Xavier had 'counseled' with him, but that didn't mean he was all sunshine and puppies, either.

"How am I supposed to make a living, then?" He had walked up without fanfare or pleasantries and launched right into his concern.

"By blacksmithing?" Clay sounded like he was guessing.

"For who?" Darrell demanded.

"Well, me for one," Clay reminded him. "I got a ton of horses that are going to always need shoes. Pretty soon we'll probably start building wagons and they'll need stuff made. For that matter, you should look into building wagons if you know how. As fuel gets harder to come by and vehicles finally quit running, everyone will be needing wagons to move stuff."

Darrell reacted as if he'd been slapped. He clearly hadn't thought of that.

"Damn, Clay," he almost murmured. "I...I never thought of that. Or about the shoeing, either. And you'll pay me for that?"

"Of course," Clay nodded. "Mind you, I hope you're reasonable, since I have a whole bunch of horses, but yeah. No one else here can do it that I know of. Maybe Charley, I guess, but that's just a guess. I've never asked her. Anyway, I expect you'll be one of the busiest people on the ranch outside of the people farming and caring for the livestock. I don't know of another blacksmith or farrier anywhere around."

"I'm sorry," the bigger man took a deep breath. "I just kind of panicked. I've been trying so hard to be a better husband and father and suddenly I didn't know how I was going to take care of them."

"Well, I get that," Clay nodded. "But you know, housing and food are still going to be available to everyone, Darrell. At least everyone that works or is willing to work. No one is going to have to start buying food. They will have to put in hours in the gardens like last year, but that's everyone. Including all of us on security and doing farm work. Those gardens feed us. They're important."

"No problem," Darrell promised. "Thanks again, Clayton."

"You're welcome."

-

"Quick thinking, Cowboy," Lainie chuckled as Clay relayed the story to her. "And, maybe, hopefully, I was wrong. I really do hope I am. I'd love to see all this go smoothly."

"Wouldn't that be novel?" Clay laughed.

-

"Clayton."

Clay turned to see Evelyn Lacey, the Goat Lady as she was universally known, walking toward him.

"Hello Evie," Clay smiled. "How are you? I haven't seen you in a bit."

170

"I've been busy," the soap maker nodded. "I wanted to talk to you about the hubbub going around concerning work and money and what have you. Got a minute?"

"Sure," Clay replied amiably. "What can I do for you?"

"Well, you can reassure me, I guess, that I'm not going to get lost in the transition around here when this whole thing gets started."

"Uh, lost how?" Clay asked. Why did people keep asking such confusing things?

"Word is you're going to start a money system here on the farm," Evelyn said. "People working for pay and what have you. How is that going to affect me, you think?" she semi-demanded.

"Ah, it should give you customers?" Clay made it seem more like a question. "People with money to buy your soaps and what not? Which you can sell in the store we're going to be building, by the way. You should do okay once you get your prices set with what the new market will bear out."

"And if I can't sell anything?" she wanted to know.

"Well, that would suck, for sure," Clay nodded. "But I'm sure there are several people who will buy your goods, don't worry."

"Well since I have to feed thirty goats, two dogs and myself, I sure do worry," she said pointedly.

"They'll be fed, Evie," Clay realized that, here again, someone was jumping to conclusions. "So will you, for that matter. We aren't going to have a grocery store, you know. Just a trading post. What food items there are will be guilty pleasures for the most part. Candy, cookies, berries and jams and the like. Mess hall will still be serving meals, and your goats and dogs will be taken care of right alongside the other livestock. No problem there."

"Oh," Evelyn lost most of her bluster at that. "I didn't realize."

"Most people don't seem to," Clay nodded, sighing. "You aren't the first, or even the second person to come to me today with concerns. You'll still have to work in the gardens just like everyone else, but what you make will be yours to do with as you see fit. Which, I assume, means selling it."

"I'll still have to depend on you for oils, though," she pointed out.

"Well, we'll be glad to sell 'em to you," he grinned. "For that matter, you should find some enterprising young woman, or man, who desires your wonderful smelling soap enough to gather what you need for you, in exchange for some of your goods. Free enterprise at work, right there," he said with a flourish.

"Hey, that is a good idea," she mused, looking thoughtful. "Well, that's all I was worried about, honestly. I wasn't sure I could make it, even here, if I was forced to have money just to eat."

"In an ideal world, that would probably be for the best, but there's just no way to do it, here. Not in the circumstances we find ourselves in, anyway," Clay explained. "We're just going to try and ease our way into some kind of return to at least partial normalcy."

"Sounds like you've got a good plan," she nodded approvingly. "Thanks for your time, Clayton."

"You bet."

-

"Well, it does look as if I was mistaken," Lainie agreed that evening over supper. "I would have sworn you'd have a good deal of bickering before this was finished. Instead, it looks as if no one will have any complaints."

"Oh, I think at least one or two will probably complain before it's over," he shrugged casually.

"Why do you say that?"

"Just a feeling."

CHAPTER SIXTEEN

"You want me to what?" Lainie demanded, her voice and eyes equally flat as she gave Clayton 'the look'.

"Manage the store," Clay smiled at her. "And maybe the bank. Not all alone of course, but you'll be in charge. What do you think?"

"I think now I know who you expected to complain," Lainie shot back, almost growling. "You know that I'm busy sewing every day, Clay," she waved her arms around her sewing area in T1. Her use of his name rather than 'Cowboy' was a warning sign. Her temper was likely to show up very soon, and very lost.

"Well, you can always sew over there, of course," Clay nodded. "But truthfully, you won't have to be there constantly. You'll have people who work for you, you being the manager and all. You'll do more supervising than anything, in all likelihood."

"And just who is going to be working for me in this little endeavor of yours?" she demanded.

"Hadn't gotten that far," Clay admitted. "I figured you'd want to have input in the decision if not outright do it yourself, anyway. I had thought about Kandi as an inventory clerk, though, and maybe Janice as a counter person. Maybe her, Millie and a couple more? We'll also have to have someone doing the banking, but we'll run that out of the store, so if someone wants to deal with the bank, other than making a deposit or withdrawal that is, they can ask whoever is working to call you."

"Sounds like you've got it all worked out after all," Lainie retorted, arms folding up underneath her breasts.

"Well, you can say no, of course," Clay shrugged. "That would leave me looking for a replacement, which would mean that I'm back to not having it worked out. I admit it's a work in progress at this point."

"This is why you were so cagey about my work experience and my degree," she accused him.

"It is indeed," he nodded. "I feel those two qualities make you perfect for the job."

"Lucky me," Lainie's tone was just short of scathing, but not much short.

"Don't be like that, now," Clay cajoled. "If you don't want to do it, just say so and I'll try and find someone else with your qualifications.

Probably be difficult, I admit, but there has to be someone, right? I'll just have to start looking."

"Don't try to guilt me into this," she warned. "This is like some kind of emotional blackmail is what this is."

"How can you say that?" Clay tried his best to look innocent. "It's just a job that needs doing, that's all. It is an important job, I will grant you that, and naturally I need someone I can trust and depend on without question to oversee it, but at the end of the day it's still-,"

"Oh, my, *God*, you are so transparent!" Lainie threw her hands up in an irate gesture. "I mean really, really, annoyingly transparent," she frowned.

"And cute," Clay added straight-faced. "Don't forget cute. Oh, and have a nice ass," he raised an index finger as if making a point. "You said that yourself."

"I hate you at times," Lainie almost growled. "Really, really hate you."

"Hey now, don't be like that!" Clay smiled broadly; arms open wide. "Don't be a hater!"

"Hate you," Lainie nodded firmly, as if reaffirming her stance. "Fine. I'll look at-,"

"Thanks!" Clay cut her off smoothly. "Listen, I gotta run, but the twins and Millie have already got a lot of the leg work done, so you can get the high points from them. They're at Operations right now if you want to go ahead and get started? And I'll see you later! Bye!" With that he almost blinked out of the sewing center in Building One he left so fast.

"Oh, you will pay for that," Lainie promised the air around her.

-

"And that's where we are so far," Leanne finished the pitch as the three teens wrapped up their 'report' on what they had accomplished thus far.

"I don't think I like the idea of selling guns and ammunition to people we don't know," Lainie mused, looking down at the notes she had made. "Be just our luck to have them used against us at some point, wouldn't it?"

"That is a possibility, but was something Clay really wanted to have," Millie explained. "Like an old-time general store. We'll sell everything someone might need or want. As far as we can procure or make it, anyway."

"And what are we going to do with the products we get from people living here on the farm?" Lainie asked. "For that matter, what will we be paid for facilitating work for those people? We should get something for working as a job referral service."

"Hm," Leon mused, looking away into the distance. "I didn't think of that last one. For products, we either get a commission, or else buy outright at a price where we can make a profit. I don't know how to figure a rate for a referral service. Not everyone will make the same, and not every job will pay the same even for those who make a higher income."

"We can always have an advertising board, and charge a monthly fee for that," Leanne suggested. "In all honesty, it's only going to be people like Mister Goodrum and Uncle Jake that will get any large jobs from advertising with us. Everything else we'll pretty much have available at the store anyway."

"That is true," Leon nodded in agreement. "What do you think, Aunt Lainie?"

"I can see it working, at least when it comes to major jobs like that," she nodded slowly. "You forgot Gary Meecham, though. And that armorer that came with Flores, what was her name again?"

"Sara Yamaguchi," Millie supplied, looking at her own notes. "Sergeant. If that still means anything," she added, shrugging.

"Depends on where you are at the time, I guess," Lainie returned her shrug. "Anyway, the two of them are sure to get some business. No one will want to try and replace a firearm in this world. Not if they can repair it."

"True," Leanne nodded. "Alright, so make it four? Unless Mister Meecham and Sergeant Yamaguchi decide to go into business together."

"Something else to consider," Millie made a note of that idea.

"I'm going to want some time to think on the bank idea," Lainie announced. "We'll need some kind of safe place to keep funds, and it's going to have to be guarded. We'll probably have to put the safe here in Building Two and start posting a permanent guard here. Should have that anyway considering what all we keep here," she added. "Operations, the clinic, apartments upstairs. If we open this place up for business, as in the farm I mean, then we're going to start getting some nosy neighbors and begin having potential crooks scoping us out. We're going to have to be ahead of that. Be sure you bring that up to His Majesty, Clayton the First," she ordered, getting to her feet.

"Uh, why don't you-," Leon began, only to be cut off.

"He and I won't be talking for a day or two," Lainie told him flatly. "You three obviously have an idea of who might want to sell items in the store, so start talking to them. You need to know what they can market, how many of them you can depend on getting per month, and how much they will want for them. I'll tell you now that I'll start thinking about what I can do as far as making clothing, though I'm going to have to make sure we can meet our own needs before worrying about anyone else. By own needs I'm referring to family," she stressed to the teens.

"Ah, I'm not really-," Millie started, but was also cut off.

"Please," Leanne scoffed. "Don't make me embarrass the two of you with Aunt Lainie standing right there."

Leon and Millie both turned an interesting shade of red at that, examining the floor for faults.

"Ouch," Lainie actually smiled at that one. "Okay, so let's get on this. If we have to do it, let's get it done, and done right. If you need me for anything, I'll be next door."

"I think Uncle Clay may be in trouble," Leanne mused once Lainie was gone.

"She did seem a little tense," Leon agreed neutrally.

"Tense?" Millie snorted. "You need a better vocabulary, Ace. That woman is *pissed*."

-

"I don't understand why you're so mad at me!" Clay exclaimed, though in truth he was trying not to laugh. "I didn't force you to take the job, you know!"

Lainie ignored him as she finished the dishes and cleaned her kitchen. That done, she walked right past him, into the bedroom, and closed the door. Clay didn't try to follow, knowing that the door would be locked. Instead, still trying not to laugh, he trooped upstairs to the loft bedroom, where he had stored pillows and blankets for just such an emergency. Actually, they had always been there, kept on hand for anyone staying with him, but he had never removed them.

Now, he'd put them to use as his significant other got her mad out.

176

-

"*Operations, Gunner, please respond.*"

"Go for Operations," JJ said at once, straightening in his seat.

"*Advise Bossman, heavy traffic moving north along the interstate,*" Zach informed him. "*Foot traffic and a few horses. No vehicles I can see, but there are a lot of people in there. No gunfire I can hear, and they aren't running.*"

"Roger that, Gunner. Will do." JJ picked up a GMRS radio and called Clay to Operations. He was there in less than a minute.

"What's up, JJ," he asked.

"Zach says there is a lot of foot traffic moving north along the interstate," JJ repeated what Zach had said.

"Okay," Clay sighed. "I'll head up there. Let him know I'm on the way."

"Will do," JJ nodded, turning back to the radio. Clay was already gone.

-

"That is a bunch of people," Greg Holloway said quietly as he lowered his binoculars.

"It is at that," Clay agreed. "We need to pull back out of sight I guess and let them pass. Hope they'll pass, anyway. Greg, go back and tell Jose we need a strong security team up here in case things don't go our way. Tell him to pick five people and send them back up here with you. Use the carts coming back since they're quiet. Less noise we make the better until this is over."

"Got it," Greg nodded, heading back to their ATV. Fortunately, it was a quieter model, and the crowd was still a good way off.

"What are they running from, I wonder?" Zach asked, a thoughtful expression on his face.

"What?" Clay asked, still studying the mass of people.

"Last time something like this happened, it was people streaming south," the teen reminded him. "And they were running from the plague. Makes me wonder what this bunch is running from." Clay slowly lowered his glasses at that as he turned to look at Zach.

"Ah, crap."

-

"Papa, we must stop soon."

Isaac Miller looked at his middle daughter, Ruth.

177

"We have to stop, Papa," Ruth repeated. "Abram and Mary will never say it, but she and the baby both need rest. And Martha does as well. Not to mention we need to rest the horses and see if we can find them water."

"We cannot afford to delay, daughter," Isaac replied evenly. "They will have to be tough."

"Where are we going, Papa?" Ruth asked suddenly.

"What?"

"Where are we going?" she repeated. At his silence, she raised a blonde eyebrow beneath her bonnet. Waiting.

"I do not know for sure," he finally admitted, reluctance in every word.

"If we do not know where we are going, what difference does it make if we delay a bit?" Ruth asked him pointedly. "Even a day will make no difference if we don't know where we are headed."

"Fine, daughter," Isaac told the ever-headstrong Ruth. "We will leave this road at the next exit and make camp for a day and rest. Happy?"

"I would be happier at home," Ruth said sadly. "But this will do in a pinch." Suddenly she raised up onto her toes and kissed his cheek, just above his beard.

"Enough!" he swatted at her playfully. "Go and tell them the news," he ordered. "Perhaps that will cheer you up. It's no wonder you never found a husband, child. Too headstrong by far," he shook his head in mock sadness.

"I simply have high standards," Ruth sniffed airily. "Thank you, Papa," she added softly before heading to tell her sister-in-law that they would be stopping soon.

"High standards," Isaac shook his head, a wry grin across his face. "Would that your mother would have lived to see you grown, girl."

-

"Uh, Boss?"

"What is it, Zach?" Clay asked, turning from where he'd been talking to Greg Holloway. The flow of traffic had slowed considerably, with most of the crowd already gone by, many already out of sight.

"I think they're getting off here," Zach replied, slowly raising his hand to point toward….

"Is that a wagon?" Greg asked, leaning forward a bit as if that would clear things up.

"No, it's two wagons," Zach replied. "Two wagons with five people, four horses, a cow and a dog."

"You got to be kidding me," Clay was shaking his head.

"They're Amish," Greg noted softly. "I think I know that guy," he added. "He...damn," he stopped suddenly. "I bet the group that hit here has hit everywhere south of here already."

"You were right it looks like, Zach," Clay clasped the young man's shoulder lightly. "Good eyes and good reasoning."

"Thanks," Zach nodded, clearly pleased with the compliment.

"Gregory, if you know this man, let's go and talk to him once he gets up here and away from the highway. Maybe he'll head toward Jordan."

"I doubt it," Greg was shaking his head. "Pretty sure this guy knows your father."

"Course he does," Clay rolled his eyes. "Why wouldn't he?"

-

"I know this road," Isaac told his son-in-law. "This way leads to Jordan, but this way will lead to the farm of Gordon Sanders" he pointed each way in turn. "I have done business with him on occasion over the years. He is an honest and God-fearing man, especially for the Yankees."

"I've heard you speak of him," Abram Troyer nodded. "Always with respect. Do you believe he might offer us a place for the evening?"

"I had not thought to ask," Isaac admitted. "I had merely thought to appease Ruth and rest for a time, perhaps even a day. The horses need rest, as do Mary and the child. It would not hurt any of us, in truth."

"That is true," Abram nodded. "I did not want to suggest it, but Mary is flagging. She is very tired, and nursing simply makes it worse for her. I do not imagine it does little John any better."

"I should think not," Isaac nodded. "We can always see if he still lives, and if his farm is still in his hands. Perhaps it is."

"Perhaps."

-

"Yeah, that's Isaac Miller," Greg said gently as he and Clay watched from cover. "I don't know who that young man is, but the girls are Isaac's daughters. I hate to think what has spurred them to leave their farm, man. It's a good piece of ground, good house and good barn. He did all kinds of different things for their community."

"What kind of things?" Clay asked, suddenly interested.

"Well, he makes wheels for one thing," Greg told him. "Wagon wheels, I mean. That and wagons too, but that's not nearly as often. Fair hand at carpentry for that matter. Helped his brother run a sawmill, I think, but don't hold me to that one. He may not have been involved in that. Builds nice furniture when he's got nothing else going on."

"What kind of furniture?" Clay wanted to know.

"Well, he makes porch furniture, dining tables and chairs, and bedroom suits. All the old-fashioned way, so it's not always popular with us 'English', as he calls us."

"Who is us?"

"Anyone who isn't Amish and in good standing with their church," Greg shrugged. "It was all I could do to get him to stop using 'Yankee'. He hails from a place in Ohio where that's what they call outsiders. Yankees. I explained how that wouldn't really fly here and he started using English, which is what the majority apparently call us. I say apparently because he's not exactly forthcoming with information about their way of living. They are a tight-lipped people for the most part."

"Looks like it's just him and his immediate family," Clay pointed out. "Not so closed off now, I guess."

"Doesn't look it," Greg nodded. "Well, he's almost to the road. Want to let him get inside the tree line, or meet him out there?"

"Let them get into the tree line," Clay decided. "That way no one else sees them and wonders what's up here."

-

"You know this place, Papa?" Ruth asked as they left the interstate and started down the small country lane. "The town is the other way."

"We are not going to the town, child," Isaac was shaking his head. "They have likely faired no better than we did, assuming the devil's minions made it this far. They will not want visitors. This way leads to the farm of a Yankee I know. As I told Abram, he is a good and God-fearing man, even if he is an outsider. He may allow us to camp for a day or two, and his farm will have plentiful water if nothing else. If he has it to spare, he will probably offer us food."

"That sounds good, Papa," Ruth replied, nodding her head. "I may like this man already," she smiled.

180

"Don't like him too much," Isaac warned. "He is still a Yankee, whatever his good traits may be."

"Yes, Papa," she replied. "What will we-," She stopped as she realized her father had stopped dead still in the road.

"What's the matter, Papa?" she asked, trying to look around him. When she finally managed it, she froze. There were two armed men in the road, facing them.

"You folks look as if you've traveled a piece," one said. "If you're peaceful, we can offer you water and place to rest. Maybe a hot meal."

"We are always peaceful, Ya-, English," Isaac replied. "I was looking for a man I know by the name of Gordon Sanders. He once lived nearby."

"Still does," the speaker nodded, his voice friendly. "I'm his son, Clayton. You'll be wanting to see him, I reckon?"

"I...if possible, that would be good, yes," Isaac replied, mind working quickly. If these two meant to cause trouble, there would be no escape for anyone.

"Okay," Clayton replied with a nod. "You want to all go up together, or just you?"

"I would prefer we stay together, if possible," Isaac admitted.

"Sure," Clayton nodded. "Y'all need any help?"

"I believe we can manage but thank you."

"Sure thing. Come on along and we'll see if we can find Dad. Probably at the barn this time of day."

Isaac followed, leading his family into what he hoped was the land of a friendly man and family.

CHAPTER SEVENTEEN

Gordon had just finished caring for his horse when he looked up to see Clay coming toward him with a familiar face.

"Isaac Miller," Gordon called, wiping his hands on a shop rag as he stepped outside the barn to meet the coming group. "Long time since I seen you, Isaac."

"Indeed, Gordon Sanders," Isaac didn't allow his relief at being openly welcomed to show. The two men shook hands, then Gordon looked past Isaac and frowned at seeing his family.

"Isaac, have you suffered a misfortune?" Gordon asked carefully. He didn't want the other man to feel offended or that Gordon was butting into his personal business.

"I am afraid so, Gordon," Isaac admitted freely. "Most of our entire community was overrun and destroyed. My home and barns are gone, as are most of my tools and supplies. We have managed to survive the winter, but there is nothing left for us where we were. We are moving north to try and start again, if possible."

"I'm sorry to hear that, Isaac," said Gordon. "All of it," he added to clarify. "It's none of my business I guess, but your daughter looks about done in, Isaac. Why don't you let us put you up for a few days to rest and regroup a bit? She's got a young one, so she likely needs a good meal or two and some rest."

"I would not presume upon you, Gordon Sanders," Isaac said formally. "If you could but let us camp somewhere near water, we will be fine."

"Isaac, it's no presumption to take care of a good man and his family," Gordon shook his head. "For that matter, it's a Christian duty even if it was to be an imposition. Now, let's have no more talk about this. Would you be willing to allow our doctor to take a look at your daughter? For that matter, all of you should see her and get a checkup. I know you don't normally use our English physicians, but you should make an exception at least this once. Meanwhile, we'll set to finding you a good place to lay your heads while Angela and some of the others get to cooking."

"I do not-," Isaac began but Ruth stepped in front of him suddenly.

"We accept, Mister Sanders, and offer our thanks," she said formally, then curtsied. "You are a good and kind man, and I will pray that the Lord blesses you for your benevolence."

"Thank you, young lady," Gordon smiled gently. "Clayton, will you see to their arrangements while I see your mother?"

"Sure," Clay nodded. "Mister Miller, there's a guest house just up the hill from here. We can corral your horses behind the buildings at the old Troy farm and have our vet check them for you. We'll keep them there in isolation from our herds. I can get a truck and some help to move your things, or you can use your wagon and then bring the horses back down. Whatever you prefer."

-

"I expected you would raise hell when Gordon offered them a place to stay," Greg mentioned idly as he and Clayton returned to the Troy farm.

"Man, that girl has an infant," Clayton complained. "I'm not that bad, am I?"

"Didn't say it was bad, now did I?" Greg noted. "I'm not knocking you either way, dude. I just figure you got something in mind, that's all."

"So, now I've gone from being predictable to transparent?" Clay snorted.

"Do you?" Greg pressed.

"Yeah," Clay chuckled, shaking his head. "Even if I didn't, I would have suggested letting them stay at least until they were rested. But, if Miller can do all you say he can, then he would make a great addition to our little community, wouldn't he? Think of what he can teach us, man. Over and above what he can do himself. How good would it be to have another carpenter, let alone someone who can create furniture like that? See what I mean?"

"I do," Greg nodded. "And don't forget that wheelwright thing, either. One day sooner than we want to imagine, we'll be needing wagons like that. Building those wheels is a dying art."

"Honestly, we probably don't need wagons like that for a time," Clay mused. "We can build wagons out of dead trucks. Use their beds, like in the old days?"

"Good idea," Greg nodded. "Be a lot easier to ride in, that's for sure."

183

EMBERS

"Right?"

—

"Would you care for more, child?" Angela asked Ruth Miller. The girl looked at her, but hesitated, glancing at her father.

"This is my table, young lady," Angela noted primly. "The only permission you need here is mine. I'm sure your father will agree to that, since this is my kitchen," she glanced at Isaac, who chuckled a bit.

"A wise man never argues with the cook," he told his daughter. "Do as you like, child, but mind your manners."

"Yes, Papa," Ruth smiled. "Thank you, Mrs. Sanders," she smiled shyly at the matriarch of the Sanders' clan.

"You're quite welcome, dear."

—

"You're dehydrated, exhausted, and on the verge of malnutrition," Lieutenant Candida Guerrero told Mary Troyer quietly. The Physician's Assistant had arrived on the farm with Lieutenant Flores' group and had never looked back, inserting herself neatly into the clinic and then into her new community.

"John is also bordering on malnutrition, but is in better shape than you are," she continued. "You were right on the verge of negatively impacting his physical and perhaps mental development, but we've caught that in time to make sure he gets the vitamins and minerals he needs to catch up. Mostly that means ensuring that you get those vitamins so that you can pass them along as you feed him. We can manage that just through a better diet than you've been getting, I feel certain. This place has good food, and some of the best cooks I've ever seen. I bet I've gained ten pounds since I got here. Mostly right here," she slapped the seat of her pants.

Mary had nodded to acknowledge that she understood what she had been told but remained silent. She managed not to show her surprise at the other woman's blatant reference to her…to herself, and her weight gain.

"You okay, sweetie?" Guerrero asked, noticing that Mary seemed to be a little off balance. "I know it can be a little overwhelming, but don't worry. You'll be alright, I promise. This place is as safe as any place in the world can be nowadays. Around here, anyway. So, try not to worry about anything except your health and the health of your baby. I promise we'll take good care of you both," she smiled brightly.

Mary managed to return the smile, albeit tiredly. She had lived in near terror for so long that she was almost completely exhausted. Spent. The release of so much tension was suddenly overwhelming for Mary, and before she realized it, she was sobbing, her face cradled in her hands.

"It's okay, sweetheart," she heard Guerrero's voice say, though it sounded dim and distant to her ears.

"You'll be fine, I promise, and so will your son," was the last thing she heard before her world faded away.

-

"I would like to see my wife and son, please," Abram Troyer said. He was standing in the clinic, openly concerned at the absence of his wife and child.

"Quietly now, Mister Troyer," Guerrero shushed him with a finger to her lips. "This way," she led him behind a privacy screen. Troyer looked almost hesitant to follow a woman not his wife to such a secluded place but did so. Behind the screen he found Mary, sleeping on a bed and holding John in her arms. She had obviously had the opportunity to clean up and was wearing a gown provided by the clinic.

"What is the problem?" he demanded.

"Quietly, I said," Guerrero reminded him. "Come with me," she ordered, and Abram Troyer had no problem recognizing it was an order. While a man grown among his own people, in the English world he was still under-age. Merely seventeen, he was easily intimidated by strong people when outside his comfort zone. That comfort zone had been destroyed a few months before, leaving him with a young wife and baby and no way remaining to provide for them.

Following the woman in the camouflage uniform, he was soon near a long bench against the wall, where the woman propped one boot up on the bar beneath the desk area.

"Your wife is suffering from malnutrition, dehydration and just pure exhaustion, Mister Troyer," Candid Gurrero informed him. "Once she figured out that she was safe, at least for the moment, she broke down in tears and passed out from exhaustion. Simple as that."

"While her situation is bordering on serious, we've caught it before it became that way," she continued. "Good food, rest, and safety will do her a great deal of good. I expect she'll be fine within a week or so, other than it will take a bit longer for her to recover from the malnutrition,

185

mostly due to her nursing John. She will be fine, however, Lord willing, so far as these problems are concerned, anyway. I can't speak to the future, of course."

Hearing the oddly dressed woman refer to the Lord had given Abram a sense of comfort he hadn't known he needed until he had it. He suddenly felt as if everything was going to be alright.

"I am indebted to you, ma'am," he bowed slightly. "Thank you for caring for my family."

"It's what I do, Mister Troyer," Guerrero smiled brightly. "But you're quite welcome."

-

"Are you going to argue with me if I offer Isaac a place here for him and his family?" Gordon asked Clay as the two leaned against a rail fence that decorated the front area of the pad in front of Building Two.

"No, of course not," Clay replied, frowning. "Why would you even ask that?"

"Clayton, you have rarely done anything we've asked of you without arguing since this all started," Gordon reminded him.

"I've argued over doing stupid shit that was destined to get some of us killed," Clay retorted, brow creased in borderline anger. "Like going to the church, where, if you recall, we were actually attacked and your gift of food was looked upon as too little, and you were told that people would be calling upon us each week for our 'contribution'. Remember that?"

"I remember," Gordon nodded, acknowledging the hit.

"At the place we're at now, there's no point in refusing someone who can be an asset to our community," Clay calmed a bit at that. "In fact, we should be searching them out, or at least watching for them to come by. I had entertained the idea of doing just that, in fact. Going out on patrols to look for people who would be a good fit for us and could offer us something in return."

"And those who can't?" Gordan asked, eyebrow raised.

"How many of them do you think we can care for?" Clay didn't rise to the bait. He'd begun to suspect that his father sometimes did this just to goad him. He wasn't going to play that game this time.

Gordon's face reflected the surprise he felt at having the subject tossed back at him like a live grenade. His mouth opened, closed, opened again, then finally closed as he looked to the ground.

"Yeah," Clay nodded. "When you have to think about it in those terms, it sobers you a bit, don't it? Welcome to my world, Pop."

"Suppose I deserve that," Gordon gave a dry chuckle. "It's difficult to see those in need and not offer them a hand."

"Look at this farm, Dad," Clay waved his arm around them. "How many people are here that honestly have no business being here? I don't mean that we shouldn't have them living here. I'm talking about how many people we've taken in other than close friends. It's a pretty big number. And don't forget the orphanage and the kids there that we're responsible for."

"I get it, Clayton," Gordon raised a hand in supplication. "Peace, Son."

"Good luck with that," Clay snorted. "I get very little peace and almost no quiet."

-

"Your friend is truly a good man, Papa," Ruth Miller said quietly as she and her father sat in the living area of the small house the Miller family had been placed in.

"He is not my friend," Isaac shook his hand. "He is a Ya-, English. Someone I know and have done business with."

"Does he know that?" Ruth asked, head tilted to one side. "Because I believe he counts you as a friend, Papa. His welcome to you was earnest and heartfelt. His concern for all of us was apparent as well. He has seen to our needs and provided us a safe harbor away from the storm. I would suggest that whether you consider him a friend or not, Mister Gordon definitely considers you one." She had gotten to her feet and crossed to him as she finished.

"Goodnight, Papa," she kissed his cheek and disappeared into the room she was sharing with Martha before her father could frame a suitable reply.

Behind her, Isaac thought long and hard about what his daughter had said.

-

Abram Troyer stepped outside of Building Two and stretched himself. The morning was brisk, a typical spring morning in this part of the world. As he stood there, two young men and a young woman, all dressed in military clothing and carrying military gear, walked by him, talking and laughing among themselves. All three nodded polite greetings to him as they passed, which he returned automatically.

"You guys be sure and check the duty roster," a voice behind him startled Abram. He turned to see another young man, also in his age range, sharpening a knife.

"Got it, Z," the girl waved as the three deviated from their course to enter the building Abram had just emerged from.

"Busy place, most times," the man called 'Z' noted Abram's interest. "You'll get used to it."

"I do not think we will be here long enough to get used to it," Abram said without thinking, making his way to where the young man sat on a cinderblock.

"Oh?" Z never looked up as he spoke. "Surprising. Most of the time people are fighting to get in here, or else to kill us all and just take it from us."

"That is what happened to us," Abram nodded gravely. "Most friends and family perished in an attack on our community before the holiday season. After Thanksgiving."

"I'm sorry to hear that," Z replied. "It's happened to a lot of places, and apparently not just around here." He paused as he checked the edge of the blade. Satisfied, he sheathed the blade and drew a smaller one, starting again.

"We were attacked here after the first of the year," he continued. "I guess about the middle of January, though to be honest I don't much bother keeping up with dates these days. One day is as good as the next anymore. Anyway, we were attacked without any warning or attempt to negotiate. We lost nine good people and had several others injured. Some likely won't ever completely recover. But we're still here, and they aren't."

"You fought?" Abram asked, though he already knew the answer.

"Of course," Z showed surprise as he looked up at Abram. "What else would we do?"

"I don't know your ways, Yankee," Abram shrugged. "It is not our way."

"What isn't your way?" Z frowned. "I'd be careful how I threw that 'Yankee' tag out around here, by the way." He stood and sheathed the smaller blade, the stone disappearing into a pouch on his gear.

"Apologies, Englishman. The term Yankee is an old one from our home in Ohio," Abram explained. "As to our way, we are not aggressive ourselves, nor do we respond to aggression with violence. We respond with peace."

"Well, that's a new one, I guess," Z mused. "How's that working out for you? 'Fore you got here, I mean?"

"I do not understand," Abram replied.

"What's your name?" Z asked suddenly.

"I am Abram Troyer," Abram replied. "I am married to Isaac Miller's oldest daughter," he added. Many people knew his father-in-law, though they had no reason to know Abram from the trees in the forest.

"Zach Willis," 'Z' nodded. The one letter form of address now made sense, at least.

"I do not understand your question, Zach," Abram repeated.

"You don't believe in fighting, so that means you don't protect yourself, your home, or your family. Right?"

"We strive to be Godly, always, no matter the situation," Abram explained. "Our beliefs do not allow us to use violence."

"Hm," Zach nodded slowly. "And I asked how that was working for you so far," he said. "What have you lost because of that policy?"

"It is true we've lost much," Abram admitted. "Our homes, farms, many of our tools necessary for our labor. But we have not lost our way, nor our souls. We cannot give in to vengeance and hatred of the man before us."

"Hatred?" Zach frowned slightly. "I don't hate anyone, Abram. I don't even hate the people who attacked us here."

"Then why do you fight them, Zach?" Abram asked. "If not for hate, or vengeance, why raise your hand to others?"

"I don't hate the people I'm fighting, Abram," Zach repeated. "I don't fight because I hate them. I fight for the people behind me. The people beside me. I fight to protect the weak. Hate doesn't have anything to do with it. I can't believe you can't at least fight to protect home and family"

"It is not our way," Abram said simply.

"Well, guess that's your decision to make," Zach shrugged. "Good luck with that."

189

EMBERS

Abram watched the young man walk away, thinking about all he had been told.

-

"I feel I must try and offer you some form of compensation before we move on, Gordon Sanders," Isaac said over the breakfast table in Angela's outdoor kitchen.

"Told you before that wasn't needed or wanted, Isaac," Gordon shook his head. "And move on? Where are you moving to, Isaac?"

"I am unsure yet," Isaac admitted. "We must find another congregation to join, somewhere."

"And do you know where one is?" asked Gordon.

"Not at this exact moment, no," Isaac admitted reluctantly. "I know where several were, but they may have met with the same fate as our own. I must go and see before I can know."

"You know, you and your family could just stay here, Isaac," Gordon said easily, leaning forward to place his elbows on the table and then resting his chin on steepled hands. "There's no reason for you to take your children and that little grandbaby out into that mess out there," he waved toward the interstate. "No to mention your daughter isn't really in any condition to travel further at the moment."

"What do you mean?" Isaac asked, looking at Ruth, then at Martha.

"Not them, Isaac," Gordon shook his head. "Mary is pretty bad off according to my daughter-in-law. Dehydrated, malnourished and exhausted. Nursing an infant just compounds all of that from what Pat said. She needs a few days of rest and a few days more of good meals and clean water before she can go much further."

"She must go where her husband goes," Isaac shrugged. "That is no longer up to me, but rather to him."

"You'd just drag her along to her death, then?" Gordon showed the first sign of anything other than friendliness. "Even after our medical people have already found out what she needs and started seeing to it that she gets it?"

"I doubt we can afford-,"

"There's no charge of any kind attached to that help, Isaac," Gordon cut him off. "For anyone. There hasn't been since this has all started. Those who are sick or injured get whatever help we can provide them. Sometimes it isn't enough, but all we can do is all we can do. Sometimes

I reckon the Lord comes calling and that's all there is to it. But there's no need to worry about cost, because there isn't any."

"We cannot accept-,"

"If you call me English and say you can't accept help from me after knowing me for all these years, doing business with me, then I may just test that no aggression clause in your religion, Isaac," Gordon warned, his voice low and dangerous.

"Gordon!" Angela almost hissed.

"You stay out of this," Gordon didn't even look her way. "You aren't the only one with beliefs, Isaac Miller. I've always respected yours, and I had always assumed you would extend that same courtesy to me. Well, my way, *our* way, says we extend assistance to all men, especially to those of the household of faith. While our strict definition of the household might not include those outside the church, that turn of phrase simply means we take care of our own first, which we have. We have also extended help to as many as possible, including an orphanage less than a hundred yards from the house you slept in last night that serves as a home for over a dozen small children who we have no way to identify. You don't suppose we charge them for their upkeep, do you?"

Isaac Miller wisely kept his mouth shut on that one.

"I risked the wrath of my son, Clayton, to make sure that you and your family would have a place here, Isaac," Gordon continued, though somewhat more calmly than just a few seconds before. "I didn't do that because I expected payment from you. If you want to repay me, then be a good and productive member of our community. We're trying to survive and to make a decent life for the children we have here. You can be a part of that. I'm sure there's a great deal of knowledge you have that could be passed along to the next generation. But I haven't asked you for anything material and won't." Gordon paused for a moment, visibly collecting himself.

"Now then," he continued finally. "Let's try this again. Isaac, you and your family are welcome here. We all help with gardens that help feed us, and those who have skills we can use are asked to contribute where and when needed. We're also trying to reinstitute a specie driven economy here on the farm proper. If someone hires you to do a job, then whatever arrangements you come to with them, that's yours. We don't ask for any of it to be contributed to the farm or farm operations. In turn, we're looking to open a general store and a bank. Your family can make products to sell in the store at whatever commission they work out with you, and you can spend the money you make there on goods you want in return."

"Meals are already provided along with housing, so those are two things you don't have to worry about paying for. Security is also provided, though we can't and don't guarantee that the farm won't be attacked or that you won't be hurt. We have been attacked more times than I can remember right off hand, and we've lost people in those attacks, with others injured or wounded at the same time. But we do have a good fighting force that's well trained and equipped and includes several soldiers that are the survivors of the group that was stationed here before the plague. Far as I know they're good people, and my son's men are as well."

"You can stay or go as you please," Gordon got to his feet. "Know that the offer is there, if you want it." With that Gordon stepped outside and headed for the barn. Behind him, Angela bustled around, cleaning and wiping down her kitchen.

"Please allow me to assist you, Mrs. Sanders," Ruth got to her feet.

"Thank you, Ruth," Angela smiled. "Please don't hold that against Gordon, Isaac Miller. We've been through a lot just trying to do our Christian duty and I'm afraid it has somewhat tarnished Gordon's halo just a bit."

"It is I who should ask that you not hold my behavior against me," Isaac shook his head slowly. "And I who must ask your husband for forgiveness. I have insulted him, though without the intention to do so. Your husband is indeed a good man, Mrs. Sanders. If you will excuse me?" Isaac was on his feet now.

"Of course," Angela smiled at him.

"Ruth, please care for your sister," Isaac ordered. "If Mrs. Sanders needs help or company, you two should provide it. I will return when I can." Without waiting for a reply, Isaac stepped out of the outdoor kitchen to follow Gordon's path to the barn.

"I fear the pressure of things is getting to him, Mrs. Sanders," Ruth told Angela once Isaac was out of earshot. "Things have been rather hard since we were attacked."

"I had a thought once that so long as your community was left alone, your people would be able to continue on with little interruption,"

Angela told the girl. "I admit that I had a great deal of naivete at the start of all this, Ruth. My son tried to warn me, as did others, but I didn't listen. I was determined that things would continue as normal for us, and I tried to make it do that by force of will. Silly, stupid, and selfish just to name a few things that describe me at the time," she sighed.

"Just as it was naïve to think that your community would be able to keep going. I should have known that someone who is a thief and bully would choose to attack a place like yours. Because your people believe in non-violence, that would seem ideal to a person such as that. I am so sorry that you all had to endure such a thing."

"Thank you, Mrs. Sanders," Ruth bowed her head slightly. "Our view is that such things are the will of the Father. Such things are tests for our faith and obedience. Just as it was God's will that we were gathering from our garden when the attack came. It is removed from the house...where the house was," she stumbled slightly before regaining her equilibrium. "We were gathering a few things that we had planted late. Kale and spinach, along with a few carrots and onions. We heard the shooting from where we were, but by the time we got home, the house and barn were burning, as were most other buildings in the community."

"Had we not been gathering food we would have died with the others. As it is, we were part of perhaps twenty-five in all to survive the attack. Out of over two hundred," she finished softly, a single tear tracking down her cheek.

"You poor child," Angela embraced the girl, holding her tightly as she began to cry.

Throughout their ordeal, it had been Ruth who had remained steadfast and strong. Whatever the need was, she had been there to meet it, whether with someone else of her family or on her own. She had held her younger sister when she cried for the loss of their home, she had helped her older sister when the duties of motherhood had threatened to overwhelm her without a home. She had labored with her father to dig through the remains of their home, barn and outbuildings to gather whatever remained of their clothing, tools and supplies. They had been extraordinarily fortunate to have a small root cellar that had remained undiscovered by whoever had attacked the farm, and that cellar had not only given them what remained of the stores inside, but a place to huddle out of the weather.

Ruth had been the resolve for her father when his hope had dimmed. She had been the inspiration for her younger sister when she was devastated. She had been the encouragement for her sister and brother-in-law when they saw their fragile start together left in ruins, and them with a newborn to care for. She had been there for them all, their strength in the face of the end of all their hopes and hard work. Through it all, she had been the glue that held them together.

Finally, the weight of all that came crashing down upon a fourteen-year-old girl who had not yet taken the time to grieve for extended family and friends that had been lost in the senseless violence that had taken their home.

Ruth shuddered as sobs wracked her body, her face buried in Angela Sanders' shoulder, safe in the strong arms of a woman who had seen her own share of devastation and knew what the girl was going through.

Soon, Martha joined them, and Angela opened her embrace of Ruth to pull Martha into the same hug. Ruth cried too, but more because her sister was crying. Angela began to slowly rock the two of them as she sat with them on the bench of the dinner table.

Providing what comfort she could in a world gone mad.

-

"I ask for your understanding, Gordon, and your forgiveness," Isaac finished, his hand extended.

"Of course, Isaac," Gordon smiled. "If you forgive me for my aggressive behavior at the table. That was uncalled for, and I apologize. I let my desire to help your family overrule my manners."

"There is nothing to forgive, Gordon," Isaac assured him as the two finished shaking hands. "And thank you for your kindness, and desire to help us."

"There is always a place here for you, Isaac," said Gordon. "You are a good man, with a good family. Strong, hard-working and honest, which are all traits that are in short supply these days."

Isaac considered all that for less than a minute before reaching a decision.

"Please tell me about your community, Gordon," he spoke quietly but with a firm voice. "Tell me what we could expect, and what would be expected of us, were we to accept your kind offer."

"Well...."

CHAPTER EIGHTEEN

"They're all suffering rather badly from PTSD."

Beverly Jackson was in the clinic with Patricia Sanders and Jaylyn Thatcher. She had sat and talked with all three of the Miller girls, including Mary Troyer. Normally they would not have been likely to speak to someone like Beverly, but Jaylyn had basically hidden Beverly's interview inside the 'welcoming' physical given to all three girls. Beverly had a way of getting people to talk to her, and after a few minutes with each girl she had a clear picture of their life over the winter.

"I'd be shocked if they weren't," Pat nodded. "Lost friends, extended family, home and hearth, escaping with literally the clothing on their backs and not much else? I'm honestly impressed that they didn't break down during their ordeal. That Ruth is especially strong, God bless her soul. Every family ought to have someone like her."

"I must agree with that," Jaylyn nodded somberly. "All of it, really. It really is surprising that they're doing as well as they are. Mrs. Sanders helped them a great deal, and then walked them over here personally. She like as not helped them as much as anything we can do."

"On that we are all agreed I should imagine," Beverly replied. "There's nothing better for them now than a feeling of safety and belonging. Safety shouldn't be a problem, barring another wide-open attack."

"You think belonging will be problematic?" Patricia frowned.

"I do," Beverly nodded. "It won't be because of us, or any of our people that I can think of. It has more to do with how isolated they were, and now how isolated from the rest of the farm they're going to feel. Atop that, the normal things we use to help with that, gatherings and games and what have you, won't work with them as they will likely avoid them completely due to religious concerns."

"Hadn't thought of that one," Pat sighed. "And no, they're not likely to participate in any of that. That means we'll have to come up with something else."

"There are several things that are going on around here that would probably seem like normal activities to them," Jaylyn mused. "The sewing room comes to mind. And they'll need clothing, anyway.

195

Especially Ruth. That girl is developing quickly and the clothing she wore here has seen better days."

"It's a start," Beverly nodded. "We can also depend on Angela to include them in things like her gardens. And the cooking over at Sander's house."

"I'm sure," Pat nodded. "Ma also has a loom and spinning wheel she's experimenting with. How much you want to be that Mary and Ruth know how to use them already?"

"No bet," Beverly smiled. "A steady schedule of familiar things, coupled with openly friendly and protective adults will go a long way toward helping them. Sooner or later, they'll have to assimilate into the community a bit better, but not right now. Not unless they show interest themselves. Too much culture shock will be just as bad as what they've already been through."

"We'll need to keep a close eye on them."

-

"Hello Ruth, Martha," Lainie smiled brightly. "I'm Lainie Harper. Welcome to the sewing room."

"It's big," Ruth commented, looking around her.

"That's true, it is," Lainie nodded. "But we make clothing for almost everyone on the farm at one point or another, so we need the room. Also, all the old clothing we have is stored here, either to pass it on to others, or else to tear it apart and use the cloth for something new. Would you like a tour?"

"Yes," both girls said at once, still looking on in wonder.

"Well, come with me, then," Lainie held out a hand to each of the girls. Each took a hand and stepped up beside the beautiful redhead, eager to see something even partially familiar.

-

"You have many horses as well as cattle," Abram Troyer said as he rode beside Gordy Sanders, checking fences.

"We do," Gordy agreed. "Even got a small herd of hogs, up near where you guys live. It's pretty much a full-time job just to keep an eye on the fences around here," he laughed.

"While we did not have so many, we raised cattle, too," Abram shared. "My family, I mean, not Isaac. My father had a small herd of about one hundred, give or take depending on the time of year. He had horses, of course. We all do...we all did," he corrected himself. "Those

FIRE FROM THE SKY

we brought with us, and the one cow, are all that remain. One livestock dog out of many. The others were shot and killed in the attack."

"I'm sorry to hear that," Gordy's comment was heartfelt. "We've got a small herd of Kangal livestock dogs, and we let them run free, but call them in if we're under a threat of any kind. We also have a large German Police and two Belgian Malinois, plus the Goat Lady has a pair of Australian Shepherds that herd her goats. We should have some pups soon out of the German Police and the Malinois, and maybe out of the Kangals not too long after that. No idea if Miss Lacey will ever let her dogs have pups or not."

"We have a female Aussie with us," Abram noted. "She is almost three years old and a well-trained stock dog. We lack stock for her to take care of, now, of course."

"Might let her be bred by Jack," Gordy suggested. "That's Miss Lacey's male dog. Some might not agree, but I say we can't possibly have enough stock dogs. We can teach them to stay shut of one another if we have to but having maybe two dozen livestock guardian dogs roaming this big old ranch would be nice."

"How big is this place?" Abram asked.

"The two farms combined come in at about four thousand acres, give or take one hundred acres. Plus, we've claimed about another thousand acres that are lying fallow to use until and unless the owner shows up. That was by order of the military commander, by the way, as part of an effort to feed his men and hopefully others. Unfortunately, he died during the plague," Gordy shook his head. "Shame, too. He was a pretty cool guy."

"Cool?" Abram asked, puzzled.

"Means he was okay. A good guy, yeah?" Gordy tried to explain.

"Ah, I see," Abram nodded.

"Well, we got a ways to go yet, so we better get to it."

-

"You ask only that we do the kind of work we have always done?"

Yes, sir," Clay nodded. He had been talking to Isaac Miller as he gave him an abbreviated tour of the ranch. "We can sometimes use a hand with carpentry and the like, and we're trying to teach everyone the older ways of doing things, especially the kids. While we still have a few modern conveniences, we know they won't last. There's no way to do much maintenance on them, and sooner or later, everything breaks.

197

So, we want them to be prepared for that and be ready to make their way in the world ever how they need to."

"A wise plan," Isaac agreed. "While we are accustomed to doing things the 'older way', as you put it, we do that from a religious standpoint. While many of us will make an allowance for the use of modern equipment, it is something of a sore spot for many. I myself sit on the fence; I believe it is called. I have always thought that if using such things meant that I did a better job, thereby glorifying God in the process, then it could not be considered wrong, at least inherently. It would be the way in which it was used that would make it sinful or wrong."

"Sounds well thought out," Clay nodded, rolling the words over in his mind. "I like it. Might be we can apply that to ourselves, somehow."

"You speak of the violence you feel forced to do in defense of home and family, no?" Isaac asked.

"I do," Clay agreed. "I understand you folks don't think that way, and why, but it's just not in me to sit idly by while others destroy so much. I've fought against that kind of thing my entire adult life."

"I understand you were in the military," Isaac stated rather than asked.

"A lot of us here were," Clay nodded.

"That is not our way," Isaac said simply.

"That is my understanding," Clay's reply was equally simple.

"We cannot assist you in defending this place," Isaac pressed on.

"Haven't asked you to," Clay surprised him. "I fought for people to have religious freedom as well as physical freedoms. I'm not going to change that when I'm on my own soil. Your beliefs tell you that you can't fight back, then you won't be placed in a position where we need you to. If you don't defend yourself, however, I can't ultimately be responsible for you or your family. We'll do our best, but sometimes that isn't enough."

"Nor would I ask of you to take responsibility," Isaac nodded slowly. "Ultimately, our safety is in God's hands, Clayton. We will depend upon Him to either deliver us from harm, or should it be His will that we perish, then to deliver us from the Evil one. That deliverance is the most important."

"I've heard that, too."

-

"Thank you for inviting me into your home, Mrs. Sanders," Mary Troyer said softly. "I am grateful to you."

"Well, I thought you might could use the chance to get out and about," Angela smiled. "I can vaguely remember when my children were so young and it's wearing on you. I figured by the time you got settled good, they'd be fighting over him," she nodded to where Dee Talbot, Dottie Greer, Evelyn Lacey, Amy Mitchell and Daisy and Jasmine Webb were fawning over little John.

At first Mary had been as hesitant as any new mother about allowing so many strangers around her son. That concern had stopped within minutes as she noted how careful all of them were, and how enamored they were with her son. She smiled very slightly at the sight of grown women in a good-natured argument over whose 'turn' it was to hold, change or play with the baby in the house.

"They seem to be of gentle hearts," Mary noted. "And yes, it has been exhausting," she surprised Angela by admitting. "We would not normally be well thought of if we said something of the sort, but…anyone who would have chastised me for it is gone, I'm afraid."

"I know, dear, and I am so sorry," Angela reached out to pat the younger woman's knee. "No one should have to endure so much. But you aren't alone. Many of us have endured much worse," she looked to the women again, where Amy, Daisy and Jasmine looked as animated as she had seen them look in some time. Amy had been doing well by all appearances, but Angela didn't doubt that she still woke up screaming on occasion.

"But that's enough about that," Angela smiled brightly. "Truth is, I wanted to ask you about something. We've been trying to learn how to do a few things since all this started, and one of them was using a spinning wheel, and a loom. We've had a few videos to watch that help teach people how to do those jobs, among others, but we still haven't had much success. Would you happen to know how to do either?"

"Yes, of course," Mary nodded at once.

"Could we impose upon you to teach us how?" Angela clasped her hands in front of her as if she was begging. "We have materials that we've stored since the harvest. Well, the linen we've broken down into strands, actually. But anyway, we would be in your debt if you would show us how to work the wheel and the loom both."

"I would be delighted to help," Mary smiled for the first time in what seemed like years. "And there could be no debt after how well you have treated us. It would seem as if I were contributing in some way."

"Oh, honey, it wouldn't just seem like it," Angela assured her. "We've been on the verge of pulling our hair out trying to get this to work. We'll let them fawn over John a little longer while I send for my daughter and then we can give it a try!"

-

"Who are your helpers, Lainie?" Beverly Jackson asked, smiling as she saw Ruth and Martha Miller working at disassembling older clothing into pieces that could repurposed.

"Aren't they cute?" Lainie bragged, winking at both girls. "They have slid right into things and are already doing work for the farm after just a week. How about that?"

"How about that, indeed," Beverly smiled. She walked casually over to the same table the girls were sitting at and took a seat.

"Are you here to talk to us more?" Ruth asked, looking at the woman before her.

"Not today, sweetie," Beverly shook her head. "This is where I work when I'm not busy with other things. I've been going through all these clothes for a while now. Mostly when I'm not helping Lainie with the actual sewing."

"You work here too?" Ruth couldn't quite hide the suspicious tone of her voice as she looked closer at Beverly.

"I do, part of the time," Beverly nodded. "Most of us have more than one job, and many of us have three or more. This happens to be one of mine. I like to pretend I'm a fashion consultant," she laughed.

With that Beverly settled in to work, careful to all but ignore the presence of the two girls. She could observe how well they were coping without asking them any questions or intruding on their sense of peace. It would let the psychologist determine their progress in a 'real world' setting, instead of the clinic.

Ruth watched her carefully for full minute, highly suspicious of the pretty woman and her motives for being there. She had to admit after that minute or so that Beverly showed no interest in Ruth or Martha, and her brief interactions with Lainie seemed to indicate that she really did work in the sewing center at least part-time.

With no reason to continue her blatant doubt, Ruth returned to her work. Every few minutes she would look up suddenly, but each time she found Beverly hard at work and essentially ignoring the Miller sisters.

Across the way, Lainie bent her head toward her work to hide a small smile. Beverly was really good at what she did.

-

"I do not understand why I am so tired," Abram complained, fighting a yawn as he once more rode with Gordy Sanders. "I slept soundly last night."

"Probably PTSD, man," Gordy told him. "Happens to most people who have been through a shock to the system."

"PTSD?" Abram repeated, puzzled.

"Sorry," Gordy laughed. "Stands for 'Post Traumatic Stress Disorder'. Something that soldiers and first responders get diagnosed with quite a bit. The body's reaction to the let down from adrenaline fueled stress, or words that sound like that, anyway," he laughed again. "Anyway, people who have been through a stressful situation often end up suffering from it. You should talk to Jaylyn and see what she thinks. If she feels like you need it, she can set you up with Beverly. She can help you, Abram. She's helped most all of us at one time or another."

"You?" Abram asked, curious.

"Yep."

-

"Got it?"

"I already said I got it," Heath replied, exasperated. Zach meant well, as did Titus, but he was hurting, and his temper was getting short.

"Easy, now," Titus soothed. "We didn't doubt you was good to go, really. Just…checking, I guess. We don't want nothing to happen to ya."

"Yeah, I don't either," Heath nodded. "I've been shot enough for a lifetime."

"If you're hurting, you should stop," Zach ordered, moving to where he could support Heath if his strength failed. Heath was currently doing pullups, trying to get to ten.

"I'm fine," Heath grunted, pulling.

"No, you're not," Titus argued, grabbing Heath by the core and lifting him. Heath released his grip on the bar without thinking and Titus put him down on his feet.

"What'd you do that for?" Heath demanded, rubbing his left arm.

"Because you were about to give out, dude," Titus replied. "Your arms were trembling, and you were pulling harder with your right than your left. You're done for the day, my man."

Heath looked as if he were about to argue when the sound of a throat clearing stopped him. He turned to see Leanne Tillman standing behind him, maybe twenty feet away, arms folding beneath her breasts as her small foot tapped the ground. The frown on her face told him she had seen and heard everything.

"Uh, hi," he smiled tiredly. "What's up?"

"'Uh, hi'?" Leanne repeated. "Is that the best you got?"

"Oookay," Zach and Titus said in a chorus. "I think we'll just be moving along, then," Zach continued as the two grabbed their own gear. "Good work, brother," he nodded to Heath. "You're improving every day. We'll see you later."

"Cowards," Heath muttered. "Traitors."

"Harsh, but not untrue," Titus snickered. "Good luck with that."

The two departed before they could face any kind of wrath from the Tiny Terror. While not truly tiny, Leanne was much shorter than any of them, by at least a foot. And her temper was famous across the farm. It hadn't taken long for the name to stick, having been coined by Corey Reynard himself.

"It sounded suspiciously to me as if you were pushing yourself too hard," Leanne accused Heath, once his friends had made their retreat.

"I'm pushing myself as much as I can, yeah," Heath nodded. "I figure as long as I don't hurt myself or collapse, then it's not really to the point of being too hard."

"I'm not sure Doctor Thatcher would agree," Leanne argued. "And I don't either," she added.

"Leanne, I have to get back into shape," Heath reasoned. "I've spent two months laid up. My arm is weak, and so is my shoulder. It's not all from the injury, either. It's partly from atrophy due to doing nothing for weeks. I need to rebuild the muscle mass and the only way to do that is to push the muscles. Yeah, it hurts, and yeah, it's tough, but it has got to be done. It's either that or just quit. I'm not going quit."

"I don't expect you to quit, Heath," Leanne's voice softened. "I do expect you to be more careful. Please. I...I'd prefer not to see you lying in that hospital again. Please," she repeated, eyes glistening slightly with unshed tears.

"That's not fair, using the puppy eyes and the tears both at the same time," Heath chuckled, and Leanne's face went red. "I promise I'm being careful. My two mother hens are being careful for me, in fact. They're with me every day for just that reason. It's going to be fine."

"Let's go see the doctor and then we can get something to eat," Leanne changed gears on him all at once. Holding her hand out, she waited for him to gather his things and then take her hand in his. They walked to the clinic in near silence, enjoying one another's company.

CHAPTER NINETEEN

Clay watched patiently as everyone gathered in front of the pad at Building Two. The tumult that had resulted in the coming money system, bank and store had reached almost a fever pitch in less than two weeks as people wondered what about this, what about that, what about something else, and so forth, until Clay had finally just called a mass meeting to both explain the plans and to allow for questions. Lainie, Patricia and his mother had all volunteered to watch the orphanage, while the men from his old unit along with Gordy, Zach and Titus were handling all the security duties.

When it looked as if people had stopped heading their way, Clay gave it five more minutes before stepping up on the trailer they were using as a stage, microphone in hand.

"Okay, folks," he held up a hand. "If we can all settle down, we can get started. Come on, now! Most of you wanted this or something like it so let's settle down and get on with it!" Noise gradually died away as everyone gave him their attention.

"Okay, so everyone here has heard some form or version of the plan, or else someone's opinion or version of said plan. While there is some truth in most of the stories I've heard, or been approached with, none have had the entire truth and most have had some outlandish lies. So, I'm going to explain what we have so far as a plan, and then take questions. I'm warning you now, don't ask me silly shit that I've already covered or that you know are silly. I won't respond well to that, and you won't like my response."

"It was my idea to open a store," Clay began. "There are things we likely want, and we can trade or barter with people to bring them in to us, which limits our exposure to whatever is outside this farm. Things like metal, car parts and the like. Also, people will have items they want to sell, or trade for something they need. The idea here is not so much to make money as to provide a couple of services and needs. The services are, as I said, to gather items we need or think we need, and to offer people a place to display their wares, for lack of a better word, when they make something, or maybe have a service to offer."

"The bank idea grew out of that, in a way, as we began talking about money. In this case we're talking about establishing a specie-based

204

economy here that we hope will spread out to the area around us as time goes on. For those wondering what specie means, it's just a fancy word for coinage or for minting coins. Metal or precious metal money. We're going to use silver coins, and to a lesser extent some gold coins, to get this started."

"The bank is a way not only for you to keep money safely in an account, but also to help get money into the hands of people outside the farm, whether through loans, or else through cashing in receipts from some of you for things they have brought to sell you."

"How do you make money? That's been a big one so far, so I'll answer that now as best I can. Many of you have talents and trades that will do well in this environment. To name a few examples, there is Darrell with his forging, Evelyn with her soaps and oils and what not, Lainie with clothes, though she's not alone there, and the Webb's with leather gear. We may as time goes on find a way to make decent candles or else a candle alternative, or maybe to create black powder, and so on."

"For those with products to sell, it can be done one of two ways through the store; either by commission, where the store gets a percentage of the purchase price for selling your products, or by selling directly to the store, providing they have a market for your things, and then the store reselling it for their own profit. You can always sell your things directly of course, and I will certainly encourage you to do so, though for the time being that will require you to work out a way to deliver your product at least as far as the store if not out to the highway because we are not in a position to allow strangers or outsiders onto the farm. We may at some point try to arrange for the store to be closer to the road, but for now it will be here close, where we can keep an eye on it. That is not open for negotiation. None of it, just to clarify."

"Jobs. There are people who work for the farm who will be put on the payroll to help us manage. It takes a lot of work to manage this place and we can't do it alone. Further, there are people who do jobs that honestly only the farm can pay for, like Operations, or the Orphanage, or Security. There will be others whose services we need to keep the farm going, and Gordon will be dealing with them, working out a fee for those services when and as the farm needs them."

"The farm will not be paying for work in the gardens," Clay decided the time had come for a bit of the bad news. He nodded at the chorus of complaints that came from the crowd in general.

"Sorry, folks," Clay held up a hand to quieten the group. "Those gardens feed you, feed all of us, and everyone will still be required to put in their hours. If you want to pay someone to do your work, that's fine so long as it's worked out in advance. If the hours aren't done then there will be a penalty assessed for the person who was scheduled originally to do the hours, which will go to the person who had to fill in when no one showed up. We'll have to appoint a manager for the gardens since there will be well over one hundred acres of garden spread over the farm this year. Everyone will answer to that manager for their hours. The rule is simple; you don't work, then you'll have to be responsible for your own meals. That's about as fair as I can make it."

"As to that, meals and lodging will remain as they always have been. There won't be any charge for either one. Remember that there is no kitchen staff, however, and that you are responsible for the cooking in your own community. If some of you want to work out a trade with a better cook, that's fine. Someone might, for instance, trade their cooking hours for garden work, freeing up a better cook for kitchen duty. That's between individuals and none of my concern. Remember to keep the people responsible for those areas apprised of your trading. Note that they have the right and responsibility to start limiting said trades if it becomes a burden when people don't show up like they're supposed to."

"We need to get paid for that!" someone yelled from the crowd, and several heads nodded in agreement. Clay didn't catch the voice.

"Okay," Clay nodded amiably. "Then I start charging you for rent and meals. If I'm paying you then you'll have money, right?"

"That ain't fair!"

"Of course, it is," Clay kept his voice reasonable. "You're working to put food on the table, but you still expect me to somehow pay you. I have to have a way to make that money back, so I'll make it charging room and board. I can't just pay you to work for yourselves. I won't last long that way."

This time the head nodding was on Clayton's side he was glad to see. He'd like to have seen all of them nodding, but it looked like he had a firm majority and he'd take that for now.

"Can we try to salvage stuff from off the farm?" someone asked. Again, Clay couldn't catch the voice.

"Not until we're sure that the plague is gone," Clay replied. "Once we know for sure that it's done, then I have no objection so long as you realize that we will not be responsible for your safety. Can't be, for that matter. I would advise against it, myself, but that's just me. No one is a prisoner here and never has been. That said, if anyone leaves before we're at least reasonably certain the plague is gone, they need to take their belongings with them because they won't be allowed back on the farm. The risk is too great for the rest of us. I know that sounds harsh, but disease running rampant through us all will be much harsher. I won't risk it."

"I think that covers the basics, at least as we have them for now," he concluded. "Do be aware that this entire thing is just a plan at this point. We do not have a timeframe for implementing it yet, as there are still terms to work out as well as logistics to deal with. We will try to give a two- or three-week warning when we're getting ready to open things up. Until then, things will continue as they have been. With that in mind, I'll do my best to answer any questions that I can, assuming you have any."

They had plenty.

-

"Good grief," Clay collapsed into his office chair, promptly emptying the water bottle that Lainie had passed him. Once it was empty, she carried it to a water cooler to refill it.

"I did warn you," she told him.

"I know, and you were right," Clay agreed.

"A lot of ingrates on this farm," Greg grumped from his chair.

"I don't think they're ingrates," Clay shook his head, smiling his thanks at Lainie as he accepted the water bottle back. "Most of the people that were complaining have been hard working since they got here. Not fair to call them ingrates just for trying to get the best situation they can, whether for themselves or their families."

"That's true, I guess," Greg allowed, face wrinkled with thought. "Hadn't really gone down the list."

"Anyway, we've still got some ways to go yet," said Clay. "Right, Miss Manager?"

207

"You really enjoy sleeping on the floor, don't you?" Lainie smiled, but it was an evil looking smile that made Greg get to his feet.

"Ohh-kay," he drew the word out slowly. "I can see I need to be...yeah, I need to be over...over there. Somewhere over that way. See you two later," he tossed over his shoulder as he was already out the door.

"Even your friends know better," Lainie snorted.

"Well, it is a well-known fact that you should never kick a sleeping dragon," Clay laughed, wrapping his arms around her before she could escape.

"And now I'm a monster," Lainie looked at him, a severe frown formed across her beautiful features.

"Everyone knows dragons are beautiful," Clay scoffed, kissing her quickly on the tip of her nose.

"And that they can burn you," she reminded him, eyebrow raised.

"Are you really that unhappy with it?" Clay asked, suddenly very serious. It caught her by surprise.

"Seriously, tell me," Clay urged. "If you're really that unhappy with things, then please, say so and just...refuse. I'll get someone else. I promise there are people who would love to have the job, or think they would, anyway. They just don't realize yet how much work it might be."

"No," Lainie sighed. "I mean yes, I am unhappy with it, but it's purely for selfish reasons. I didn't want to give up my little kingdom in T1, that's all."

"Uh...kingdom?" Clay was confused now for sure.

"My sewing center," Lainie nodded. "When I'm over there, I can lock everything else away and just sort of...forget about it, I guess. Just for that time that I'm working. I love to create things and working in the sewing center is very rewarding from a helping others standpoint. I feel like I'm doing a good thing and that in doing so, I'm really helping the population here. That, plus that isolation feeling I would get make it a wonderful job."

"I'll find someone else," Clay said at once, never hesitating. "No problem."

"No," Lainie shook her head. "Like I said, it's selfish. Others can sew just as well as I can. Not many others have the business experience that I do. Or an ownership stake, either. No one else would be allowed to shirk something they were good at. I shouldn't be able to either."

"That's very self-sacrificing," Clay complimented. "There also aren't a lot of people who would take that route when another was available. I knew there was a reason I liked you," he smirked, kissing her again on the nose.

"Liked?" she raised an eyebrow, looking him in the eye. "Like is the best you can come up with?"

"Well, it sounded better than 'tolerate', so I thought I'd-*OW!*" he stopped, grabbing his rapidly bruising arm.

"Jackass."

-

Clay studied the organization table on his desk, trying to find any holes or other problems before he shared it with Jose for his input. Most of the people on medical leave after the battle were now returning to duty, which was good news indeed. Losing such a chunk of their qualified security personnel had hurt, in more ways than one. Getting those who could recover back to work would ease the strain that had been felt over the past two months.

After a lot of thinking on the subject, Clay had decided that the remainder of his old team along with Gordy, Zach, Heath, Titus Terry and Kurtis Montana, would remain separate from the rest as a force that could be deployed away from the farm when there was a need. Should Heather Patton and Carrie Jarrett pass the course, they would be added to that team and be classified as full-time security. This group would still be part of the farm's defense and would help stand watches with the others but would remain separate from the rest as their own group.

Of the people who had arrived with Flores, only the three military police offices could honestly be considered combat personnel. Rather than add the military police officers to the security force, however, Clay was considering using them as an actual police force on the farm. Sienna Newell had been an MP and would make an excellent supervisor, and Greg was still the sheriff of Calhoun County, appointed by the military commander at the time. With the three MP officers led by Greg and Sienna helping where needed, there would be a proficient police force to deal with any domestic or home-grown disturbances, should the need arise. All of them would still be available to help defend the farm in an emergency.

The remainder of all combat forces on the farm would be combined into one united defense force covering all defenses and watches.

Leaving Jose as his second in command as well as commanding the old group, Clay slotted Faron Gillis in as commander of defensive forces for the entire farm. That would leave Flores in charge of all non-combat related defense functions, such as supply and training.

While it would not be her job to do actual training, it would be her responsibility to ensure that all defense forces had passed their training and were all current on their qualifications. Flores would be responsible for supervising those assigned to work in areas of firearms care and maintenance among any others. This would give Clay someone to yell at when things didn't get done properly or on time. Their supply situation was ably managed by Kandi Ledford with support from the twins and now from the supply specialist that had arrived with the rest of the Headquarters Group.

It had been a simple decision to place Gordon in charge of farm operations since he was the single most experienced farmer on the entire place. Dee Talbot and Terri Hartwell would fall under his supervision, as would Gail Knight, Charley Wilmeth and Samantha Walters. Anyone assigned to farming or livestock operations even part time, such as Ronny Tillman and Clay himself, would also answer to Gordon when working those positions. For the gardening supervisor he had chosen Dottie Greer, though placing her, and the gardens, under Gordon's overall supervision as well.

Mechanics would be Jake's area, supported part-time by Sienna Newell and including the new military mechanic, Pacifico Aroha. There would be others assigned to them on an as needed basis for extra hands and labor, but those three would be the primary mechanics, at least to start.

He decided to leave other operations the way they were for the present, since they all were currently functioning without difficulty. There might come a time when changes would need to be made, but he felt that he was already going to be upsetting the workflow enough by making the other changes, since they would be done rather quickly and all within the same week. In fact, he-,

His thinking stopped at a knock on his door. He looked up to find Xavier of all people, standing in the doorway.

"X, come on in," Clay leaned back in his chair. "How's it going?"

"I believe things are going well for the moment," Xavier replied, taking a seat across from Clay. "Tomorrow is a new day, of course," he added drily.

"Ain't it though," Clay snorted. "I noticed you and Leanne sparring yesterday but couldn't get over there to watch. How is she doing?"

"She hip-tossed me yesterday, alone and unassisted," Xavier bragged slightly. "She is remarkably determined for one so unaccustomed to violence. She is doing well not only with me, but also with Tandi. A true fighter, that one."

"Well, you've met the rest of the family," Clay snorted. "No other way to survive around here."

"I suspect that to be true," Xavier laughed.

"I saw you with another student a couple days ago," said Clay. "How is Amanda doing? Getting back into shape?"

"Funny you should ask," Xavier smiled, and Clay groaned.

"Now what?" he asked, resting his forehead in his cupped hands.

"No, no, nothing like that," Xavier waved the coming complaint aside. "She is doing rather well, especially considering the damage she suffered. It was fortunate for her that Doctor Thatcher was here or else she might not have recovered. We are indeed smiled upon by Fickle Fate to have your sister-in-law with us, but I do believe repairing Amanda's damaged abdomen might have been beyond her skill set."

"Might have been," Clay nodded slowly. "Can't ever be sure with Patty. She worked a lot of ER shifts at Vandy, so I'm sure she saw her share of gunshot wounds. But that was a while back, too. So, what about Amanda, then, if she's not causing problems," he chuckled.

"She noticed Miss Patton and Miss Jarrett preparing for their training to attempt wearing the Skull and Bones," Xavier replied. "She is...interested in following them, once she has recovered her conditioning. I warned her it would be an order of magnitude more difficult than what she has been through already, and that you would have the final say. That mistakes such as the one she made the day she was shot would never be tolerated among our ranks."

"That didn't dissuade her?" Clay frowned.

"It rather seemed to harden her resolve," Xavier shook his head. "I believe she sees this as a way to find redemption for her past mistakes and also to prove to you that she can be a worthwhile asset."

"What do you think?" Clay inquired, watching his friend closely.

"I feel certain she has the desire and the fortitude," Xavier looked thoughtful. "My only concern at this point would be if her actual physicality would prevent her from making it. I do think she would be worth the investiture in training if only to see if that is true."

In other words, Xavier felt like she could make it, but only the actual doing would prove him right or wrong.

"I take it you don't believe she can make it at this point?" he checked.

"Doubtful," Xavier's voice sounded regretful. "With another two weeks, knowing what was at stake, I think she would surprise us, but she doesn't have another two weeks."

"That is true, but we could likely stall for that amount of time," Clay mused. "Heather and Carrie are waiting on Heath, who should be ready in about two weeks himself, so it's not like it would be a big deal to wait for her. If Amanda can be ready in the two weeks you suggest, or by the time Heath is ready, then we will allow her to try as well, if she still wants to. Sound fair to you?"

"It does indeed," Xavier smiled. "Very much so. I thank you, Clayton," he inclined his head slightly.

"Don't thank me until you're done, brother."

212

CHAPTER TWENTY

Clay had begun to wish he had left the idea of banks and stores and pay a mystery. The last three weeks had consisted of people trying to charge for every little thing they did and complain loudly if they were refused. He had listened and explained patiently for the first week. For the second week he had still explained, but with much less patience.

The third week was the straw that broke the camel's back. He called another 'assembly', and this time didn't spare anyone's feelings.

"I felt sure I had made this clear before, but since it appears I was in error, I intend to make sure this time. No one gets paid for their garden hours. Period. Gardens are our own breadbasket. We all get our meals from there and our stores for the winter. We will all participate in the gardening, or we will not eat. If that sounds too harsh for you, feel free to pack your belongings and go find another place that offers as much as we do with so little effort on your part."

"I don't intend to argue about this, nor will I explain it again. Everyone does garden duty, and you will not be paid for it. Period. Remember that the farm still provides meat for the table, and everyone eats for free. That's because we all work to make sure we have something to eat."

"Housing is still free and will remain so. Yes, it may be cramped at times. We're trying to make sure that's not a problem, but until we can, things may be a bit crowded. Deal with it. You aren't being charged any rent and you won't be in the future, so there are no real grounds for you to complain about. Again, if you don't care for that, pack up and mosey on down the road to Utopia, where everything is free, and no one has to work. This isn't it."

"The store will not open until we have everything ironed out and ready. We need to have a firm guide on how to price things, how to charge commissions for work or products, and rules by which we will operate. Things we can't effectively run a store without. We will do our best to make it as soon as possible, but that's not a date or a time frame. Just our best effort."

"Same goes for the banking. We're working on it, but there are a lot of rules in banking and money handling, and we aren't going to open any type of bank until we have a solid set of rules to run it by. That's

213

also a period. When it comes to money, no one is going to accept rule changes on the fly, and we wouldn't expect you to. So, everything must be ready and waiting when the operation opens. We haven't arrived at that point yet, but we are trying. Remember that the people trying to work all this out also have jobs to do, including working in the afore mentioned gardens."

"In case you aren't getting the message, I've had it with the complaints and the pissing and moaning about why you can't get paid for work that no one else is paid for. There's not even a place to spend it yet! If you refuse to work, then you will not be fed at the farm's expense, nor at the expense of your neighbors. We've never had a problem with this until I mentioned trying to make a return to normal. Now all of sudden, everyone 'needs' to get paid."

"I made sure to tell you who would get paid by the farm, and for what. The gardens, just as a for instance, are not a case of you working for the farm, but rather working for yourselves. Even the security forces and those who have other essential jobs still do their share in the garden labor, and they don't get paid for it. This has been the way of it since we began. It's not going to change."

"If it does change, it will be that everyone has their own garden and prepares their own food. That will probably be a lot more difficult for some, but that would be your problem and not mine. People don't get paid for their garden at home, or didn't before the Storm, anyway. I don't imagine that's changed any."

"I'm not going to answer any questions this time because you've got all the answers you need. Make sure your garden hours are recorded, and that you do them, or feed yourself somehow from now on. And I'm not kidding about finding a new place to live, either. We will not have any kind of uproar or trouble stirring on this farm. We've got too many problems as it is to allow more. Make your decisions and let me know what you're going to do. That's all."

-

"Well, that was direct and to the point," Greg commented as he took a seat in Clay's office.

"I hate to say I told you so," Lainie sighed.

"But you told me so," Clay held up a hand to ward off her comment. "I know. I expected difficulty, but this is beyond me. It's not everyone, thankfully, but it's enough."

"Well, if this didn't put an end to it, nothing else will I suspect," Greg noted, his hands raised to his sides in a gesture of helplessness.

"I'm tempted to cancel the whole thing," Clay grumped. "At the very least to suspend it for a while. I shouldn't have mentioned it at all, and if I had seen this much difficulty in it, I wouldn't have. This all started with me wanting a store and trading post where we could trade with people outside the farm."

"We can still do that," Greg shrugged. "Just have the trading post set up to do business with outsiders and leave it at that. Trading them stuff we have for stuff we want. I know Leon wants more alternators and generators from cars. I'm sure Darrell would want more spring steel, too. For that matter, I imagine that Gary and Sara would be interested in any firearms that aren't working. Between the two of them I'd guess there isn't much they can't repair."

"Wouldn't that just inflame the complainers even more?" Lainie asked.

"We'll blame the whole thing on them, though without calling them by name," Clay shrugged. "We'll still pay the people working for the farm but ask them not to bandy that about. There may come a time when they'll be glad to have the silver."

"Asking for trouble with that last one," Lainie sighed. "Again."

"That's true," Greg sounded like he hated to say it. "But the idea is sound. The store idea I mean," he clarified.

"I'll think on it."

-

The traffic going northward had trickled to a halt just days after Isaac Miller and his family had stopped at the farm. While there was no way to absolutely establish that the travelers were trying to escape further predation by the kind of gangs that had attacked the farm during the winter, Isaac himself had spoken to at least three households who had the same idea as he did; find somewhere else to be. A purely luck of the draw decision had led Isaac to the Sanders' farm, where he and his family had found a new home. Others had kept going, hoping for greener pastures further away.

With the Second Exodus, as it was now being termed, over, life on the farm returned to a semblance of normal as the Sanders and their 'employees' prepared for planting season. There was also an influx of new piglets and new chickens. Finally, both Bella and Petals were getting close to delivering litters of puppies sired by the giant Bruce. New protectors of the people on the farm. It was sure to be a busy time and that was despite the turmoil started over the store and the bank and 'pay'.

"I hate to say-," Lainie started, almost in singsong.

"Then stop saying it, okay?" Clay sounded somewhat exasperated. "I get it. You told me so."

"Somebody's grumpy," she teased. She felt completely justified after the way Clay had dumped the whole *'golly, if you don't do the bank and the store, who would I ever find better'* routine on her.

"Somebody is fed up is all," he corrected her. "Somebody also has to prepare for planting season. We're about a week-and-a-half away from it, and there's a lot more land to prep and plant this year. Not to mention security to plan for the operations."

"Sorry, Cowboy," Lainie was genuinely contrite after hearing all that. "That is a lot to worry over. Anything I can help with?"

"No," he shook his head. "Thanks, but most of it will be Ronny and I driving and Dad and Robert supporting. Dee can drive, too, so she'll probably be helping, and I think both Moses and Cliff have a little experience, but all that is up to Dad. I just go where he points and do what he says," he chuckled.

"Glad not to be in charge, are we?" Lainie laughed.

"You have no idea."

-

"So, what did you end up doing?" Clay asked as he and Lainie met with the twins and Millie Long.

"We bought items from people on the farm who make different things, mostly clothing at the moment, but also wooden toys, and soap from Miss Lacey, of course," Leanne began.

"The Webbs have a ton of stuff they wanted to market, and they should do really well," Leon continued. "Leather gear like gloves and pouches, ammunition bandoliers and even one backpack. Daisy and Jasmine are making home remedies for aches and pains, sore feet and treatments for corns and what not as well as some other stuff I'll let these two fill you in on," his face reddened a bit.

"Better get over that, Ace," Millie warned, and for once wasn't joking. "They're making women's needs, and doing a pretty damn good job, too," she then told Lainie. "I'll show you," she nodded to another part of the building and the three women headed that way.

"Got something you wanna tell me, Deuce?" Clay asked. "Or should I say Ace?"

"Not yet," he muttered. "But maybe soon."

"Do I need to get a place ready for you and Millie to live in?" his uncle asked.

"I don't know, yet," Leon admitted. "Have you thought about having a honeymoon shack or something?" he asked suddenly.

"I have not, in fact, I don't think anyway," Clay frowned a bit, trying to remember. "But it sounds like a fine idea to me."

"It's just…there are a lot of people starting to hook up around here," Leon shrugged. "That's going to continue, too. People will eventually want a honeymoon as well as their own homes. Just human nature."

"You're right, it is," Clay almost hummed. "That's given me a lot to think on, Leon. Thank you."

"You bet," the nephew smiled. "I wouldn't think on it over long," he added as a last warning, face red again.

"Then I won't."

-

"Yeah, I've thought about that," Gordon nodded. "Surprised it hasn't come up before now, really."

"Everyone is too busy surviving," Clay shrugged. "Or has been, anyway."

"That is true I suppose," Gordon admitted. "Got any ideas?"

"A couple," Clay replied. "I thought we could build a smaller version of the Square up around the Plum farm. The well there is a good one and there's other water there for horses and what have you. We keep the post manned around the clock so that gives them some security no matter who lives there. As for a honeymoon shack?" he snorted. "That I got no idea for, really. I mean I do for the house, just not for where to put it? You know of a good place?"

"Before the attack in January I would have said yes and told you to put it along the pond in Number Eleven," his father nodded. Number Eleven referred to Pasture Eleven.

"Yeah, that's a little too exposed," Clay mused. "Maybe somewhere along the creek?"

217

"Where would you put it that it wouldn't be just as exposed if someone came on us from the north?" Gordon questioned. "Might never happen, but if it did and someone was there, it'd be bad."

"True," Clay sighed. This was much harder than he'd expected. "Hey," had a thought suddenly. "What about Ladybug Spring?"

"What about-, oh, yeah," Gordon caught himself, nodding. "Yeah, that would work okay. Take a bit of work to get it in shape for something like that, but once finished it would be easy to keep up. We've kept the water clean over the years, too."

Ladybug Spring was an old home place that was so old not even Leon the Elder had known who was there before the Sanders had arrived. The home was long gone, of course, but the spring remained, and had been watering Sanders' cattle for years. Decades, even.

"Would we need to block the cattle out, you think?" Clay wondered.

"Just around the one side," Gordon informed him. "Fence down either side to leave part of the spring open for the love birds," he chuckled. "We can even get Ronny to dig it out a little and make a small wading pool for it. You know, when no one is newly married, that would be a fine reward for people who are doing good work, or else you could rent it out. Or both," he shrugged.

"Let's get it built, first," Clay laughed lightly. "Then we can worry about becoming landlords."

-

"We'll try to make this meeting short and sweet, though that's never worked before," Clay snorted. Jose Juarez, Greg Holloway, Sienna Newell, Faron Gillis, Triana Flores, Jaylyn Thatcher and Kandi Ledford all sat around the table, tablets in hand. This was their weekly supervisor's meeting. Gordon had decided that he and Dottie need not attend, and that had been that. Sienna was representing the 'garage' in this instance, Jake being elbow deep in an overhaul.

"Jose?" Clay started.

"Security is set the way we planned it, with the towers all manned and equipped and the roving patrols beefed up as well as the response unit. We've got enough people to run three shifts, and even allow for time off in ones and twos. We're considering splitting each shift into threes to allow a twelve-hour shift, with four hours for each team on patrol, on the towers and on response. If we did that, then each team

218

could get a full day off, or maybe even two days, as the teams rotate. We're still studying the details on that."

"I like that, if it can be done," Clay nodded, thinking it over. "Allowing for some steady time-off would lend a sense of normalcy that we're sorely lacking right now. If I can do anything to make that easier, let me know."

"Will do," Jose nodded. "Otherwise, our gear and equipment are stored properly and in good shape."

"Greg?" Clay called on his friend next.

"We have a steady patrol on call, ready to answer any kind of law-and-order issue, though there haven't been any so far. Still, our walking patrols are being seen and doing a good patrol, so it's a start. I am using a couple of people who signed up for the old Sheriff's patrol to help pad the numbers, by the way. At some point we need to start getting out to the radio stations we set up and see how they're doing. Otherwise, we're good."

"We'll try and work that in somewhere," Clay promised. "Not a bad idea at all. And using who you need to from the old patrol is fine. Just make sure any duties it takes them away from are covered."

"Got it," Greg promised.

"Cece?"

"Jake and Paci are overhauling a 939 right now," Sienna reported. "I've been stripping the transmission from an old pickup, a Chevy, that runs but won't pull right. If we can fix it, we can either use it or trade it. Thanks to our own efforts and the new arrivals we are in good shape for parts and tools both. All vehicles that are listed as ready for use are up to date on their service and so are most of those that are listed out-of-service. They're down for other reasons that we're working on, but if you needed them, they're ready to go. The only real issue is covered storage for all the vehicles, and you have plans for that."

"Great!" Clay smiled at that. "Faron?"

"As Jose said, we're set," Faron replied at once. "Other than examining the new shift, or at least the potential for it, our patrols are mapped out and in service, with alternating routes every two or three days, but never in a pattern. The towers are equipped with heavy weapons and if we ever face an attack like the one in January again, they will be able to blast it with 40 mike mikes as soon as contact is made. The big bunker is also now equipped to handle pretty much anything that can be thrown at us and constantly manned by people who know how to use everything in there. They are, by definition, not part of the regular rotation. That is their permanent assignment when they are on duty. We're fully equipped and have no shortage of any kind right now."

"Good idea with the bunker," Clay complimented. "I like it. Not everyone knows how to deal with that kind of equipment. Good deal. Let's see…Triana?"

Triana Flores blushed slightly as everyone turned her way. She had worked very hard since her arrival to make up for her attitude when she'd first visited the farm. Everyone had gradually accepted her presence and slowly learned to trust her as time wore on. She still walked on eggshells as the saying went, but she was becoming more comfortable with each passing day. Meetings like this one were helping her.

"I feel like my reports are redundant," she chuckled, and the others laughed with her. "There are no major problems to report, anywhere. There are always problems, of course, but they are simply the normal and run-of-the-mill sort of problems we'd have to deal with even in peace time. Things like the overhaul on the niner-three-niner," she nodded at Sienna. "We now have a complete inventory, but I will let Lieutenant Ledford speak to that, since it was her work. For now, we have sufficient man, or woman, power to accomplish all of our tasks."

"Good news. I love good news," Clay smiled again. "Jaylyn?"

"All wounded are now out of the clinic, and all are doing well. Several are already back on duty and the rest are almost to that point and working hard to finish their rehab. We are good for manpower and supplies, thanks in no small part to the arrival of Lieutenant Flores' folks, but as always, whatever you can find when you're out and about is always welcome."

"Everyone has that word," Clay promised. "And saving the best for last, Kandi!" Clay made an elaborate flourish, causing Kandi to turn beet red while everyone else chuckled, except for Sienna Newell, her roommate and best friend, who just flat out laughed at the blonde's discomfiture.

"We completed our inventory on all supplies and equipment outside of food stores, which was already finished," Kandi studied her tablet closely. "I'm sending you a copy of everything," she tapped her screen with a stylus and the two tablets connected with a radio signal and exchanged information.

"While there are a few gaps in that inventory, that's to be expected and is completely normal, even when the world was still working," Kandi finally looked up, careful to avoid looking around her. "For now, we are completely able to meet all expected needs, and all contingencies that we've planned for. In fact, we have packages ready to go for each of those contingencies, including a scramble to put a patrol out. Sergeant Winfield and I review some part of those plans each day to try and anticipate what needs we might be called upon to meet. We are caught up at this time and with the part-time assistance in place, we are sufficient on manpower," she concluded.

"Thank you, Kandi, and I apologize for embarrassing you that way," Clay told her, genuinely contrite. "I was simply glad to be almost finished, and hoped you were going to have a good report as well."

"It's okay," she smiled brightly, showing everyone why Shane Golden was enamored with her.

"Well, with that all done, I think we can safely adjo-," he stopped short as a shell-shocked looking Leon walked into the meeting.

"Leon?" Clay asked, concerned.

"We...we have a problem," Leon told him softly. "We have a big, big problem."

"What kind of problem?" Clay asked, instantly on guard.

"You'll need to hear it for yourself," he waved toward Operations. "It's still playing."

"What is 'it'?" Greg asked, getting to his own feet to follow.

"Better for you to hear it yourself, I think," Leon replied. As they neared the door, Clay could hear what had to be a radio transmission.

"-heavy fighting is still raging outside of Chicago where rebels are dug in and seem determined to destroy the historic Windy City. Meanwhile, in other fighting, government units have encircled the last group of resistance in Pittsburgh and hope to have things there under control soon.

Efforts to re-establish communications and control with the rest of the nation are still under way, and our signals are reaching further and further with each passing week as our repeater network is repaired and expanded. Soon, all our citizens will be able to receive the news, as well *as alerts and updates from the government. We know you are all as pleased by this as we are.*

This has been a newscast of the National Salvation Government Public Information Office. Stay tuned in for all news updates as well as orders and announcements issued for the citizens by the Government."

Suddenly the air waves were filled with the soft sound of big band music, the likes of which hadn't been played since probably the forties.

"Is this some kind of joke?" Jose was the first to speak.

"If it is, it's a dangerous one," Triana Flores was the first to answer him. "Radio was one of the ways the mass attacks seemed to choose their targets. If this is just a joke, they're setting themselves up for a hit."

"I don't like the sound of 'National Salvation Government', myself," Greg noted, looking around at everyone else.

"You're wise not to," Jaylyn surprised them all by speaking. "It's been used through history more than once, and it never means anything good. Mostly it represents an autocratic junta replacing a failing or overthrown legitimate government. It has never been anything less than brutal." Silence reigned in the room for a few moments, the silence finally broken by Clay himself.

"Well, crap."

TO BE CONTINUED

AFTERWORD

This book was difficult to write for several reasons, and I apologize for the long wait. I hope you will find the book worth that wait. Embers presented me with problems at every turn, including tonight as I write this when I realized that somehow, I had written an entire line of characters into the Dramatis Personae that had no business being there. I kept thinking 'I don't recognize that name' over and over as I typed. Well, there was a good reason for that. They weren't in the book, nor were they supposed to be.

I have appreciated (and continue to appreciate) the encouragement and support I receive from you, the readers. More than you will probably ever realize at that. I love you all and want to always do my best to give you quality material, wherever it is or whatever the subject might be. As always, I will let you decide how successful I am.

If you do think I've done well, then please consider leaving me a review. Reviews drive the search programs that will make recommendations to new readers. Your review is worth far more than simply making me smile, though they do, indeed make me smile (the nice ones do, anyway). Also, a share on social media is always appreciated. Several new readers have written to me that they only initially looked at my books because one of you out there recommended me to them. Your help is always appreciated.

In addition to thanking all of you, I need as always to thank Dan Edwards and the crew at Creative Texts Publishing. No matter when I call or e-mail, he gets back to me ASAP, and is continually looking after my best interests even as he does his best to make me look like a real writer. Thanks Dan, for sticking with me ☺

Last but in no way least are thanks to my wife and nephew, who serve as my conscience, sounding board, editors, and chief complaint takers (my complaints, not readers). I honestly don't know what I'd do or where I'd be without them.

A couple of notes about things that have been brought to my attention. First, that my books were not showing up as available in print, or on audible. The publisher contacted Amazon and spent a good bit of a day ironing out whatever glitch caused that, so it should be solved. In truth, everything was available all the while, but you had to be on another web page to access it. An identical web page, but still separate. How that happened is anyone's guess, but no one is perfect. I appreciate very much those of you who wrote me for taking the time to send me a note letting me know something was out of kilter.

Second, something I should have known all along, but didn't even think of. A veteran who reads my work informed me that the narrator who read the Fire Novels onto Audible was continually pronouncing such titles as MRAP by their acronym, rather than simply saying 'm-rap' like the rest of us. After consulting with that veteran and a few more, we decided that it would not take away from the book for me to simply go ahead and write m-rap in the manuscript. So, if it looks a little strange, that's the reason. I don't think it will fool any of you, but it might help the audible go better.

Added to that is references to 'Mark' this and 'Mark' that, which is normally written either as 'Mk' or just 'M', I am now spelling those things out as well, rather than just use the 'Mk', again trying to avoid any confusion for narrators that have no military background or familiarity at all. If I missed any this time, being new, then I ask your forbearance, please.

These are things I should have considered earlier, but since I was a wee laddie, it's been 'Mark such-and-so' and so forth, so to me it was familiar, and I think I kind of assumed it would be to everyone. Sorry about that, and a big thanks to the people who were kind enough to point the problem out to me. I can't thank you enough.

In closing, I do hope you enjoy Embers. It is a big book for this series, with many, many changes and more coming. Hopefully, you'll all enjoy them. As you read this, if I've made you laugh, cry and cuss all in one sitting, maybe I did something write (see what I did there? Little righter humor. Oop, there it was again! Am I not hilarious? I mean seriously.)

Anyway, the book is yours, and by the time it reaches you I will probably be elbow deep in another. Don't let that stop you from dropping me a note, just realize it may be days before I answer. Thank you all, from the shores of Pickwick Lake,

NC Reed

More Books by Author N.C. Reed

Book Series
Fire From the Sky
Book 1: The Sanders Saga
Book 2: Brotherhood of Fire
Book 3: Trial by Fire
Book 4: Home Fires
Book 5: Friendly Fire
Book 6: Hostile Fire
Book 7: Hostile Fire
Book 8: Hell Fire
Book 9: Brimstone
Book 10: Damned Nation
Book 11: Ashes

The Black Sheep of Soulan
Book 1: Parno's Company
Book 2: Parno's Destiny
Book 3: Parno's Gambit
Book 4: Parno's Peril
Book 5: Parno's Gift

Stormcrow
Stormcrow: Book 1
Stormcrow: Book 2

Stand Alone Titles
Odd Billy Todd
Roland: Reluctant Paladin
Tammy and Ringo
Friggin Zombies
The Kid

THANK YOU
FOR READING!

If you enjoyed this book, we would appreciate your customer review on your book seller's website or on Goodreads.

Also, we would like for you to know that you can find more great books like this one at www.CreativeTexts.com

Made in the USA
Monee, IL
28 May 2022

97165461R00142